KICK BALL SLAY

An Introduction to West Coast Swing...
<u>And</u> a Murder Mystery

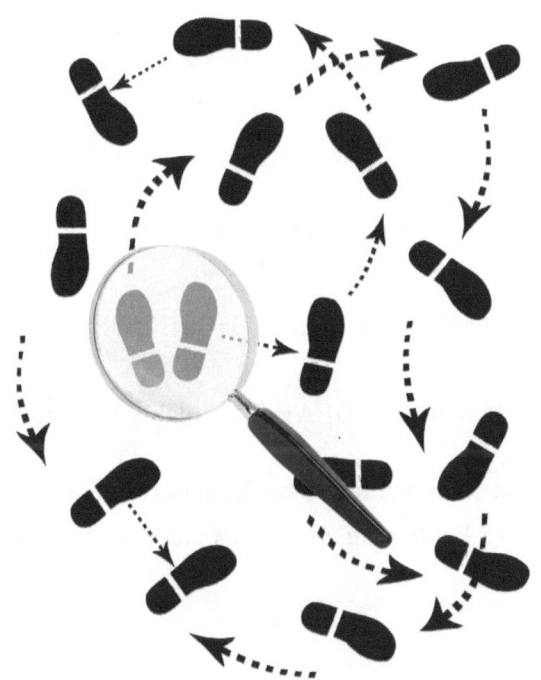

Also By Doug Dorsey

NEVER ALONE

•

BROKEN HERO

•

THE DECEPTION

•

THE RED LEDGER

•

THE BETRAYAL

•

ROCK STEP TRIPLE HOMICIDE

•

QUICK QUICK SLOW DEATH (Available January 2026)

For a complete list of books available from
Studio 15 Publishing, visit www.studio15inc.com

KICK BALL SLAY

A NOVEL BY DOUG DORSEY

STUDIO 15 PUBLISHING, INC.

Ponte Vedra, Florida

Printed in the United States of America
First published as a Studio 15 Publishing paperback in 2022

For information about permission to reproduce selections from this book, visit our website www.studio15inc.com or contact us at (904)874-4856.

This book is a work of fiction. Names, characters, businesses, organizations, places, events, and incidents either are the product of the author's imagination or are used fictitiously. Any resemblance to actual persons, living or dead, events, or locales is entirely coincidental.

The Library of Congress catalogue of the paperback edition is as follows:

Dorsey, Doug (Douglas A.)
Kick Ball Slay / Doug Dorsey - 2nd ed.
ISBN - 13: 979-8-9856953-3-5
ISBN 10: 8-9856953-3-5

Edited by Robyn Zomorodian.
Artwork Contributions by Madison Dorsey.
Promotional Items by Phoenix & Sunrise.

Studio 15 Publishing, Inc.
Ponte Vedra, Florida
www.studio15inc.com

PRINTED IN THE UNITED STATES OF AMERICA

1 3 5 7 9 10 8 6 4 2

Second Edition

This book is dedicated to Stephanie Hitchcock.
Je t'aime tellement et toujours, mon âme.

REVIEWS OF KICK BALL SLAY

"An incredible murder mystery wrapped up in the world of swing dancing... loved it & highly recommend. Five stars."
-Kathy Stickles, *ReaderViews*

"Twist-riddled, character-driven, un-put-downable whodunnit... Dorsey's twisty tale of murder and intrigue will stay on the reader's mind long after they turn the final page. An absolute stunner."
-*The Prairies Book Review*

"*Kick Ball Slay* is a fascinating whodunnit thriller with a unique setting & a compelling cast of characters." Winner - Gold Award.
-Thomas Anderson, *Literary Titan*

"Dorsey excels at creating tension & suspense... deviously delicious."
-*Bookview Review*

"Rumors, suspicions and fierce dance steps coalesce in the shadow of imminent danger... sly humor adorns the pages and is apparent in everything from the cheeky cover to the detective's dry sense of humor. Five stars."
-R.C. Gibson, *Indies Today*

"Full of suspense, heart and intrigue, *Kick Ball Slay* is the perfect murder mystery with charming characters and a strong start to a new series."
-Audrey, *OceanWriter Reviews*

"*Kick Ball Slay* is more than a thriller, it is a peek behind the stage of competitive dancing, a specialized domain not well known to the general public. This fiction with end-chapter cliffhangers will keep the reader up at night."
-Carol W., *Authors Reading*

"Five stars. A captivating sleuth tale that hooks you in from the first page & keeps you glued until the end."
-Pikasho Deka, *Readers Favorite*

Miss you, brother!

In Loving Memory Of:
Richard Lennon Foxworth
September 29, 1973 - May 15, 2020

BOOK 1 IN THE ADVENTURES OF
DETECTIVE EVANN MYRICK

PROLOGUE
Two Weeks (& Several Refrains) Earlier

A light breeze blew across the ninth floor balcony, catching a wisp of Trisha Beck's long brown hair; she brushed it out of her eyes, only to reveal a tear rolling down her cheek. Until this moment, the alcohol had kept her tormented thoughts at bay, but that feeling of numbness had begun to wear off. In turn, the repressed emotions were starting to flood back in, forcing her to grapple with them once more - this time with a vengeance.

Lively music wafted out from just inside the hotel room door, accentuated by her friends' distinctive laughter. They reveled in the second night of their weekender together, unaware of Trisha's inner conflict. Tomorrow was a new day, but it also brought with it more rounds of grueling competition, and Trisha found herself almost paralyzed with anxiety at the thought of having to go back out on the dance floor to perform once again, especially in the midst of the worst slump of her career.

Alone, she hammered down the last remnants of alcohol from the cup in her hand, consuming it in a single gulp. Then, reaching clumsily over the banister of the balcony, she let go of the red plastic container so that it fell haphazardly toward the ground below. It wildly drifted back and forth in the wind, analogous to how her own life felt at the present moment.

Eventually losing interest in the plight of the cup, she turned her eyes to the Boston skyline. Her thoughts were back on the death of her friend Yves, another gifted dancer who'd passed away only a few weeks earlier at a dance conference in Sacramento. The rumors were that he'd been struggling internally with his own demons just before taking his life. Yet, Trisha wasn't entirely convinced there wasn't foul play involved. Yves had made a cryptic statement to her the day of his death, intimating that he'd made an enemy of someone. The more she dwelled on his vague comment, the more it haunted her that she hadn't pressed for more details instead of chalking it up to paranoia and the immense pressure they were all under.

Frightened that she was about to go down the same morbid path as her friend, reason finally set in, convincing Trisha that it was best to head back inside. Only, as she turned around, it became instantly apparent that she was no longer alone; a figure was standing behind her, wearing a dance hoodie so that the person's facial features were mostly concealed amidst the dim moonlight.

"Oh, hey," Trisha quickly attempted to wipe the tear off her cheek, suddenly wishing the bangs of her hair were back covering it and embarrassed to be caught out of sorts like this by one of her contemporaries. "It's good to see you," she continued, doing her best to hide the fact that she wasn't feeling very social at the moment.

"Is it?" a cold, less-than-pleasant voice responded.

"Um, I don't…," Trisha fumbled her words and her soft brown eyes widened in confusion, "I don't understand. Why wouldn't it be?"

"You should've stayed out of this." There was a pause, allowing the import of the statement to sink in. "But you're involved now. Which, unfortunately, has also forced me to do something I don't want to do."

The breeze that had blown so wildly along the balcony suddenly stopped and there was a persisting stillness that took over, as if even the elements were waiting on edge. Unsure what to make of this conversation, a chill went up Trisha's spine and she decided that she wanted no further part of it. Still clearly inebriated, she stumbled back toward the hotel room, hoping to rejoin her friends who were partying inside.

Yet shockingly, as Trisha walked by, the edge of a hand came swinging toward her throat, colliding violently with her windpipe. Trisha doubled back from the force of the impact, gasping for breath and clutching at her neckline. Her eyes went wide in disbelief, completely stunned at what had happened. Before she could react, her attacker was on her, forcefully shoving against her chest and pushing Trisha back toward the balcony's edge.

Attempting to cry for help, Trisha found that she could barely talk, her trachea having been fractured by the precision blow. In an instant, her body was pressed up against the railing, the speed of her attacker shocking, and leaving her no time to react. Before she knew it, she was bent over the side of the rail, perilously close to falling over it.

"Please noooo!" she spoke in a weakened voice, simultaneously gasping for air.

But her words had no impact, and it soon became apparent they would be her last ones. Her attacker gave a final thrust and Trisha went careening over the side, desperately flailing for the rail, but unable to seize a grip. With a frozen expression of sheer terror pasted on her face, Trisha fell backwards and down toward the depths below, seemingly enveloped by the darkness. Unlike the red cup, her body went straight down, unaffected by the howling winds.

The killer observed the entire fall from the balcony above, sullen but aware that it was necessary. While not an originally intended victim, Trisha Beck's intuition had led to her downfall; her attacker couldn't risk being revealed. Trisha was a casualty of unfortunate circumstance. And now that she'd been eliminated, the next - and in the killer's eyes *more deserved* - murder could take place, that of the powerful and iniquitous Warren Steyn.

CHAPTER ONE
Connection Happens Through the Body

A light snowfall, the first of the season, was coming down in delicate flurries as Detective Evann Myrick pulled his vehicle along the emergency lane of the airport hotel. It was getting late, close to midnight, and this was the last place he wanted to be on his day off and at this late an hour. He'd been woken in the middle of the night, having received a call from Police Chief Clark, himself. The Chief had explained that there'd been a death, *likely homicide*, at the Silver Moose Lodge and Conference Center, and that he wanted Myrick to go check it out. Myrick had protested. There were two other homicide detectives on duty that could thoroughly investigate the matter. But the Police Chief had insisted that Myrick be the one to take the lead, as Myrick was his best investigator; and more importantly, it had been a longtime friend of the Chief's that had been the apparent victim of this heinous crime.

Myrick had eventually acquiesced, understanding that this was more of an order and less of a request, and so he'd quickly thrown on a change of clothes and made the trip over to the lodge, which was the largest one in Colorado Springs. Upon arrival, one of the first things he noticed was a young man and woman sitting on a bench, and an elegantly dressed woman pacing back and forth in front of them. Still sitting in the driver's seat of his SUV, Myrick cut the ignition, switched off the headlights and then sat patiently in the dark of his vehicle for a measured few minutes while he surveyed the scene.

He noticed that the beautifully dressed woman was puffing away nervously on a cigarette, pausing every so often to say something to the two sitting on the bench, as if expressing a train of thought. Intrigued, Myrick pulled out a small worn notepad from out of the pocket of his jacket, then fumbled inside the glove compartment in search of a pen. Once he found one, he began flipping through the notepad until he'd reached a clean page near the end, as he'd been taking notes in it for quite some time. On it, he began scratching out a few initial impressions, with abbreviated writing almost more cryptic than a waiter's when recording a customer's order.

Once he was finished, Myrick tapped on it three times with his forefinger (three being his favorite number), placed the notebook neatly back in the pocket of his wool grey herringbone coat and then proceeded to exit the driver side of the vehicle. Up ahead, the woman in the evening dress had stopped pacing, apparently aware of the approach of someone new and hoping it was the police detective she'd been promised would arrive soon. The woman sitting on the bench was decked out in all black attire: black leggings and a black low-cut shirt that read, "**I BUST MINE SO I CAN KICK BALL CHANGE YOURS**". Her clothes were almost as dark as her hair and the smoky, deep-colored eyeliner along the waterline of her eyes, gave her the perfect goth appearance. Myrick found it interesting that the girl was currently barefoot, although she did have a peculiar black bag in her hand that contained what Myrick guessed *might* be her shoes.

The young man next to her on the bench was dressed in casual clothing: faded jeans and a t-shirt. Myrick noticed the man's eyes were almost as red as the shirt he wore, as if he hadn't slept in quite some time. The man's face was round and boyish, and Myrick guessed he was no more than twenty-three, *maybe* twenty-four. He looked shaken, as if he'd seen a ghost, and Myrick noted that his foot was tapping nervously on the ground.

And then finally, there was the impeccably dressed woman, whose evening gown was as sophisticated as her overall visage. Now that he was standing only a few feet away from her, Myrick got a better glimpse of her and the luxurious diamond-studded dress she had on, which Myrick guessed (rightly) must've cost a small fortune. The flamboyance of her attire was matched by the magnificent jewelry that she wore along her neck, wrists and earlobes. As if to accentuate her glamorous look, there was even a hint of glitter evident along her cheeks and neckline. The woman's hair too was also neatly done in braids, beginning in the front and then gradually twisting into a spiral shape along the back of her head so that it had a flower-like form, a single diamond stud placed in the center to accessorize it. And on her feet she wore fancy suede boots, giving her the appearance of a southern belle, proof that such mythical creatures still existed.

Myrick also noticed that the woman with the perfect features and attire was attempting to wipe a tear from her eye; in the process, however, wisps of smoke from the cigarette dangling loosely between her fingers blew towards her so that it irritated her watery eyes even more. Suddenly, as if disgusted by the unhealthy habit, she tossed the completely spent cigarette to the ground, flashes of burnt-orange cutting through the darkness as it bounced along the curbside cement. Meanwhile, in her distracted state, she'd done a poor job wiping away the evidence of her sorrow. Now there was a noticeable dark-colored smear just below her eyes, as if her tears had blemished the mascara that had been meticulously (and heavily) applied earlier. And no matter how beautiful her attire… and hair… and jewelry… and boots were, they were no distraction from the stark remnants of mascara, which the woman seemed completely unaware had affected her appearance.

"Are you the lead detective?" the woman in the elegant gown demanded almost immediately, her voice nervous and scattered, and Myrick instantly could feel she had a chatty nature. "Because the other two bumbling fools your department sent over are already messing up the investigation."

"Be patient, Ellen," the girl in the goth attire cut in, referring to her friend by her first name, "let the man do his job. No one's messing up things. I know you're upset. We all are. I'm sure they'll get this figured out." The girl then turned to Myrick, and her eyes widened slightly as she spoke. "You *are* going to figure out what happened, right?"

"I hope so," Myrick answered. "But I do have a few questions for the three of you that might at least get me off to a good start." And as he spoke, Myrick reached inside his coat and pulled out the weathered notepad once again.

"Fire away." The girl in the stark black clothing was matter-of-fact; and Myrick glanced over momentarily with a smile, aware that the girl, despite likely being in her early-twenties, possessed both a maturity and determination unique for her age.

"Ok, before I begin," Myrick had his trusty notebook now in his hand as he spoke, "let's get everyone's names… *because if names are not correct, language will not be in accordance with the truth of things*," Myrick emphasized the words that he'd heard his father speak many times growing up on their simple dairy farm in Julian, North Carolina. Advice that had seemed to Myrick quite dull at the time, but which had gained powerful meaning as he pursued a career in police work.

"Confucius, right?" the girl immediately guessed.

"Yes." Myrick was impressed, again noting that the girl was quite sharp. "*And* my father," he added.

"My name's Ellen," the woman in the diamond-studded dress spoke up quickly, apparently eager to evidence how cooperative she was in the investigation, "Ellen Cromwel. This is my event. It's a weekend of West Coast Swing competitions and workshops… plus we've added a retreat to the hot springs for anyone who can stay over until Monday."

"Oh good." Myrick was a bit surprised that the woman in the frantic state was also responsible for having put together the entire dance event, as Myrick had been informed that close to five hundred people had traveled to Colorado Springs just to be there for it. "Well, in that case, you'll likely be a great help to me."

"I hope so."

"And you?" Myrick turned to the only male in the group. He had a boyish face, large wide set, almond-colored eyes and his head turned slightly at an angle as the question was asked, giving him the appearance of a harmless Labrador puppy.

"Jonathan Scott," the boyish man offered.

"And are you one of the co-producers of this event also?"

"No." Jonathan's eyes widened in apparent amusement, although they still possessed a level of nervousness. "No, I'm just the videographer for it."

"That's helpful to know also," Myrick nodded his head pensively, simultaneously recording a quick thought in his notebook. "I take it then you can provide me with the recording of the evening, as I've been informed the victim died inside the ballroom."

"Sure," Jonathan answered back quickly. "Although, Warren died while sitting down at one of the side tables. I haven't had a chance to review the footage so I'm not certain if we were on a wide shot or a close up when it happened. Our attention was on the competition that was taking place; it's difficult to capture all of the action with forty or so dancers out there at the same time."

"I'd imagine it is," Myrick's eyebrows inched upward as he considered the point. Of course, this subject was also entirely outside his expertise; he'd never danced a day in his life. Well, except for one poorly considered attempt at a friend's wedding shortly after graduating college; and that decision hadn't ended well, as he'd stepped all over the girl's feet and he didn't have another date with her after that. "And you," Myrick finally continued, his attention now on the girl in the goth attire, "could you tell me your name?"

"It's Jayde... spelled with a 'y'," she added, as she could see that Myrick was jotting everything down. She was also intrigued to know what he was writing, given she was curious by nature, not really saying much, but also paying attention to what was going on around her. "Jayde Ch'en."

Myrick was an incredibly quick study of people and he had an innate ability to size them up pretty accurately; guessing that Jayde was not only an observant person but that details mattered to her as well. He noted to himself that she'd likely be a good source of information, and that he should definitely follow up with her later, given it was possible she had seen and heard things that the others perhaps hadn't; possibly some of which she might not be comfortable sharing out in the open.

"Let me ask you this," Myrick decided to get down to the heart of the matter, "where were you sitting when the victim died?"

"I wasn't," Jayde replied, purposely phrasing her responses cryptically. She liked to keep people guessing. It added an element of suspense to things.

"Then where were you standing?" Myrick was willing to play this game, but only because he was trying to get a read on the personalities of the people around him.

"Actually, I was dancing," Jayde revealed. "I was competing on the dance floor."

"So the competition had already started," Myrick replied, although his attention was back on Ellen, who he knew was also the director of the event.

"Yes," Ellen chimed in, "but it's more complicated than that. There are different levels of competition - Novice, Intermediate, Advanced, All-Star..."

"And the victim died *watching* the competition?"

"Yes, that's correct," Ellen explained, somberly. "It happened while the Advanced dancers were on the floor."

"How many people were competing?"

"There were forty-two out there at that time."

"And so that means you can at least rule out forty-two potential suspects," Jayde cut in, excited to play a little detective herself.

"You would hope so, but we'll see," Myrick added, and Jayde was less than happy with his response, having assumed he'd give more credence to her supposition.

Myrick jotted down a few more thoughts in his notepad, then folded it back up and placed it inside his jacket pocket, indicating that he was done with his questioning of the three… at least for now.

"Could you direct me to the deceased… and to those two bumbling officers you mentioned earlier?"

"Yes, of course," Ellen replied quickly, and it was clear that she was going to be staying as close to Myrick as possible during the investigation, especially given this was her event and the last thing she needed was bad publicity among the dance community. It was already incredibly gossipy by nature, almost to a high school level. "They're in the ballroom. I'll take you there."

Ellen walked past the bench, leaving both Jayde and Jonathan behind. And, as he went to follow Ellen, Myrick noted that Jayde had broken out a pack of cigarettes - menthols - and was lighting one up, exhibiting that her nerves weren't quite as calmed as she might have originally let on.

Once through the glass entry door to the hotel, Myrick could see he was now inside the conference center's expansive hallway. Exhibitor booths were set up all throughout; some selling dresses, some dance shoes and there were even massage stations set up in the far corner. It was a quick introduction to Myrick on the unique needs of the dance community, given he had very little prior experience with it. He also noted that the hallway was full of people milling about; all of which appeared antsy and confused, but also not yet willing to return to their rooms, as many - maybe most - of them preferred to be the first in the know and wanted to be there when the officers emerged from the ballroom with any updates.

Ellen pushed past the multitude of dancers, beckoning Myrick to follow close behind, which he readily did. It was impossible to entirely ignore the stares of the people all around him. Most of the participants at the event knew Ellen; her position as the director came with a level of celebrity status. It was the person who she was currently escorting - the hastily dressed, plain-clothes detective with the three-day stubble beard and the dark circles around his eyes - that the attendees at the event were curious to find out more about.

The double doors to the ballroom were shut tight and there was a volunteer out front, sitting on a stool, and ensuring no one entered without permission. But, as soon as she saw Ellen approaching, the volunteer opened the door and allowed Ellen and Myrick to proceed inside. Immediately, Myrick could see that the ballroom was relatively empty. There were rows and rows of chairs in front of him and then in the very center of the room was a large wooden floor, which Myrick guessed was where all the theatrics had taken place that evening. Glancing around, he spotted the two officers he was looking for. They were still muddling their way through their investigation just as Ellen had explained, and so Myrick made his way over to them.

Myrick turned to the nearest officer, Detective Stephen Reynolds. "What can you tell me so far, Steve?" Myrick pressed.

"Not much really. It's too early to tell what happened. Might have been a spiked drink. Might have been a sudden heart attack as well," Reynolds explained, stroking the edge of his thick mustache as he spoke, as if that gave depth to his thoughts. "Medical examiner will be able to tell us more."

"It's murder," Ellen chimed in unexpectedly, unable to keep her opinion to herself. "I know, it is. This is the dance community's third death in over a month. Something terrible is going on."

Detective Reynolds decided it might be best at that point to escort Ellen out of the room. Emotions were running high, understandably, and it was oftentimes best in those type situations to remove any undue suggestibility so that the facts could speak for themselves.

Seeing Reynolds take a step toward Ellen, Myrick understood why Reynolds was doing so, but he had a contrary thought about the value of Ellen's interruption and so he threw in his two cents. "It's all right, Steve... let's go ahead and hear her out."

"I'm sorry," Ellen added, immediately regretting her outburst. She'd not intended to interfere with their investigation, and she knew the officer was right in his assessment, emotions *were* getting the best of her. "It's just... Warren and I used to compete together. I've known him for most my life. He was the most amazing person. He was so talented. We even won a U.S. Open Swing Dance Championship together... and now he's gone."

"Any reason why someone would want to kill him, ma'am?" Myrick asked in a concerned tone.

"No," Ellen answered back emphatically. "He was liked by everyone. Sure there's a level of politics to these events… and even backstabbing… that's going to happen in a high-stakes environment like this… everyone wants to reach pro status even though only so many can be. But Warren…" Ellen stammered with her words, "he was the *least* political of all of us. He'd reached the pinnacle in dance long ago, but it wasn't what made him happy. He didn't want to compete anymore. He didn't want to be treated like a celebrity. He just came to the events, danced and enjoyed being around his favorite people. They were his extended family."

"I'd assume traveling to all these events around the country gets expensive," Myrick pointed out.

"It does. But most dancers… the good ones… they obtain sponsors… or earn free entry fees and hotel stays by winning events. So that's how they can afford to keep competing on the circuit."

"And Warren Steyn? You said he didn't compete anymore."

"Warren was wealthy. I mean, he didn't brag about it. He wasn't extravagant. In fact, just the opposite. But it was still obvious he had money… maybe even more than he knew what to do with. In fact, he'd just announced he was going to renew his sponsorship of the Colorado Springs WestieFest."

"Which is this event, correct?" Myrick looked over at a banner-type sign hanging on the far wall which read, "Welcome To The Eleventh Annual CSWF" and connected the dots from there."

"Yes."

"And so Warren Steyn was the one who bankrolled your event."

"He was. What's your point, detective?" Ellen's tone changed and she became suddenly defensive. "Because if you're considering me a suspect, I'd be the *least* likely to kill the man who was financially helping to make all this possible."

"There's no need to get upset, ma'am," Reynolds interrupted, revealing his unique ability to be both courteous and condescending at the same time. "We don't even really have a reason yet to be sure this was a homicide."

"Maybe I should go ahead and take a look at the body now, Steve," Myrick interrupted, deciding this was a good time to change the subject; his eyes trained on the covered victim lying along the very edge of the dance floor and just a foot away from where he'd been sitting before keeling over instantly in death.

After agreeing with the suggestion, Detective Reynolds instructed Ellen to remain where she was as he and Myrick went over to inspect the victim together. Once there, Reynolds knelt down and lifted the cover up slightly, careful to do so at an angle that kept Ellen from seeing the face of her deceased friend. Myrick then scanned over Warren Steyn's body, searching for any sort of clues."

"This is interesting," Myrick noted eventually. "You see the extensive swelling and the redness near his Adam's apple... what do you make of that?"

"Yes, looks a bit like a nasty bug bite," Reynolds guessed, assuming that it would've taken a particularly venomous spider or wasp to create such an intense level of irritation to the skin and in such an unfortunate spot.

"Perhaps. But wasps and spiders don't leave a stinger... and if you look closely, there's clearly something lodged in the exact center where the redness is centralized. I do agree the irritation was caused by an external toxin," Myrick conceded, "but not from an insect. I'm willing to bet Warren Steyn has been felled by a poison-tipped needle of some sort."

"That's a heck of a leap there, Maddog," Reynolds called Myrick by his nickname. He'd been given it by an instructor in the academy who was confounded by the unique spelling of Myrick's middle name - Madocs - and so he'd simply started referring to him as Maddog; and the nickname stuck, especially given it also seemed to perfectly match his dogged determination when solving cases.

"Maybe not as much of a leap as you think," Myrick went to elaborate. "Look at the scratch marks along the side of his neck."

"The bite probably itched. He dug into it."

"I don't think so. I'm willing to venture that was his last desperate act, feeling the sting on his throat and trying to claw it away." Myrick then stood up, his focus changed, and he walked back to Ellen, speaking to her as he walked over. "I'd like to go ahead now and take a look at the video footage. Do you think your videographer... Jonathan Scott... can set that up for me?"

"I'm sure he can, Detective," Ellen was quick to confirm. She'd positioned herself on the far side of a table so that she couldn't see Warren's body, and her eyes were purposefully averted to the side as she spoke. The whole event had been beyond traumatizing, and she was ready to be anywhere other than in that room with the detectives - so the suggestion to go elsewhere was readily received by her.

"Very well. I have a feeling we'll know more once I've viewed it."

Ellen pulled out her cellphone, placing a call to Jonathan, who she was certain was still sitting outside on the bench, keeping Jayde company. Sure enough, after picking up the phone and hearing Ellen's request, Jonathan let her know that he'd be right in and suggested they meet in the video booth. Ellen then hung up her phone and asked Myrick to follow her, which he did, fascinated to see what the video would reveal; or perhaps any clues as to who could have set up in a place hidden from the camera's view, which Myrick was aware a clever killer just might do.

CHAPTER TWO
Video Is Helpful in Self-Evaluation

The editing room wasn't actually much more than a minimalist boardroom in the back of the conference center, and felt like anything other than a space for creatives to work. In the center of the 12-by-18 foot space was a single table with a gray and white tablecloth draped haphazardly over it. The table was surrounded by four sleek black mesh chairs, like those seen often in a commercial workspace. The only other decor in the sparse setting was on the wall: a 65 inch flat screen TV, which had already been cued up and which had on it a freeze frame of an empty dance floor and two officers standing next to a now-deceased Warren Steyn.

"This is where the recording was cut," Jonathan explained. "We'd accidentally left camera number one rolling so it captured everything up to this point."

"Better to have more than we need, than not enough," Myrick noted, grateful. He'd taken his tweed flat cap off for the first time, herringbone in pattern like the coat he wore, and placed it on the edge of the diminutive table, revealing his unkempt hair, which was salt and pepper colored like the tablecloth. He was scratching the top of his head, as if in thought, when he went to speak again, "Can you take me to about ten minutes before our victim suffers his unfortunate death?"

"Sure, just give me a moment," Jonathan answered back, happy to accommodate but also satisfied and relieved to know he was a help in the investigation. In front of him was a metallic laptop. It was already open and a mirrored image of the dance footage was presently on the screen in front of him. Below the video clip were playback controls and so Jonathan used them to scrub through the footage.

At the same time, Myrick watched as a sea of dancers walked backwards, flooding into the ballroom again, and at high speed. Some were returned to their tables... some to the dance floor... and some to a crescent shaped line of chairs at the front of the room. Jonathan kept scrolling back until the data below the footage read, "ECC 03:02:04", and which Jonathan explained represented Error Correction Code memory and a timestamp of three hours, two minutes and four seconds into the footage.

"This far enough back?" he finally asked, as he reached a stopping point in the recording.

"I believe so," Myrick answered, and as he studied the frozen image on the screen, he sized up the group that he considered to be his primary suspects. "Who are the sixteen individuals in the chairs at the far end of the room?"

"Those are the judges... the pros," Ellen cut in. This was her event and so Jonathan had no problem deferring to her while she explained the particulars. "They're watching the competition; scoring the dancers who are on the floor."

"Would these same sixteen have been at the other events... when the two other deaths occurred?"

"It's possible. The pros make their money by traveling to events, but there's also a level of jockeying for those coveted judging spots... and each event coordinator decides who will or won't be invited. But all you have to do is go online to see who was present at the various venues. The details of each sanctioned event are archived by the World Swing Dance Council."

Myrick had his trusty notepad out again and he went to jotting down that information. It also occurred to him how little he knew about the dance community; and its eccentricities were far more complex than he'd originally understood. A realist by nature, Myrick quickly came to grips with the fact that his unfamiliarity with dance culture was going to be a handicap in his investigation. Fortunately, Ellen was doing a good job of filling him in on the more idiosyncratic details; and her chatty nature was proving more beneficial than he'd originally expected.

"Pardon my unfamiliarity, but what exactly is the World Dance Swingers Council?" Myrick humbly asked, making no attempt at false pretenses, and fumbling both the order and the *meaning* of the organization's title.

"It's where all West Coast *Swing* events and results are recorded throughout the entire dance circuit. You'll hear people refer to this dance as 'WCS' a lot, which just stands for 'West Coast Swing'. Colorado Springs WestieFest is a WCS sanctioned event. The dancers that you see on the screen before you are all competing in the Advanced Level. If they do well enough, then they'll eventually become All-Stars. Most of the pro level dancers are at the All-Star level."

"So, sort of like a minor league baseball player trying to make it to the Majors," Myrick used his favorite pastime as an analogy.

"I'd imagine so," Ellen answered back, although not entirely familiar with the hierarchy of baseball. "If you work hard enough, you can get to the pro level in just a few years."

"Or for some of us, it takes a lifetime," Jonathan jested, a hint of self-deprecation in his humor. "West Coast Swing is not for the faint of heart."

"So you're a pro also?" Myrick remarked.

"No, no..." Jonathan quickly replied, as if a bit embarrassed. The features of his face turned downward, along with his gaze, and he was no longer making eye contact with the detective as he spoke. "I'm just a small fish in a big pond. The real pros are the ones sitting in those chairs at the head of the room."

"You're being too modest," Ellen chimed in. "Jonathan's got a lot of potential. He'll eventually get there. He's in the Intermediate Level," Ellen explained to the detective, although her words seemed to be doing little to alleviate Jonathan's uneasy self-consciousness.

"Well, I'm sure you could spend hours getting me up to speed on this West Swing..."

"West *Coast* Swing," Ellen corrected.

"Yes, West Coast Swing. So let's just go ahead and play the video from here, if you don't mind. See what we can see."

Jonathan obliged, cutting the lights off in the room and then pressing the play button on his laptop. Myrick, in turn, watched in fascination as the dancers, who were currently depicted on the video screen, spun and twirled and dipped and did all sorts of other smooth maneuvers. There were forty-two of them, just as Ellen had explained earlier, and he was impressed by how perfect their timing and routines seemed to be. He could also see the soon to be deceased, Warren Steyn, sitting at a table no more than a foot or so from the dance floor. Because of the positioning of the camera in the rear of the room, Myrick only had a shot of the back of Warren's head, but based on the way he was bobbing his shoulders to the music and talking to the people around him, it appeared Warren was in high spirits.

"This is a partner dance? Myrick asked over the music on the video: a TobyMac song, *Feel It*.

"Yes," Ellen simply replied.

"It all looks choreographed."

"It's not though. These dancers come from all around the country. They're then randomly assigned to perform together right before the competition starts. They don't even know what the song will be. The DJ starts the music and then they begin dancing."

"Quite impressive," Myrick replied, and he truly meant the compliment. Artists, in all their various forms, amazed him, particularly as Myrick functioned best when things followed a predictable pattern. In fact, Myrick was certain he did not possess a single creative bone in his body. He was unmatched when it came to processing facts and figures and numbers and all things *known* quantity. But the free flow nature of artistry was one of the concepts that he couldn't quite wrap his mind around. So when he watched others that possessed that unique skillset, he was always intrigued by the nature of it.

The video continued to play on the flat screen monitor, and they were just two minutes into it when the music stopped.

Suddenly, the lead dancers were instructed to rotate six positions to their right, so that they were all standing in front of new partners.

"And what just happened there?" Myrick asked.

"To keep things fair, the leads are randomly assigned to new follows during the competition. They'll now all be dancing to a new song and with someone completely different, maybe someone they've never even met before."

"Sure enough, the music started again, this time a Blues song, with a completely different vibe: *Fifth of Whiskey, Case of the Blues*. Whereas before the dancers were moving around in quick fashion, this time they were slower and cooler in their footwork, and it allowed Myrick to really appreciate their timing and technique.

No more than a minute into this second song, and just as the music phrase was hitting a 32-count break, Warren could suddenly be seen clutching at the front of his throat. As Myrick had guessed, the scratch marks along Warren's neck were also clearly caused by him clawing at whatever was irritating him along the region of his Adam's apple. Despite the music still playing, those closest to Warren began glancing over in concern. Even the dancers on the floor stopped some of their routines, confused at the commotion taking place. The judges in their crescent-shaped circle at the head of the room, stood to their feet, desperately trying to see over the crowded dance floor and toward what was happening on the other side of it. And then, within a very short fifteen second period of time, Warren could be seen keeling over and out of his chair; tragically gasping for air, as he lay dying on the floor.

"Pause it here," Myrick cut through the quiet, and instantly Jonathan stopped the footage from playing.

The image on the screen was frozen in place again. This time on a room full of panicked and confused faces. Myrick got up out of his chair and walked over to the flat screen TV, wanting to get a closer look, studying each and every face visible on it, searching for any sort of clues. But all the expressions of the dancers seemed appropriately expressed. There were no "mysterious woman in a white dress standing unaffected on a grassy knoll"-type figures that stood out to Myrick.

Of course, that fact alone, however, didn't mean that Myrick couldn't make some important deductions from what they were seeing. He was still curiously studying the frozen feed on the screen when he went to speak again: "I'll need a list of the competitors who were on the floor during this particular timeframe. I'd also like to talk with each of them and the sixteen judges. Can you help me arrange that for tomorrow?"

"Of course," Ellen replied. "We're a close knit community. I'm sure everyone will be glad to cooperate."

"Good." Myrick's attention was still on the frozen screen shot, his focus on the sixteen judges at the very head of the room.

"What about the rest of the attendees?" Ellen pressed. The conference was scheduled to end tomorrow at four o'clock. Most have flights lined up shortly thereafter. Should we send out an email that everyone needs to make plans to stay an extra day or two so you can conduct your investigation?"

"No, that won't be necessary."

"Are you sure?" Ellen replied, confused.

"Yes, quite sure," Myrick replied as he finally turned around, finished examining the still frame and ready to wrap up his investigation for the night. "I'm relatively certain our victim was hit with some sort of poison dart in the front of the neck. Given where he was facing at the time and his position in the room, that eliminates the vast majority of those in attendance, as they would all be sitting behind him and wouldn't have a line of sight to exact the mortal wound. The murderer has already done us a favor and limited the pool of potential suspects. Anyone in this video not on the dance floor or judging those same competitors is free to return home."

There was a visible show of relief on Ellen's face as Myrick explained his theory, as she figured it also meant she'd likely been eliminated as a suspect as well. Still, she did her best to conceal that exuberance and instead nodded calmly. "I'll reach out to everyone and let them know."

"Much appreciated," Myrick replied, already walking back over to the table and picking up his tweed cap, then placing it back on his head, tilting it slightly downward over his forehead just as he liked to wear it. "One more thing, Ms. Cromwel," he then stopped before exiting the room. "Where were you when Warren Steyn was killed?"

"I was, um, backstage of course. I'd done the introduction before the Advanced Level competition... and I went behind the curtained area again afterward. Why?"

"Just making sure I cover all the bases."

"Of course," Ellen mumbled back, concerned.

"Very well. Let's commence interviews tomorrow morning at 7:30 sharp. We'll meet back here... You included, if you don't mind, Ms. Cromwel."

"Um, of course," Ellen agreed, shaken that she'd not been eliminated as a suspect after all.

"This particular room will work fine for them. Thank you both for your assistance, it's been invaluable. I'll have Detective Reynolds come by to pick up this video from you so that he can get it over to the police station and placed securely into evidence."

And with those final instructions, Myrick nodded, simultaneously tipping his cap to his accommodating host Ellen and the equally helpful videographer Jonathan, wishing them both a pleasant evening. Knocking his knuckles against the surface of the table three times out of habit, he then turned and exited the room.

Just as before, curious attendees were still wandering about in the expansive hallway, and Myrick correctly guessed that many hadn't accepted the inevitability that the weekend's festivities were over; and so he pushed his way through their numbers and out of the building, leaving them to their own devices. The night air was cool, but the snow had stopped falling. He looked down at his watch to see it had neared 1:00 a.m. Myrick hadn't been on scene for more than an hour or so, but already he had many of the answers he needed and his short time there had proven crucial. The Chief had been right to assign him to this one; their culprit was clever and it was going to take an equally brilliant mind to catch the vile perpetrator of Warren Steyn's death - which was a challenge uniquely suited for Myrick's remarkable ability to unravel mysteries. This is what he was born to do.

CHAPTER THREE
Roll Through Your Feet As You Dance

The front door to Myrick's quaint house creaked a bit as he pushed it open, and he fumbled around for the light switch while stepping hesitantly inside. The time was now an unconscionably late 1:30 in the morning; Myrick was spent but - now that his mind was racing - he also knew it would be entirely impossible to go back to sleep. One of the hardest things about being a homicide detective was the difficulty in setting work aside when off duty. The ability to do so was a highly coveted skill that they didn't adequately explain at the police academy, despite it being one of the most important for any law enforcement officer to possess. The cases, even the run-of-the-mill ones, oftentimes became all-consuming in nature. The detectives that got themselves in the most trouble were the ones who thought about their investigations 24/7, unable to have a life outside of work.

Myrick had learned this lesson the hard way, and understood better than most just how fleeting life could be. As he walked through the narrow hallway, there were pictures hanging all along the walls. In them were a younger version of Myrick with an absolutely stunning woman, possessing a glowing smile, standing alongside him. Each of the pictures were of the two and the various adventures they'd shared together, including their wedding day. Yet, Myrick knew these pictures were nothing more than distant memories at this point and times he could never have back, no matter how desperately he wished and prayed otherwise. And while the pictures did make him smile every so often, they also haunted him as well; reminding him of how much he'd lost with the passing of his wife, as Riley held his heart like none ever had before - or would again.

At the end of the hallway, Myrick turned a corner and was once again fumbling for a light switch, this time the one to the kitchen. It flickered as it came on, reminding Myrick that he needed to check the bulb on the light fixture that hung above the circular kitchen table. Making his way over to the stove, he took the steel kettle that was sitting on one of the burners. Myrick filled it with water, the running of the kitchen sink the only sound in the room and it had a soothing effect, like a cascading waterfall. Once filled, Myrick placed the kettle back on the stove and then went over to the kitchen table to sit down, almost collapsing into the cushioned seat.

As the steam rose in the room, it brought to mind the memory of better times, especially those with Riley around. She'd been his soulmate and things had never been the same after she'd passed away. Myrick felt it impossible to move on, although he'd made almost no effort to try, not willing to even risk the thought of letting the memory of her fade, including keeping the steel pot that she'd loved to make tea in. It'd been three years since she'd last been in the kitchen but little had changed in that passing of time and that was the way Myrick wanted it to remain.

Still, Myrick had his regrets as well, and those gnawed at him. He'd been relatively young on the police force back in those days, a rookie detective trying to make a name for himself. The hours were long and the cases were demanding. But with youth comes an extra level of vigor and Myrick had always been the prototypical cop - constantly on the job, even when he wasn't technically on the clock. His motives were admirable, even if the end result was particularly tragic. People needed him. Countless families were depending on him to solve crimes that had left them and their loved ones devastated. It was a heavy burden to bear: meeting with the family of a victim, sympathizing with their terrible loss, and hearing them voice heartfelt pleas for justice to be served; and Myrick found it impossible not to give *every* ounce of what he had and who he was to their cases.

Making matters more complicated, Myrick truly was one of the brightest minds ever to graduate from the academy. It was as if he was created to solve crimes; seeing the world through a completely different lens, capable of deciphering clues faster than most and possessing an uncanny ability to read other people. All of those were traits that made him the perfect crime-fighting detective, but not so much the ideal husband. That said, Myrick had loved Riley more than any man ever loved a woman; and so even though he'd been consumed by the demands of the profession, he'd put everything else he had into making sure she knew how important she was to him and how grateful he was for her patience with his career.

Riley had been an avid gardener. She could spend hours toiling away in the yard, growing vegetables, and herbs, and spices... and so many green-colored things; none of which actually interested Myrick, but all of which he'd enjoyed simply because he knew how much those things meant to her. So, in the midst of solving cases, on his days off he'd spend more than a few sitting in a quaint Adirondack chair in the backyard, talking with Riley and watching her garden. The peaceful setting also allowed his mind to wander; and so as he would sip his coffee, his thoughts inevitably would revert to his most stubborn of cases allowing him to unravel many of them, devoid of distractions.

These particular times were the ones Myrick loved to recall. The ones he didn't, however, revolved around Riley's wish to travel more. In college, she'd gone to Mexico City and stayed with a host family there, and she would recount the tales of all the adventures she went on and the wonderful people she'd met. She had longed desperately to return and she'd made that wish no secret to Myrick; so, in turn, he'd promised her they'd do so eventually. The plan was for him to work his tail off, establish himself in the detective division and then they'd take time away to travel the world. It was the perfect plan, until it didn't happen. Not long afterward, and one horribly fateful day, Myrick had come home to find Riley crying at that same kitchen table. She'd been diagnosed with a malignant cancer.

Three anguished months later and Riley was gone. There would be no travel to exotic locations, just hospital visits and long nights full of suffering. Myrick had never left Riley's side during that time. All the leave he'd accumulated at the police department did go to good use, at least; he'd spent every ounce of it at home caring for the person he loved most in the world. But even having every second of that time with her wasn't enough, and when she passed away, so did a part of Myrick. There'd been no one else in his life since then... and, more importantly, he didn't want there to be.

Myrick now leaned back in his chair, and then did the one thing he'd promised himself he wouldn't do anymore; he spent his time at home thinking about a case. It was a hard and fast rule that he'd determined never again to break during those last few months he'd had with Riley, as he'd suddenly understood what was most important in life. The rule, though, had lost most of its import once she was gone and he was left alone in the one bedroom townhome that they'd shared. It was hard for a man to find solace in such a place, especially one whose mind was capable of incredibly complex problem solving and endless contemplation, as his clearly was.

Fortunately, for him, Myrick had one other respite in his life, and it lay dead center on the cedar table in front of him. As he leaned back in his chair, Myrick glanced over at it, as if pondering its meaning and what to do with it at the moment, unsure if he wanted to remain in his work thoughts, running through the possibilities of this newest mystery, or turn his attention to something that in many ways was equally pressing and important, and which would also distract him from work. Finally, Myrick made his decision, sitting forward and reaching over to pick up the lone book.

This was Myrick's nightly ritual, and it was his most important one. He'd lost Riley, but she'd made sure he hadn't also lost his faith in the process. Riley had left him a book in her final months, and she'd even had it monogrammed with his name in small, gold letters in the corner. The book was a Bible and she made him promise that he'd read it and keep it with him, even after she was gone. Of course, religion wasn't really Myrick's thing. Cold hard facts, not human-based conjecture, had far more meaning to him. Still, he kept the Book... and because he did so, he kept one of the most defining aspects of Riley with him as well.

Each night he'd sit at the kitchen table and read it; originally thinking that he was doing Riley a favor, but soon learning how much she'd saved his life by insisting he keep it with him. It was a two-fold gift, and Myrick wondered often if Riley had known all along it would be particularly so for someone like him. The passages of the Bible were far more intricate and held a deeper meaning than Myrick had thought. He'd studied them fiercely; sometimes trying to disprove a point and sometimes trying to detect an underlying brilliance in what was recorded in the thin India paper pages, and which would be missed by most. And the more he did so, the more he'd become transfixed by delving into it, as if trying to solve perhaps the greatest mystery of all; meanwhile, a sense of peace would oftentimes replace the anxiety that would've otherwise consumed him.

Eventually, although it wasn't easy by any stretch, Myrick was able to stop thinking about this latest case long enough to pick up the Bible and transition into reading it once more. Flipping through it, he came to one dog-eared page and opened the Book to it. He was on *1 Chronicles... 15:29...* and laughed to himself a bit as he looked down and read the passage, intrigued by the timing of the words that were written:

> *As the ark of the covenant of the Lord was entering*
> *the City of David, Michal daughter of Saul*
> *watched from a window. And when she saw King*

David dancing and celebrating, she despised him
in her heart.

"Dance can trigger some strong emotions," Myrick muttered to himself, "and equally fascinating behavior."

After contemplating the dramatic circumstances of David and Michal, and also wondering if it wasn't more than mere coincidence that he'd happened upon that particular passage, Myrick went back to reading. Before long, he'd forgotten about the case and Warren's apparent murder. He no longer found himself sizing up each and every detail of the video he'd seen, his incredible memory able to recall each frame, as if he had the entire video available for playback before him. And he was even able to stop thinking about the wink he'd noticed between one of the pros sitting on the far end of the room, as she'd clearly looked in the direction of, *and right at*, Warren Steyn only seconds before he was killed.

Thirty minutes (and a steaming cup of Chamomile tea) later and Myrick started to feel the first waves of drowsiness mercifully come over him. Eventually, he folded the cherished Bible up, placed it neatly back in its spot at the center of the table, and made his way out of the kitchen and over to his bedroom. The aged wood of the floorboards creaked noticeably with each step he took down the hallway, and the noise stood out starkly in the otherwise eerily quiet house, a subtle reminder to Myrick once again of just how alone he was.

Entering the bedroom, Myrick kicked his shoes off at the edge of the bed and sat down, exhaustion starting to take over. He then remembered the tweed cap on his head. Taking it off, he looked over at the dresser on the far end of the room, which was no more than a few feet away, but felt like a vast distance given his weary state. Myrick had no energy to get up once again, so he tossed the cap across the room and it spiraled through the air, like a frisbee. He watched as it landed perfectly on the top of the dresser, coming to a stop just where he would've wanted to place it, and he knew he couldn't have replicated that feat even if he'd tried. Which made Myrick wonder... *was it possible? Could one of the dancers have pulled off the shot that killed Warren even in the midst of competition? If so, it was a brilliantly conceived cover for the murder,* he considered for a brief second, but then just as quickly dismissed the thought; he needed the rest. Tomorrow, was going to be a long day, full of unexpected twists and turns.

*****

Myrick was a man possessing many quirks and habits. They helped him maintain a sense of sanity in a profession marked by constant turmoil. Over the years, he'd responded to the scenes of some of the most horrific crimes imaginable: homicides, sexual assaults, home invasion robberies, child abuses and other unthinkable acts. And in that time, he'd had to come to grips with the unassailable fact that evil existed and it did take its fair share of innocent victims more times than he wanted to admit. Witnessing so much grief, many would've lost hope, but not Myrick. It inspired him to do even more good. That was the beauty of being in law enforcement, it was a tangible way to restore people's faith that justice would ultimately win out.

Warren Steyn's death was yet another example of that tragic juxtaposition and the war between immorality and virtue, and Myrick was convinced he'd have to act fast, certain that more potential deaths were on the horizon. In fact, as his cellphone rang, and he spotted the number on it, he had a gut feeling that he was about to receive more bad news. Reaching for the cellphone by his bed, Myrick noticed on the table side clock that the time read 5:17 a.m.; he'd only been asleep for a few hours. He was kicking himself for not turning the ringer off before passing out for the night, but that was more evidence of his exhausted state and why he needed the rest so desperately.

The number on the phone was not one he'd saved in his contacts, but judging by the out-of-state area code, he was pretty certain it was from Ellen Cromwel, as he'd given her his number to call in case of emergency. So, when he picked up, and heard her frantic voice, he wasn't entirely surprised.

"There's been another murder!" Ellen exclaimed in a panic. "Jill is dead!"

"Calm down, Ms. Cromwel," Myrick replied, wiping the tired from his eyes and realizing he had no choice now but to wake up. This wasn't the first - and it wouldn't be the last - time that he'd gotten a homicide call in the early morning hours and so even that tragic news didn't faze him much. Instead, he kept a level head about him as he began to push for more information: "Who's Jill?"

"Jill McKenna is one of the pros," Ellen answered, doing her best not to get too flustered again. "She was found shot in her hotel room."

"Who discovered her there?"

"Me," Ellen revealed, and by the silence on the other end of the line, it was clear that even Myrick was a bit taken aback.

"You found her at…" Myrick paused to glance over at the clock again, assuming he must have read the time wrong, but instead saw it now read 5:19 a.m. "You found her at 5-something in the morning?" he continued, clearly perplexed.

"Yes, well you have to understand the dance community," Ellen tried to explain, only to be interrupted by Myrick on the other end of the line.

"Clearly I do not."

"Dancers are mostly nocturnal by nature, especially the pros. We come to these conferences, compete, nap in between and then spend all night social dancing. It's just what we do."

"Well, I'm pretty certain we shut all that down once the investigation commenced," Myrick noted.

"And your officers did." There was a moment of dead air before Ellen continued. "But that just meant that we all bounced between rooms talking and drinking. There's a lot of nervous energy going round right now. There was no way any of us were going to sleep. And like it or not, there are aspects of these conferences that are very much like high school… so once the rumor mills start swirling, there's no stopping them or the gossip."

"Okay, hold on for a minute," Myrick cut Ellen off again. He was now resigned to the circumstances, and aware of the seriousness of the situation; and so, pulling his weary body out of bed, he made his way back down the narrow hallway and toward the kitchen area. A single console table was the only furniture in the hallway and on it were just three items: a ceramic Carolina Mudcats coffee mug, a baseball so worn that the red stitching was starting to visibly fray and a picture frame with a teenage Myrick and his dad at a minor league baseball game.

Myrick swiped two of the items off the table - the coffee mug and the baseball, then turned the corner into the kitchen. The coffee cup he placed down on the kitchen counter. The baseball he kept in his free hand and began tossing methodically up in the air. Meanwhile, now that he was in a place to think better, he continued: "Tell me more about the gossip that was taking place."

"Well, there was all sorts of talk. And we were all in Deion's room... about seven of us; and Deion says that he heard Jill murmuring about how she had a hunch who the killer might be and how she couldn't wait to talk with you in the morning," Ellen was back to racing a mile a minute, her voice hurrying more and more with each spoken word; still Myrick let her ramble on, not wanting to interrupt her train of thought, "And then I figured I should go to her room and find out whether the rumors were true. This is my event so I thought it was only right she told me. But when I got there, she was just lying there on the floor, dead... caught between the doorframe and the hallway, as if she'd peeked out to see someone and then was shot."

"Any witnesses? Anyone say they heard anything?" Myrick pressed. He'd stopped tossing the ball into the air, but only long enough to get the coffeemaker going, needing some caffeine in his system so he could be thinking sharp. As soon it began brewing, he went back to tossing the baseball again with his free hand.

"No, nothing. Which is so strange because that entire floor, that block of rooms, was all dancers. But nobody says they heard or saw a thing," Ellen paused before continuing, as if overcome with emotion yet again. "I'm sorry, detective. I didn't want to call you so late. I just didn't know what else to do. Can you please hurry here?"

"Yes, I'm heading that way now," Myrick replied. "Keep things calm until I arrive, Ms. Cromwel."

Ellen agreed to do so and then Myrick hung up the phone. A few minutes later and he could hear the steady drip of the coffeemaker slowly cease so that he now had a full pot to work with, and which he very much needed at the moment. Myrick poured himself as much as he could into the ceramic coffee cup, then took a healthy sip from it as he made his way outside into the bitter cold. There was a thin layer of frost on his windshield, and so he sat behind the wheel of his vehicle for a few moments while he let the defroster do its job. The thin line of ice slowly faded away, leaving him a small hole to peer through, which Myrick would soon learn was about the same size window of space the killer had to work with when the fatal shot was discharged and Jill's life was tragically taken.

CHAPTER FOUR
Create a Center-to-Center Connection

"This is exactly how we found her, Maddog," Steve explained. He'd still been on call when the *10-54, Possible Dead Body*, went out over the radio, as he had the entirety of the grueling late night shift, given he was the newest detective on the homicide team. He also looked even more tired than Myrick, and Myrick genuinely felt for him. Steve had young kids. He'd hooked up with a cute blonde, ten years younger than he was. Next thing he knew they were married and starting a family. It was common knowledge around the police force that Steve was juggling more at home than he was at work, knocking out his 1900 to 0700 shift, then heading home just as the little ones were starting to stir. The man got maybe four hours of sleep in a day. It sounded brutal, especially to Myrick, who had no desire to have kids this late in age.

"Her hand must've been on the door, propping it open when she was shot," Steve continued with his preliminary findings. "I'm thinking the shooter was someone she knew for her to answer it at that late hour."

"Good thinking," Myrick agreed, as he slid on a pair of vinyl boot coverings over his shoes, similar to the ones that Steve was wearing and that were used to protect the crime scene from contamination. "Although, I speculate it was also someone she wasn't so sure she wanted inside her room either. Must've been a brief conversation between her side of the door and the perpetrator's... maybe to limit witnesses... and then the killer shot. I don't imagine this encounter lasted more than a few seconds or so."

"Medical examiner should be here soon. He may have some initial thoughts," Steve explained, but he could see that Myrick was no longer listening and that he was more fixated on a search for clues.

Myrick noted the position of Jill McKenna's body, which was wedged up between the door and a nearby wall. She had what appeared to be an inch in diameter bullet wound just slightly to the left of the breastbone, and where her heart would be located, which had likely killed her almost instantly, meaning there had been no struggle or movement of her body after she was shot. The white tank top she wore was saturated by blood that matched in color the red of the yoga pants she was wearing. The only other notable clothing she had on were black scrunch-shaft bootie shoes that Myrick noticed had suede on the bottom and were unlike the soles of any pair he'd seen or worn before.

The room itself was in surprising disarray as well. There was clothing scattered all over the floor and several suitcases were open, as if they'd never been unpacked but simply dug through in a rush whenever an item was needed. On the mirrored counter was a hairdryer, flatiron and a dizzying array of makeup products; all of which were scattered across the counter in haphazard fashion, *surprisingly* fitting for the overall feel of the disorganized room. Myrick chalked all this up, not to a struggle, but to the fact that his victim must've been rushing around all weekend, likely busy between competitions and judging... and apparently even frequent wardrobe changes.

Eventually though, Myrick spotted an item that did interest him and that he figured would shed more light on the murder that'd occurred. On the bed, as if tossed there at some point, was a cellphone. Myrick picked it up and pressed along the side so that it sprung to life. Looking down at the blueish-hued screen, he could see that the phone was locked, but that it did have a couple of missed calls and a message on it.

While the entirety of the text wasn't visible, he could see the beginnings of what it read, "See u downstairs in 20..." it started off, but that was all Myrick could read without having the passcode to access the rest of it. The text was time stamped at 5:06 a.m. and displayed that the sender was a "Dee" and which Myrick guessed was likely short for Deion. Seeing this, Myrick realized it was probably a good time to begin his interviews... and he was going to start with a man who's name had already been highlighted on his list - Deion Mitchell. The same Deion who Ellen had first mentioned on the earlier phone call and whose number happened to be the last message sent to Jill before her death.

There was an evidence technician now on scene and she was taking pictures. Myrick knew that her name was Rosa and he'd worked with her many times before. She was meticulous in nature and more often than not, the photos she took and the evidence she collected ended up being pivotal in solving a case. Myrick decided it was time to walk over and get her input.

"Let me guess, this one is a favor for the Police Chief," Rosa spoke perceptively before Myrick had even reached her.

"Yeah, I really need to get better at saying no to things," Myrick smirked.

Rosa nodded her agreement and then glanced down at the female victim; the camera she held and had been using to document the scene now dangling in front of her chest attached to a neck strap. "I heard she was a dancer... one of the pros."

"She was. I'd seen her on the video footage."

"She was a beautiful girl too. Looks young, I'd guess maybe mid-thirties. I always have the hardest time with victims like these. Young, talented, and so much life left to live... but now gone. Hard to believe sometimes that things like this happen."

"It is," Myrick mused, and Rosa immediately picked up on a hint of wistfulness in his reply, aware that Myrick's wife had died in the prime of her life as well.

"Anything in particular you want a picture of?" Rosa wisely changed the subject.

"Yes. Yes, there is. Could you take a close-up of her shoes?"

"Sure, but why the shoes?"

"Just a hunch," Myrick explained. "And do me a favor... get a close-up on the soles of them also. I'm going to leave you with this for a little bit. There's a few people I need to interview before they leave town."

As Myrick was walking out of the room, he could see that the medical examiner had arrived. Myrick briefly explained to him that once Rosa had finished collecting any evidence and was done taking photos, the ME would be free to transport

McKenna's body to the morgue. After that, Myrick put in a quick call to Ellen and asked that she start getting some of the conference attendees ready for interviews, starting with Deion Mitchell.

The interviews took place in the same spot as Myrick had watched the replay of the video. Like before, in the sparse room, there was a square-shaped table situated in the center; only this time there were only two chairs, one on each side of the table. Myrick took a seat in one of the chairs and then placed a case file neatly in front of him, a case file which came from the police station and which contained not only the reports regarding the investigation into Warren Steyn's death, but also those of the two potential homicides that preceded him.

Alone in the room, Myrick glanced once again through the reports that had been provided from the other two jurisdictions. One death had happened in Sacramento just a month prior; the victim's name was Yves Lavigne. Lavigne was a renowned dancer, who'd flown in from Paris for the conference. His wife was a dancer too, and usually they traveled as a pair, but they'd become recently separated. Police had spoken to her over the phone, informing her of her husband's death, but they did very little follow up on the circumstances of their split, especially since the original thought was that the death was due to suicide; the victim having died of an apparent drug overdose. But Myrick was beginning to second-guess that finding and noted this was an issue that he wanted to follow up on.

Then, two weeks following Lavigne's death, the dance community suffered another tragic loss; Trisha Beck, a single woman in her late 20s was killed. Police had ruled it an accident, although Myrick could see signs of sloppy police work from the get-go. The Waltham Police Department had responded to a report of a woman who'd fallen over the rails of her ninth floor hotel balcony. Upon arrival, they learned that a party had taken place that night and that Ms. Beck had been drinking heavily, apparently in an attempt to drown her sorrows. Beck had competed earlier that day in the All-Star division, and hadn't made the finals; and witnesses explained that she was particularly distraught over it.

Studying the report, Myrick could see that police had provided an approximate interval for her time of death - between 0130 and 0140 hours. There were technically several witnesses to it, as it'd happened while many of the conference participants had gathered together in one of the hotel rooms, although none of them were with Beck when she'd fallen over the side of the balcony. All police had to go on was that the victim had been downing jello shots, her mood had seemingly improved and that she'd told a friend that she just wanted to step outside on the balcony for some fresh air. Eventually, that same friend had gotten concerned and went to check on Beck, only to realize she was no longer there. It was then that she'd glanced over the railing of the balcony, spotting a lifeless body on the ground below.

"Good morning," a voice broke the silence, disturbing Myrick from his thoughts, "you asked to see me, Detective?"

"Yes," Myrick looked up from the file in front of him to see an individual with a long, lean frame enter the room. The man wore trendy jeans and an earth-toned shirt, which conveyed a subtle coolness like the mesmerizing hazel color of his eyes. "You must be Deion Mitchell. Please take a seat. I'd just like to ask you a few questions. Nothing too formal."

"Fire away," Deion returned as he sat down in the chair across from Myrick, indicating his complete willingness to help however he could, his demeanor surprisingly relaxed despite the serious nature of the interview. "What is it that I can tell you?"

"Well, for starters, I heard you were one of the last to talk with Jill McKenna... *and* that she told you she knew something about Warren Steyn's murder."

"She did mention something like that," Deion began, the whites of his eyes bloodshot, a dark red in color like his hightop shoes, and Myrick guessed he hadn't slept the night before, "maybe not in so many words, but she did hint that she knew something. We were down in the pro area getting in some practice but I could see she was distracted so I asked what was up. I think she was even going to tell me, but then Jonathan walked in. Jill suddenly got all squirrelly... and I think she just didn't want anyone to overhear anything."

"If I remember correctly," Myrick thumbed through his notepad and found the page he was looking for, then continued, "Jonathan is an Intermediate level dancer. So what was he doing in the pro room?"

"Private lesson, I think, with Victoria Monroe. She's an instructor. He'd gotten there before her... but I remember Victoria also arriving just as Jill and I were wrapping things up."

"Tell me about Jill McKenna. Did she have any enemies in the dance community?"

"Who doesn't?" Deion's dark eyebrows rose as he smirked, and Myrick noted it odd that Deion seemed surprisingly unaffected by McKenna's death. "But Jill did have more than most. She had a special talent for getting under other people's skin. It was part of her game, especially pre-comp. I can recall plenty of times right before competitions her saying or doing something to play mind games with another dancer. It worked like a charm. I used to call her the Dennis Rodman of dance. She *hated* that." Deion grinned again.

"I take it she won't be missed then," Myrick purposely threw out the morbid (but apparent) truth, as he was more interested in Deion's demeanor than his actual answer.

"By some," Deion conceded. "But others of us are going to miss her like crazy." And as he spoke, Deion's voice suddenly turned a tad wistful. Despite the sudden change in tone, it possessed a level of flatness, making it hard to tell if Deion's sentiment was contrived or genuine. "I'm definitely going to miss her. I'm not even sure I'd be where I am without her. Jill was incredibly gifted... and gifted people do sometimes run hot and cold. I guess it's fair to say you either hated or loved Jill... there was no middle ground. Me... I loved her."

Being a seasoned detective, Myrick had interviewed countless suspects over the years. Lack of concern was a good indicator of deception, and sometimes more telling to him than mannerisms alone. But Myrick wasn't so sure that Deion's original aloofness was entirely indifference. Deion seemed to have assumed a certain persona, as if a shtick of some sort. And while he hadn't been in the dance community long, he wondered if Deion's original cool nature wasn't part of the celebrity-like image he'd assumed. Looking at him, Myrick got the feeling that Deion might be more conflicted than it appeared on the surface, and that he was finally revealing at least a hint of his repressed emotions.

Yet almost as soon as Myrick started to convince himself that might be the case, Deion began to perk up again. "I can probably guess who did this," he suddenly changed the subject, as if realizing Myrick was sizing him up and on the verge of seeing through his act.

"Really," Myrick's eyebrows inched upward and his eyes widened, "that'd be helpful. Tell me what you think happened."

"Well, I'm not sure you'll like my answer, but I'd venture a guess that you have *two* killers out there." Deion leaned forward and lowered his voice a bit before continuing, as if not wanting to be heard. As he did, Myrick got a better look at his face, which seemed more youthful at a distance, but upon closer inspection had a couple of faded scars along his chin, and which Myrick considered might be evidence that Deion hadn't lived the pampered life he casually attempted to portray. "Have you met Claire and Kendall yet?"

"No, I can't say that I have."

"You may want to. They're a mother and daughter team. Mom - Claire - she's the talent and the brains... but she's also got a reputation for being conniving. She'd do *anything* to ensure the family name and legacy carries on. Kendall has no business being at the Advanced level already. She doesn't have nearly the heart or talent of her mother. But she does idolize her mom... and we all know she'd do anything to please her. Jill was vocal about that conflict of interest. She competed against Kendall a few times in Open Strictlys and Showcases... and I can assure you that Kendall wasn't in the same league as Jill. Don't tell that to the judges though. Kendall beat Jill more times than not... and we all know that Claire had something to do with it."

"That might be a motive to murder Jill, but it doesn't explain Warren's death."

"Oh, I haven't gotten to that part yet," Deion leaned forward even more, so that there was very little distance between him and Myrick. Deion had an intense stare, as if determined to convey his point. "Claire was once married to Warren. It only lasted a year, but it was a torrid affair and created an exceptional amount of drama. Warren didn't like the strings Claire was pulling to fast track Kendall to the top. While he rarely said anything, his mannerisms gave it away. He liked Jill. He thought she was the future of West Coast Swing. And he had the prestige and money to make it happen. It was Warren that funded most of Jill's travel. He was a silent sponsor of sorts."

"I noticed on the video from the competition last night that Jill had winked at Warren right before his death." Myrick was strategic. He deliberately revealed this important fact, aware that Deion might be able to elaborate on it.

"No surprise. Kendall was on the dance floor competing at that time. Jill probably knew how rigged it was. I remember thinking Kendall's timing was off... her footwork was lazy... her spins weren't tight... and she was still going to make finals. My guess is Jill and Warren both knew it also and what you caught on film was probably just the two of them mocking the system."

"Seems to be a lot of politics and in-fighting at the top."

"More than you could imagine. It's like high school on steroids. I'm as guilty of it as anyone, I guess, too. But what's really fascinating was that really none of it could've happened without Warren. Claire was a legend... but her time in the spotlight had come and gone. Like so many other pros, she might have been put out to pasture long ago if not for Warren. He was the one with the deep pockets. He even sponsored a few of the dancers, paying for their hotels and travel expenses. My guess is there was a power struggle behind the scenes as to which direction to throw their combined weight... toward Kendall or Jill."

"Your theory seems like a stretch," Myrick interjected, sorry to tear down Deion's illusions so summarily. "The mother and daughter aren't likely to kill the one person who was giving them the ability to influence Kendall's ascension up the ranks, even if they had to share the limelight with another dancer or simply wait their turn."

"Maybe, unless of course they only had a small window of opportunity to make it happen. It was no secret that Kendall had other aspirations outside dance and that Claire was concerned her daughter would lose interest in it altogether. In fact, if you think about it... Yves Lavigne was one of Warren's favorites also. Those two were thick as thieves. Some even said that Yves was Warren's voice in judging and that Warren's opinion of scoring went through Yves. Kind of peculiar that those two are both gone and out of the picture now."

"Interesting point. I wasn't aware of the connection between him & Mr. Lavigne either... so I'll certainly do some followup on that."

"Anything else you need from me, Detective? If not, I'd like to head out. It was up to me to call Jill's family. I broke the news to them. She wasn't close to her parents... they never understood why she didn't go into banking or law or some other *worthwhile* profession. But they did still love her. And they were devastated when I broke the news. I live in the same hometown as them and I don't want to miss my flight. I'd like to be there for them."

"That's quite admirable," Myrick offered back, weighing the sincerity of Deion's words at the same time, somewhat persuaded that they were genuine. "You're free to go. Please make sure Ellen has all your contact information. I may need to call you for follow up."

"Of course," Deion replied, getting up from the desk. As he walked out, Myrick could see a second interviewee waiting just outside the door, and so he waved her to come in.

Glancing down at the handwritten list Ellen had provided him, Myrick could see there were a good fifty-eight potential suspects, most of which would prove to be as intriguing to interview as Deion Mitchell had been. The entire day of questioning would not disappoint, and Myrick learned a great deal from them, not the least of which was just how nuanced and fascinating the West Coast Swing community really was.

CHAPTER FIVE
Develop Your Own Unique Style

It'd been a full day of interviews and Myrick was mentally exhausted as the hour neared five o'clock. Some of the dancers had been forthcoming, some had not, but all of them had been full of secrets and gossip, and Myrick found himself more intrigued at every dramatic twist and turn. It was going to be hard for him to sift through it all and figure out the truth. The last of the interviews was one that he particularly relished, as it was with Kendall Callaway, the girl who Deion had insisted was getting all the favoritism.

But the interview started off much different than Myrick had anticipated. Kendall was polite and reserved. She had an understated style, presenting like the type of person who could easily disappear into a crowd. Kendall sat down across the table from Myrick, her hands placed in her lap, her posture perfect, as she went about answering any questions Myrick had, even the more uncomfortable ones.

"You know," Myrick began explaining, having gotten most of the background questions out of the way and now wanting to move on to the more pressing ones, "there are some that say you had a rift with Jill."

"Um, no... I didn't," Kendall returned, and there was a sad look on her face, more so than Myrick had noticed on any of the others he'd interviewed so far.

Myrick had spoken to no less than fifty people, all of whom knew Jill McKenna, professing to be almost best friends with her, yet at the same time harboring their fair share of bad blood as well. Over and over, Myrick heard about how tragic it was to lose someone that had such an unparalleled gift. Watching her dance, even for those competing against her, was awe-inspiring and it commanded respect. But she also possessed a fiery temper and had a way with words that didn't go over well with the rest of the pros; and by the end of the day, Myrick could confidently say that it was nearly impossible to rule out any of them as being a suspect, as they all (admittedly) had motives to wish Jill McKenna gone.

"But I know she didn't like me," Kendall continued. "And I didn't blame her. She had good reason to hate me... or at least what I represented."

"That's a pretty bold statement to make. I find it hard to believe you could've deserved such misplaced anger," Myrick observed, and he did mean his words. Myrick had never had any children, but that wasn't by choice, and he did have a paternal type nature about him, which kicked in from time to time.

"How would you feel if you kept getting passed over for promotions at work because the Police Chief's kid had a path to the top paved out for him already?"

"I'd imagine I wouldn't like that," Myrick admitted, but he had a very hard time imagining such a thing happening, as he knew the Police Chief's son well, who just happened to be a petty thief, and was lucky to stay out of jail for any length of time, and had no aspirations to be a police officer (or obtain any job at all.)

"That's what Jill had to deal with in me. She was at the prime of her career when I came on the scene. Not that I wanted to," Kendall confessed. "I wanted to go into medicine. But this is the family business. This is what Callaways do. We're born Westies."

"Westies?"

"West Coast Swing dancers."

"But that's not actually what you want to do with your life, correct?"

"It's sort of a love-hate relationship. I do enjoy it. I just don't want it for a full-time career. I think when your hobby becomes your primary source of income, it steals some of the joy from it."

In the relatively brief time Myrick had been talking with Kendall, he'd been able to size her up pretty well, finding her to be much wiser than her age, which he could see from the file in front of him was nineteen. It helped that Kendall was being so transparent about her own shortcomings, and so Myrick had hopes that Kendall would be the same regarding her mom. Instead, he learned she was quite the opposite once he broached this subject.

"I was also told that your mom was once married to Warren Steyn."

"She was. They divorced about a year later, but that's not their fault. Romance is tough on the competition circuit. You have so much pressure to succeed... and so much temptation thrown at you by others… and they just couldn't figure out how to make it all work. I'm not sure how any couples do in this environment."

"So, I hope you don't mind me asking… it's just part of the job… but was there an act of indiscretion that led to their split?"

"No I don't think so. Sure, Warren was hounded by women. Think about it… he was good looking… and incredibly successful… *and* an accomplished dancer. He had all the things going for him and so, of course, there were a lot of girls in love with him. But he only had eyes for my mom. I really believe that. It just tore at the two of them trying to navigate so much and so many who didn't want to see them succeed."

"So you blame the dance community then?" Myrick wondered aloud, not really expecting an answer, so when he got one he was a bit surprised.

"I do. I think my mom could've had a long, happy marriage. The two of them should've gotten to enjoy that," Kendall offered, and there was a protectiveness to her voice, evidencing that her own negative experiences had not affected her loyalty to her mother.

"Then I'll finish with this, mostly because I think you may have the best insight into who might have killed Warren… and now Jill," Myrick began, genuinely believing that Kendall had a good pulse on things. "Who do you believe did it?"

"Well, I'd imagine that I'm suspect number one in Jill's death," Kendall answered, matter-of-factly, giving very little additional thought to her response, and Myrick's eyebrows raised in intrigue as she did so. "But as for Warren…" There was a more perceptible air of consideration before she answered as she reflected on the possibilities, "I'd have originally told you it had to be Jill." Kendall paused for a moment as if disappointed that would've been her response. "But now I'd say it was probably Jayde. She was never a favorite of Warren's... and he did hold a lot of sway in who made it into the inner circle. Jayde may be a phenomenal dancer... maybe even as talented as Jill... but she's rough around the edges and doesn't look the part and that was an unspoken factor."

Fascinated by Kendall's response, Myrick knew he was really only starting to scratch the surface of what was going on behind the scenes; and so even as he was wrapping up his questions for the day, he was certain there would be far more to come later as the mystery continued to unravel. He let Kendall know that he appreciated how forthcoming she had been and then indicated that she was free to go for the time being. Kendall, in turn, thanked him, explaining that she and her mother needed to hurry over to the airport to catch their flight, as they were already running late.

In fact, that had been the mantra throughout the interviews, dancers who were rushing back to jobs and responsibilities in their hometowns, juggling two distinctly different lives. Unfortunately, those same hectic schedules had even meant that Myrick hadn't actually interviewed everyone he was hoping (or needing) to, including two of the pros - Alexander Kozlov and Natasha Levin. The couple had caught a red-eye flight to Moscow late that prior evening for a weeklong boot camp they were scheduled to attend. As he'd learned during the interviews, both of them had their run-ins with Warren over his decision to cut back on travel expenses.

Regardless, those interviews would have to wait (if they even happened at all), as the Police Chief was unlikely to pay for a follow up investigative trip to Moscow. Fortunately, Ellen did mention that there was another dance conference in Santa Fe, New Mexico coming up and that Kozlov and Levin were scheduled to attend; and it was only a few hours' drive for Myrick to get there, so he could always wait and interview them at that location, if still necessary.

Ellen was the last to leave the hotel. She was talking to some of the volunteers, who had packed up a few final boxes and were loading them into a van. They were going to drive all the supplies down to Durango, which was Ellen's hometown. Before leaving, Myrick took a few minutes to get her up to speed on what he'd learned so far, and to let her know that she needed to remain available for follow up interviews, at least until he had the case solved.

"I wouldn't rule out Alexander," Ellen noted one last time. "He's got some anger issues. I once saw Natasha come out of their hotel room with a huge bruise below her eye. They literally changed up the costumes for their routine to cover it up, dressing in burlesque masks that didn't quite fit the music, even though they insisted it was an attempt at exaggerated parody. Months of work go into preparing for those performances. Last minute wardrobe changes don't just happen. They were covering for what he'd done."

"I haven't ruled anyone out just yet," Myrick replied, subtly implying that he'd meant even *she* was still a suspect.

"I have faith in you, Detective Myrick. I don't usually trust law enforcement. I've had my share of bad experiences. But I do have confidence you'll solve this case."

"I appreciate that, Ms. Cromwel. I'll try to make sure your trust isn't misplaced."

"Thank you. And should you need me, please call at any time. You have my cell number still?"

"I do."

And with that, Ellen reached out to shake Myrick's hand, then turned and left out of the building, walking over to a nearby taxi that the hotel had summoned for her. It was then that Myrick realized the volunteers would be the ones driving the van with supplies the long road all the way to Durango; and that Ellen would be taking the more direct route by air. Evidently, that was one of the perks of being possessed of money and working in an industry where others were willing to volunteer just to pay their dues.

As Myrick watched both the cab and van drive off, he found himself now alone in the expansive hallway of the conference center. It'd been a long day, more demanding than he'd even expected. Worse yet, it had only magnified the work ahead of him. He had a laundry list of potential suspects now. Any of them could've been the culprit, or perhaps even multiple suspects were working in tandem. Still, he'd uncovered some crucial details and he'd even developed his first theory of who might just be responsible for these reprehensible crimes. And in Myrick's estimation, the case was off to an intriguing start.

CHAPTER SIX
Remember, the Woman Is Always "Right"

It had been two weeks since the deaths of Warren Steyn and Jill McKenna. In that time, Myrick had pushed the forensic division hard to finish testing and for the medical examiner's office to provide reports. He had his theories about what had happened, but it would give credence to them if the evidence matched up with what he suspected. The autopsy report on McKenna's death came back first. It was a detailed, fourteen-page finding, indicative of homicide.

The ME noted that Jill McKenna had suffered a perforating gunshot wound to the upper chest cavity, and that the single shot had been fired at close range. The gunshot wound was located two inches right of the midline and nine inches below the top of the head. The bullet had traveled right to left, front to back and upward, entering at the four o'clock position and exiting at 10 o'clock. Both soot and stippling were present. Jill was recorded as being 35 years of age at the time of death, with a weight of 128 and a height of 5'8".

After perusing the factual report, many of Myrick's initial suspicions were confirmed, allowing him to eliminate several potential suspects. He had also requested, and received, a report from the Forensic Division regarding a scuff mark on the base of the door, which had been preserved using an electrostatic dust print lifter. Analysis revealed that the impression had been caused by the sole of a shoe that had been forcefully pressed up along the bottom of the doorframe. Unfortunately, the shoe print was not indicative of individualized characterization, as the marking came from the smooth carbon rubber along the toe of the culprit's shoe and had no notable markings or defects.

Still, the combination of the autopsy report and the shoe print analysis did narrow the field of potential suspects considerably. Myrick could now be certain that the killer had stood a relatively short distance from Jill McKenna when she was fired upon, and that there had at least been a struggle (even if relatively brief) by Jill to keep the killer from getting in her room. Myrick surmised that Jill had no doubt tried to force the door shut while the assailant placed a forceful foot against it, keeping it ajar just long enough for the fatal shot to be discharged.

Those reports alone, however, weren't enough for Myrick to make any arrests and so the next logical step was to patiently wait and see if the findings from Warren Steyn's death might provide more certainty. The specific forensic pathologist assigned to conduct Warren's postmortem examination was known for being more painstaking in detail and Myrick had worked with her on several of his most difficult to solve cases. He was also acutely aware that there was no rushing her results.

Myrick had at least been present for the initial external examination of the body, which was an unfortunate but sometimes necessary part of his job. It wasn't the sight of a corpse or blood or the examination itself that bothered Myrick; it was the smell… the gut-wrenchingly awful odor… and how it lingered in his senses and within the material of his clothes long after he'd exited the autopsy room. Myrick couldn't stand it, and so he was only present at the autopsies of his victims when absolutely necessary. This, Myrick decided, was one of those particular instances.

And so Myrick had emphasized to the pathologist, Dr. Hendricks, that he was curious as to the unusual swelling and redness around Warren's throat and that he'd appreciate a tissue analysis of that region. Hendricks, being the expert that she was, noted to Myrick that she'd already picked up on the specific area of concern and proceeded to cut a small sample from it, observing it under a microscope and then noting even more abnormalities to the skin, including a tiny needle-like object embedded in it. She agreed with Myrick that poison was a strong likelihood in the cause of death, and she even went so far as to predict it would be a neurotoxin of sorts, given the sudden, violent nature of Warren Steyn's demise. The two continued to talk over their theories even as the internal autopsy was conducted, which lasted a good three hours. At the end, and just as expected, Myrick left the coroner's office reeking of death and knowing that he'd need to burn the clothes he was wearing.

When the toxicology report was finally returned, less than three-tenths of a gram of batrachotoxin was detected in Warren's bloodstream. There was also a small hint of that same poison substance found in the droplet residue on the tiny dart. This, Hendricks had explained, comported with the findings in her preliminary report that the cause of death was homicide. The manner of death, she continued, was a powerful neurotoxin, causing arrhythmia and ventricular fibrillation in the heart muscles, and ultimately leading to acute cardiovascular arrest. In short, Hendricks' expert opinion was that Warren Steyn was indeed murdered, and she could further say, with a relative degree of certainty, that it was the result of a poison needle discharged at a distance of no more than sixty feet.

Two deaths committed at the same hotel in less than twenty-four hours, but also committed in completely distinct ways. Warren Steyn died at the hands of a skillful assassin, who clearly planned out his death using a rare poison, and did so in a manner that would be hard to trace. The other, Jill McKenna's death, seemed to have been carried out in a far less calculated manner, as victim and assailant had stood practically inches away from each other at the time of the shooting. The circumstances of McKenna's death definitely had more of a rushed, impulsive aspect to it, and it made Myrick wonder if perhaps there weren't two suspects, working in concert and with different methods of killing.

Lastly, but perhaps the most important piece of evidence, a laptop had been seized from McKenna's hotel room and submitted to the computer forensics division for analysis. An engineer had extracted most of the files and had turned these files over to Myrick. Most of it, as Myrick could tell from the disks, were dance-related projects that Jill had been working on. A perusal of her internet history also revealed that she'd spent hours before her death searching flights, which Myrick guessed went along with her need to travel for regional events. None of this was particularly helpful in solving her death, or the motives for it, but there was one file that Myrick clicked on and which he did find quite revealing.

Jill had recorded the results of the past few competitions, including the ones that had taken place in Colorado Springs, Sacramento and Boston, on her computer. Those files also included the judges' names and the specific competitors from each flight, and a brief account of why the participants had been scored in the way they were. Myrick broke out his notepad to remind himself of the dates and the names of the prior dance events where the two other deaths had occurred. Sure enough, those two deaths coincided with events that Jill had attended as well, and the detailed results of which were recorded on her laptop files.

Myrick went to work using this invaluable information to create a spreadsheet of his own. He listed out the names of all the dancers he'd interviewed at the Colorado Springs event. He then created two separate columns: one for the Sacramento conference (where the victim died of suspected drug overdose) and one for the Waltham County event (where the victim met her end after falling from a ninth floor balcony.) By doing this, and referring to Jill's previously recorded list, he was able to quickly tell which suspects had attended all three events. Suddenly, he'd gone from fifty or so potential suspects to less than thirty, most of which were judges, although some of the advanced dancers who'd been competing the night of Warren's death were also at all three events.

Interestingly, though, one of the suspects that the other dancers had pointed to as possibly involved - Jayde Ch'en- had not attended the Sacramento conference. As such, Myrick could cross her off his list as well, simultaneously noting that he needed to be careful not to let the gossip of the various people he'd interviewed influence his detective work. Although, he did note scrolling back through scores in Jill's computer files that the ones that predated Sacramento had Yves progressively scoring Jayde lower, as if she was regressing as a dancer in his eyes.

On the other hand, his other primary suspects: Deion Mitchell, the Callaways (Claire and Kendall), Alexander Kozlov, Natasha Levin, Jonathan Scott... and even Ellen Cromwel (Myrick hadn't quite ruled her out yet) had all attended the three events. And it was interesting to note from the files in the computer that only one judge had given low marks to Kendall in her Sacramento and Boston competitions. While all of the other judges had given her high marks at those events, indicating that she was among the top in her group of competitors, Jill had ranked her far lower. In fact, it was evident from the scoring that Jill didn't even think Kendall belonged among the finalists in her advanced grouping. Myrick guessed this had caused some angst, and maybe had led to an argument or two. The only question was, *who would've been more upset about those low scores from Jill: Kendall or her mother?*

Myrick had a feeling though that he had overlooked an important detail, and he wondered if some of the case's most intriguing clues weren't actually right in front of him. He'd watched the video from the competition over and over so many times that he'd lost count. Possessing an eidetic memory, he could instantly recall where each of the dancers were exactly at the moment Warren keeled over in his chair, including the level of difficulty it would've been to shoot the poison dart accurately, yet without being noticed. In fact, as an unintended result, the song from the competition, itself, was stuck in his head. In dramatic fashion, he could recall how it seemed that at the very crescendo of the music - and just as Warren snatched his hands up to his throat at being hit with the projectile - the music reached a fevered pitch, almost as if the scene itself had been perfectly orchestrated.

But no matter how many times he watched the video or how much effort he put digging through his notes of the interviews, Myrick still found himself at an impasse. It was late, the collector's edition *Cool Hand Luke* wall clock in his office read 7:32, and he was growing weary. The desk he sat at was an old wooden one that had been passed down from Riley's father, who'd also been a police detective. He'd been a tremendous mentor to Myrick, and so to honor the man after his death, Myrick had placed it in his office. But the drawers on it stuck, and if you pulled too hard on one, it would actually come out, falling to the floor, along with all its contents. Still, the desk had a timeworn character to it, and fit Myrick's unique personality, and so he preferred to remain working behind it even into the late night hours.

Reaching over to the far end of the desk, Myrick pulled the chain cord on an antique, brass-finished lamp and the bulb cut off. The office was dark, other than the moonlight that streamed in from a nearby box-shaped aperture high up on the brick wall. Myrick had one of the few offices in the building with a window, which happened to be one of the coveted perks of his seniority at the police department. Sighing, he pushed his chair back from the desk, stretched his weary bones and got up to walk out the door. There was a coat rack, and both his cap and jacket had been placed on one of the rungs. Taking both, he threw them on and continued through the door, all in one singular motion.

Clearly at a crossroads in the investigation, Myrick realized he needed to take a step back from things. Sometimes it was wise to stop pressing for answers and instead let inspiration come to him. For five years, he'd been going to the same dive, a speakeasy just a few blocks away and within walking distance. He ordered the same beverage every time and the routine nature of that ritual allowed his mind to have space to ponder the great mystery of things... or sometimes just to do some intriguing people watching. Both were admirable uses of his time, in Myrick's estimation.

A fifteen minute walk later through the chill night air, and Myrick was finally standing in front of the bar. He spotted a police car parked out front, and wondered if there hadn't been an altercation inside. The italicized name and badge number on the side of the patrol car read, "*C.R. Nichols, #1529*". Myrick knew instantly upon seeing the name that the officer was with the DUI Unit, and was likely parked outside because there had been an intoxicated patron who'd caused a disturbance. Sure enough, as Myrick got closer, he could see inside the tinted windows that there was a man locked up in the barred backseat of the vehicle. He was the only occupant, and Myrick guessed Nichols was inside the speakeasy getting some information from the staff about what had happened.

There was a neon sign attached to the building that telecast the name of the bar - *The Basement*, and Myrick proceeded through a dingy red door that led inside. As usual for a Wednesday night, the place appeared rather empty, and so Myrick easily made his way between the brick interior corridor and over to an antique-style bar area. Fortunately, his favorite barstool, he could see, was unoccupied at the moment, and so he quickly made his way over. No sooner had he done so, than the bartender came over to him.

"Same as always, Maddog?" the bartender asked, her voice was as smooth as the slim fit vest and shirt she wore, sleeves rolled up and top two buttons undone.

"That'll do, Tessa."

"Okay, I'll be right back," Tessa answered, both winking and snapping her fingers as she did so in a lickety-split type indication.

Myrick sat down onto the leather of the barstool and placed his heavy coat over the seat next to him, partly because he had nowhere else to put it and partly to signal he did not have any interest in company. On the far side of the expansive bar, he could see that the bartender was working on his drink: an Irish coffee with an extra hint of malt extract and vanilla bean to give it a maltier taste. It was the same drink he'd ordered for five years, and Tessa had mastered the art of making it just as Myrick liked.

As he waited, Myrick stared into the glass mirror on the other side of the bar, and ultimately caught sight of a group of patrons coming in through the front door. In true detective fashion, he couldn't help but size them up immediately, noting that he didn't recognize any of them. With each passing minute, more showed up, until there were approximately twenty or so, doubling the number of people who'd already been at the bar. They also all wore distinctive vintage clothing. The guys wore a wide array of tweed vests, bowties, skinny ties and newsboy-type caps. Some also came decked out in vintage black and white Charleston shoes. The girls wore mostly short sleeved belted retro swing dresses, in a variety of pastel and plaid colors, and carrying embroidered handbags in their stylishly gloved hands. Myrick wondered if someone needed to explain that they didn't need to actually *look* the part in order to frequent the speakeasy bar.

Soon though, he began to realize that the group was there for a social event, with one particular man at the front of the room beckoning them all together. He was standing in a sectioned-off area of the room, but still visible from where Myrick sat at the bar. The area was an open space with a long wooden floor that creaked when you traversed it. Suddenly, Myrick noticed the genre of the music in the bar change from the usual contemporary songs he'd heard when he walked in to more of an early 1920s feel. The song currently playing was an Ella Fitzgerald duet with Count Basie, and the group immediately went to dancing to it.

Their movements were lively and quick, and Myrick found himself entranced by it. Glancing to the side, he could see he wasn't the only one transfixed by what was happening around him, as the few patrons situated inside the speakeasy had turned in their chairs to watch as well. Myrick had been coming to the bar for years and had never seen this before. As he was watching, Tessa returned, placing the drink in front of him.

"This is new," Myrick spoke, not turning around.

"Yeah, that was the owner's idea," Tessa explained, a hint of confusion in her voice as well. "He wanted to attract some new customers, especially on the weekday nights. This guy says he has a bunch of dancers who want to go out and he said he'd also offer free lessons if we allowed them to use our space. What do we have to lose, right?"

Myrick looked around the bar as Tessa was speaking, noticing just how empty it was and instantly agreeing that the owner probably did need to come up with something new to drum up business. He then glanced back at the dancers, they were halfway through their song and still spinning and twirling and dipping, with huge grins on their faces like they were having the time of their lives.

"It looks easy," Myrick muttered aloud, as if to convince himself that he too should be out there.

"Or maybe it's just that *they* make it look easy," Tessa returned, almost as if to warn Myrick not to get any crazy ideas. Myrick, in turn, shrugged his shoulders in agreement.

The song finally ended and then the same man as before stood at the head of the room. He made a quick announcement, intended not only for the dancers already on the floor, but also the patrons who were originally only there for a drink or a meal.

"Okay, one more warmup song and then we begin tonight's lesson," he beckoned, his hand up in the air as if to pull everyone out onto the makeshift dance floor. "My name is Terrance and I'll be your instructor for the evening. Trust me, you're going to love this."

The other dancers began to line up with partners. Terrance then glanced around the room still trying to pry people out of their seats, hoping that they might be in for some adventure. It was evident at the tables that some of the women were eagerly hoping that their dates might pull them out on the dance floor, but as the seconds ticked by, none took the bait.

The couples had already gathered together in pairs, except for one lone woman who didn't seem to have a partner yet. She stood there, alone, for a determined minute, and then

Myrick made the mistake of making eye contact with her. Almost immediately, one side of her mouth rose slightly in a coy smile at him, simultaneously biting the bottom of her lip gently in an almost flirtatious way. If there was one thing that Myrick was, he was a sucker for a damsel in distress. He couldn't believe what he was about to do, but before he could consider the consequences, Myrick was up off his barstool and walking over to her. By the time he was no more than a foot or two away, her smile had widened even more.

"I don't actually know how to dance," Myrick fumbled with his words, "but I'll try."

Without saying a word, the girl took her cue, sliding forward so that her right hand was in Myrick's left and then guiding his other arm so that it was around the back of her waist.

"The key is not to think *too* much," the girl winked, and Myrick could tell she was the type who could easily light up a room.

"That's going to be hard for me," Myrick nervously grinned back, although also entirely serious at the same time, wanting desperately to warn the girl about what was coming. "Hopefully I don't step on your feet."

"Then start on the left foot. I'll start with my right. In dance, the woman is always *right,*" she quipped, but with hidden meaning.

"Okay, I'm trusting you to make us look good." Myrick nervously replied, more so to reassure himself that this hadn't been a terrible idea, although aware there was also no turning back now either.

The girl nodded back to indicate that she had this and the two swayed back and forth together. The music, though, called for something livelier and so she lifted her right arm up (while still holding onto Myrick's left), took a slight step back and then spun underneath it in a perfect 360 degree turn. It was so smooth that Myrick wasn't sure if he'd even led the move or not. Then, once again lifting his arm up, she sauntered along his left side, then did a turn so that she was now facing him on the other side, as they'd somehow done a 180 degree change of positions. In that entire time, all Myrick could remember was how to rock back and forth, his mind racing a mile a minute in a mixture of fear and excitement.

Somehow the dance was over before he knew it and Myrick realized he'd survived the experience without stepping on his dance partner's feet (too much). At the end, she hugged him and thanked him for the dance and then told him that her name was - Susie - and that he needed to *save some more dances for her*. Myrick agreed to do so, although if he'd have been truthful he would've told her that he was so shocked to have pulled off the first dance that there was no way he'd be venturing back out on the floor the rest of the night.

Walking back to his barstool, Myrick glanced over at the men sitting at a nearby table, their dates still wistful in their wish to be pulled out onto the dance floor, and Myrick couldn't help but grin slyly at the fact that he'd had the courage to do what the rest of them hadn't. But as he was just taking a sip of his Irish coffee, turning to watch the dancers do their thing, Myrick suddenly noticed that the organizer of the event - Terrance - was walking over to him.

"That's some nice footwork you had there," the edges of Terrance's mouth edged upward in a sort of half-smile/half-chuckle.

"Oh, you noticed that," Myrick laughed back, heartily. "I call that my *perpetual* sway move."

"Very cool, man. And very smart to set the girl up so she can show off. That's all most follows are really hoping for anyway."

As he was talking, Myrick reached over to the barstool next to him and took his coat off of it. He was now intrigued by this whole dance world and decided he was okay with conversation after all. He then ventured to ask a few questions as Terrance was sitting down.

"West Coast Swing is a fun dance. I didn't even know it existed until recently," Myrick offered up.

"That's actually East Coast Swing that you just did. And you nailed it... you're a natural."

"East Coast? There's an East Coast version of this thing?"

"Sure. And it's entirely different than West Coast. East Coast Swing has a little hop to it. It's a bouncy dance. You kick it off with a rock step. West Coast Swing... it's smoother, more grounded."

"And here I was thinking I'd learned a thing or two already," Myrick jested, taking another sip of his coffee as he spoke, now aware of just how foreign all this really was to him.

"Hey, look at it this way..." Terrance asserted, "what line of work are you in?"

"Police work... detective."

"Alright so, imagine I show up one day at your job... even if I'm talented enough to become a good detective... you think I'm going to ace it right off the bat?"

"Nope," Myrick added, matter-of-factly.

"Exactly, so don't think you have to be an expert tackling this on day one either. It took me years to get to this point... *years*. We all had to start somewhere."

"I doubt there's too many dancing cops out there."

"Oh really, I think you'd be surprised man. There's all types... even attorneys ... I mean, you just danced with one," Terrance laughed as he indicated over to the woman he'd just been out on the floor with and who was now showing off with another lead (who happened to be a little more experienced at it, himself.)

"Interesting. I didn't see that coming." Myrick glanced over his shoulder to watch and marvel that the same free spirit he'd just shared a dance with was also one of the prim and proper lawyer-types he had to deal with in courtrooms all the time.

"Yup," Terrance patted Myrick on the shoulder. He then stood up from the barstool. "So keep coming back and trying this thing out. I think you'll like it. We're here every Wednesday night, starting at 8:00." Terrance then reached his hand out and shook Myrick's, as if to seal a promise that he'd be back again.

Terrance then walked back over to the group, simultaneously looking around at all the other tables as if to survey if there were any other takers. Finally, another couple joined in. Then another. Myrick watched in amusement as the brave couples fumbled with their footwork and timing. They were definitely in over their heads, but also having the time of their lives, wisely not taking it too seriously. Meanwhile, Myrick thought back on what Terrance had said and the ramifications of his earlier attempt. And then it hit him - *that was what he was missing and why he was struggling to solve his case.* He didn't truly understand the dance culture... or really *any* of the unique aspects of it. There were probably clues all around that he was overlooking and it was becoming evident what the only solution was - he'd have to completely immerse himself into its nuanced world if he was going to spot them. Fortunately, things were falling into place quite perfectly so that Myrick would get just the ideal opportunity to do so soon enough.

CHAPTER SEVEN
Maintain a Strong Frame

"I need to attend a dance conference this weekend, Chief."

"You what?" Police Chief Clark sputtered, completely perplexed and wondering if Myrick was trying to pull a prank on him, running his hand along his straight edge goatee in evident consternation.

"A dance conference. I need you to approve the travel. It's necessary... for the homicide case."

"Okay, twinkle toes. I know I run a more laidback office environment than most. But this is pushing me too far. The Department is *not* going to send you to a dance event." The Chief was sitting at his desk, a cup of hot coffee in his hand, and entirely expecting that this was the end of the ill-considered and unsolicited request by his otherwise rational thinking detective.

"Then just approve my leave," Myrick persisted. "I'll pay for this out of my own pocket."

"You're serious, aren't you?"

"When have you known me to be otherwise?"

The Police Chief paused, and there was an unmistakable air of judgment as he stared down his detective, not sure what to make of all this nonsense. Finally he continued, "You want to fund this adventure, that's your call. I'll approve the travel, but only if you promise this is *solely* for work."

"You know me better than anyone. My methods aren't always the most orthodox... but there's a reason behind them."

"I did *think* I knew you," the Police Chief leaned back in his executive-style swivel chair. He then kicked his feet up on the desk, his arms folded across his chest, and a look of seriousness pasted over the entirety of his countenance. "How long will you be gone?"

"It's a few hours' drive to Santa Fe. They say these things typically last a weekend, start on Friday and wrap up by Sunday."

"Oh good. You'll have to show me some of your fancy new moves when you get back." There was now a smirk on Chief Clark's face, and it was evident he was suddenly getting a kick out of the situation, resigned to the fact it was going to actually happen and realizing he might as well have some fun with it.

Myrick, however, was doing his best to remain all business. He knew this was only the beginning and he was going to be the butt of jokes around the police station for the foreseeable future. The force was known for being merciless when a shot at humor was at stake - and this particular assignment was ripe for prolonged office banter at Myrick's expense. Still, despite knowing what was in store for him, he remained focused, convinced - to a degree - that this field trip was the right decision.

"I'll come back with information... but expect it to be case-related only."

"Fair enough," Chief Clark replied in a surprisingly concessionary tone, as he pulled his feet off the desk and leaned forward so that he was looking his detective dead in the eyes. "Warren was my friend. We grew up together. I know you won't believe this but we both had a lot in common, just not dance. That was Warren's thing... and he was great at it. So, yes, I want my best detective on this case. I want it solved. Don't make me regret my decision on this."

"I won't let you down."

"Good," the Police Chief replied, "then your travel is approved. I'll even throw in a pool vehicle and *per diem*. The hotel, though, is on you. Or you can sleep in the backseat of the car. That's your call."

"Thanks, Chief," Myrick simply replied with sincere and simple gratitude. He then turned and walked out of the office, the frosted glass door closing behind him and concealing the (still mystified) stare of the befuddled Police Chief.

Myrick then made his way quickly down to the motor pool, aware that he needed to get on the road if he was going to make it to Santa Fe before sundown. He'd anticipated Chief Clark's approval and had already packed lightly for the trip. There wasn't much he needed anyway, other than a single suit, a few t-shirts and a pair of jeans. He'd stuffed it all hastily in a handheld duffle bag, while placing his one suit carefully on a hanger, and then threw everything in his squad car on the way to the Department.

The police department motor pool was lined with vehicles and on the far end a mechanic was busy working away on modifying one of the undercover vehicles so that it had an upgraded suspension for high speed chases. Myrick called over to the mechanic, although his voice was drowned out by the audible clicking of a torque wrench that echoed inside the building. So Myrick went over and, almost immediately, he could see the lead mechanic stand up, a set of headphones covering his ears. In his hand, he held a dirty rag and was wiping grease off his hands as he noticed Myrick's approach.

"Hey there, Baryshnikov," the mechanic joked, as he took the headphones out of his ears; and Myrick knew instantly that not only had the Police Chief called down to secure him a vehicle, but he'd also let out the secret that it was for Myrick to go to a dance conference. The wisecracks were already beginning and going to be even worse than Myrick had anticipated. "Chief said you needed a shop vehicle. Said you were going to be on Dancing With The Stars."

"Cut it out, Ox," Myrick called Nick Oxworth by his nickname. The name fit too, he was a big, strong man, standing at least 6'4", with a broad frame. He was also one of the most beloved members of the Department, and for good reason. Patrol officers had a hazardous job, oftentimes leading to vehicle wrecks, and Ox was the man who could get them up and running again. He also imagined himself the "Q" of the police department and was constantly fiddling with undercover cars to equip and modify them with things to assist out in the field.

But Ox wasn't just admired for his unmatched mechanical skills, he was a man with a genuinely noble heart. He knew all of the officers, each of them had to stop off at the motor pool at some point, and he was always up for a good chat. Officers, unfortunately, found themselves in their fair share of bad relationships and their off-duty lives were notorious for drama. Many chose police work because they liked the idea of saving others, which sometimes meant they were also attracted to people who might not yet have their own lives in order. The results were far too often predictable, and the mental toll of a demanding job and equally hard relationship was significant.

One by one they talked to Ox, treating him like some sort of psychiatrist that doubled as a mechanic as well. Even Myrick had spent hours and hours hanging out in the motor pool and talking to Ox about the hardships that followed him after Riley's death. And Ox was always ready to listen. Myrick was a man of few words and so it surprised him how much he'd divulged to his friend. Eventually, after Myrick had gotten everything off his chest, it was Ox's turn to talk... and his advice had been sage.

The best way to honor Riley now that she was gone was to keep her memory and the things she found most important alive in his heart. Tragedy, unfortunately, was inevitable in life; anyone who worked as an officer knew that particularly well. There was no denying that evil existed and the world was essentially a constant battle between right and wrong. Life was not supposed to be perfect, but there was a beauty in the struggle, and in the knowledge that God would never forsake him. Myrick and Riley *would* meet again, and in a better place; of that, Ox was certain. Until then, it was more important than ever for Myrick to keep his heart right. Riley was counting on him to do so.

After close to a year of surprisingly deep talks with Ox, Myrick went from a man that harbored more anger and resentment than any one human could seemingly bear, to a deep realization that he'd been blessed to have had his time with Riley. In turn, he wasn't going to let her or God down with what he did with the rest of his life. If the battle was real - and Myrick had seen enough from life to know that it was - he was going to use all his gifts to represent the hope people desperately needed.

"Look, I'm just saying," Ox wiped a smear of grease from off the back of his bicep, only making it worse. He then swiped his hand, which was covered in that same grime, across his mechanic jumpsuit, which was dark gray in color, like the stubble all along his chin and neckline. "You were already the most eligible bachelor in this town, brother. You come back from this trip a dancer and women are going to be all over you. The guys in the Department may give you grief, but they'll all be secretly jealous... even me."

"Oh you too, huh?" Myrick didn't believe Ox for a second. The man was happily married with three kids who he doted on constantly.

"Alright you got me, I pity you," Ox laughed heartily. He had a huge grin on his face that was visible evidence of the exuberant man on the inside, a smile that exhibited more life in it than most men possessed.

"You should. I've got a four hour drive on my hands. I need to get on the road."

"Well, I got you then."

Ox led Myrick out of the garage and behind the building to a fenced in lot. This was where many of the vehicles that had been seized in crimes had been kept. Oftentimes, the Forfeiture Division notified the motor pool that the vehicles would be put up for auction, and that there was no need to do any work on them. However, there were some that could be repurposed for other Department uses, including undercover drug buys, and those were the ones Ox loved to sink his teeth into, coming up with modifications like reinforced steel doors, hidden lights and sirens and other tactical improvements that he felt confident would keep his contemporaries safe in the field.

"Please no," Myrick spoke, suddenly realizing which vehicle Ox was leading him to.

"Yep, you're getting Ol' Blue," Ox pointed to the dilapidated Tahoe that was sitting along a dirt-lined section of the compound.

Myrick knew the history behind Ol' Blue. Most of the officers in the Department did. It'd been seized from a drug kingpin out of Louisiana, who had been just passing through Colorado Springs. Over the next five years, it'd been put to use in multiple sting operations and had gained an almost legendary status. Eventually though, drug dealers got wise to the vehicle and that it signaled undercover cops and so it was put out to pasture, only being used sparingly - and for good reason.

Opening up the side door, Myrick got an unwanted whiff of the mildewed smell of the interior. The seats were lined with worn tan leather, and Myrick could read that the mileage was now at an impressive 178,204. The vehicle was never going to make it out of the lot, let alone to Santa Fe, New Mexico and back.

"You can't do better than this?" Myrick asked, practically begging.

"Relax, she may not look like much, but I promise I've got her running to perfection."

"Does the radio even work?"

"That's right, you're a dancer now. You're gonna want your tunes on the way to Santa Fe. I feel you." Ox winked as he spoke, then finally answered Myrick's question. "Yes, it works. Gets *at least* three stations."

"Just give me the keys," Myrick sighed. He didn't find this whole situation nearly as comical as Ox did. Still, he was determined to make do with what he was given, regardless of the daunting obstacles before him.

Tossing the keys over, Ox watched Myrick snag them out of the air as he almost simultaneously slipped inside the vehicle and into the driver's seat. Myrick then punched the keys into the ignition, turning it over until the vehicle finally sputtered to life.

"See, purrs like a kitten," Ox laughed and Myrick shook his head in dismay without answering back.

Ox then put his hand on the frame of the open door and leaned down a little into the vehicle as he spoke, "Listen brother... you know I'm serious when I say this, stay vigilant. This isn't an environment you walk into unprepared. There's going to be temptations coming at you from every direction."

"I'm an aging widower with two left feet. There's a reason they don't write romance novels about guys like me."

"You're more than that, brother. We've had this talk before... and I know you know that... but stay in the Word. The enemy has many tools in his arsenal, and you're dangerous, so he's going to come at you with everything he's got."

Myrick was listening now, and he'd turned to look his friend in the eyes as he answered, "I really appreciate you, Ox. It's rare to have a friend who's not afraid to speak truth. I'm not sure who else I would talk to if not you."

"It's a guy thing," Ox interrupted - and there were few bigger and manlier than Ox - so the statement had a pronounced effect coming from him.

"But you're right. It's been tough without Riley. I'm not sure if I'm holding on more to her memory or just afraid of the thought of starting over again with someone new. I'll try to keep my wits about me. I won't water down my faith for any job or anyone else."

"That's the detective… and future celebrity dancer… I know." Ox reached inside the interior of the car and hammered his fist against Myrick's. "Alright, brother… I've said my peace." Ox offered up a huge smile again. "You've got my blessings to drive Ol' Blue. Take good care of her."

Myrick waved Ox off, summarily dismissing his affection for Ol' Blue and making it known that he still wasn't happy that Ox hadn't loaned him out a vehicle like the Porsche 911, with the red leather interior, that had been seized a couple of weeks earlier for leading police on a chase down the Interstate. Instead, he'd have to make the long trip in less comfort and style than he'd hoped. At least he had a full tank of gas and a government-issued gas card. And if things went south during the investigation - or if he found himself a lovely potential bride at the dance conference - the undercover vehicle would work nicely to get him across the border and into Mexico where he could start a new life. Those things though, Myrick knew *weren't* going to happen. Instead, and what he couldn't guess, is that events had already been conspiring to make his adventure to Santa Fe way more dangerous than he'd expected.

CHAPTER EIGHT
Dress Up for Themed Events

"Do you need a weekend pass or a day pass?"

"Neither," Myrick replied. There was a pretty girl sitting at the desk of the check-in counter, and she'd peppered him with questions almost immediately, trying to get the rush of attendees all registered.

"Are you a competitor or just here for social dancing?" The girl asked the followup question as if she hadn't understood his first answer, and as she spoke she was doing three things at once, pinning a bib number on a fellow competitor (which read, "153") while rifling through a stack of paperwork for a dancer who was insisting he'd already pre-registered for the event.

Myrick didn't want to have to do it, he'd hoped to stay relatively incognito, but it appeared he wasn't going to be able to get the girl's full attention without at least explaining better who he was and why he was there. Pulling out a leather flip wallet from his pocket, he showed the girl the shiny badge recessed inside it, and as soon as he did, he could see he had her entire attention (as well as the curious stares of a few of the onlookers around him.)

"Wow, that looks real," the girl behind the registration desk spoke, genuinely impressed. "Nice costume, Detective. Cool that you went all out for the Halloween theme tonight."

"Costume?" Myrick stammered, confused. He glanced around to see that there were others in attendance nearby who had on creative attire, and which he'd originally chalked up to the flamboyant preconceptions he had of what dancers wore. "No, this isn't a costume. I'm here to see Ellen Cromwel," he explained. "Is she around?"

"Ellen's backstage," the participant with bib number 153 chimed in. "She's the emcee for the weekend, Justin backed out last minute. Ellen's been in a panic ever since he told her. We're totally behind schedule already." Competitor number 153's voice was hurried, as if she was just as flustered as Ellen was by the sudden change. "I think she's about to walk out in a minute to kick things off for the showcase routines. So unless it's an emergency, it may need to wait Detective…"

"Evann Myrick. And it can definitely wait."

"Thank you. I know Ellen will appreciate that. I'm actually heading back there now. My partner and I are expected out on the floor soon."

"Oh, so you're one of the competitors."

"Yes." Participant number 153 held out her hand to shake Myrick's. "I'm Isabelle. I'll be dancing with Deion."

"And you'll be dancing with him in about fifteen minutes," the girl who was assisting with the safety pinning of the bib number explained, looking down nervously at her watch. "You need to go… *now*."

"Oh wow, well nice to meet you Detective," Isabelle fumbled as she hurried away. "Hope you like our performance."

Her voice drifted off as she turned a corner and entered the ballroom.

Myrick figured he'd do the same and so he took the same path as Isabelle, only in a far less hurried state, and entered an expansive ballroom, much like the one he'd seen at the Colorado Springs event. Immediately, he noticed the oak floor was flooded from end to end with dancers. There were also a myriad of tables set up all around the outskirts. Myrick spotted one in the far back corner and decided that was the best place to discreetly take a seat and survey his surroundings. His talk with Ellen could wait, particularly since his complete unfamiliarity with this type of environment felt more pressing at the moment.

Just as he had previously done in the bar as it was his habit, Myrick took off his coat and placed it in the chair next to him. He then placed his tweed cap neatly on top of the coat so that both appeared in orderly fashion. The lights were dim and he'd found himself almost hidden in the back of the room, which was just the way he wanted it while he tried to get a better feel for his surroundings. There was a DJ at the far left side of the room up in a booth and carefully choosing music for the dancers. This particular song must've been a favorite, as almost everyone in the room was out on the dance floor at the moment.

While most of those present in the ballroom were dressed in casual-type attire, Myrick did notice a small contingent of dancers huddled over in the far corner of the room next to the DJ booth, all of whom were wearing mesmerizing outfits. He could also see that Isabelle had joined them and that the green and gold dress she wore matched the similar colored attire worn by the man standing next to her, Deion Mitchell. The two were talking and Myrick guessed that they'd chosen to coordinate their costumes for the routine that they'd soon be performing. In fact, it seemed that all of the participants lined up next to the DJ booth had done so, each of the dance couples dressed so that their styles and colors were a perfect match.

Myrick was so entranced by what was taking place at the other end of the ballroom that he hadn't noticed someone sidle up beside him, and he was a bit startled when she went to speak: "I know you, don't I?" a girl spoke, catching Myrick's attention.

Glancing instinctively over, Myrick could see that it was Jayde Ch'en, and while he'd preferred not to have company, he was at least grateful to see a familiar face in the otherwise foreign surroundings.

"You're the detective from Colorado Springs, right? Are you here to do some follow up in the investigation?" she asked, astutely. "Or did you come to social dance?" Her eyes squinted in a curious fashion, as she knew that wasn't the case, but found it amusing to ask.

"Just here strictly on work. Waiting for Ms. Cromwel to have a free moment to talk."

"Then you'll be hanging out for quite a while. I think she's a little overwhelmed right now. Not sure if you heard but our emcee backed out."

"I did hear that," Myrick acknowledged. "Seems like there's never a dull moment at these events."

"So true. Which is one of the things I like most about it actually," Jayde revealed, and Myrick found himself believing her, as he guessed that she was capable of stirring up a little trouble herself from time to time. He also noticed that she had on a subtle costume of sorts for the Halloween-themed event, a black shirt with a blood-red image in the middle of four men who appeared to be singers in a band and whose images seemed to be painted in blood. There were also rips and tears in the shirt along the midsection and side as if it had been shredded by a clawing predator.

"Interesting costume by the way," Myrick noted.

"You like it? I decided to go all out this year. I'm a former groupie who suffered a psychotic episode after being rejected by a band member on Singles Appreciation Day."

"Hmmm, was I supposed to get all that from the shirt you're wearing?"

"You're a good detective, right?"

"Better than most, I'd say."

"Okay, well then yeah, you probably should've," Jayde shrugged her shoulders, convinced she was correct in her logic.

"Of course, it might have been a little more convincing had you added a broken cupid arrow placed near your heart and the other broken half sticking out from the back." Myrick winked as if to indicate he knew exactly who she was trying to portray with her costume.

"Maybe," Jayde said dismissively, although it was evident she was impressed with Myrick's knowledge of Indie bands.

"Well, since you're here, maybe you can help me understand a few things," Myrick decided it was time to change the topic.

"Of course," Jayde answered back readily. She then carefully lifted up his coat and cap and placed them neatly in another chair nearby so that she could commandeer the seat next to him as she spoke, "fire away." And Myrick, in turn, wondered to if she hadn't deliberately used the double-meaning term in her reply.

"What are those people gathered over there in the corner for? I see a lot of familiar faces from the interviews, including Jill McKenna's former partner... Deion Mitchell."

"Showcase routines are coming up. Most of these couples have been working on them for months and they debut them at the dance conferences. Deion is performing with Isabelle.

"I thought Deion and Jill were partners."

"They are... or were... for some things. But Deion is dating Isabelle. And while she isn't a pro... or even a good dancer in my opinion... she insists on performing some with him. The routines don't affect overall Tier Points in the Registry so it's more for fun and notoriety than anything else."

Myrick was about to speak again, he had so many questions, but then suddenly noticed the lights turn on and the dancers, as if on cue, all vacated the dance floor, returning to their respective tables. A split second later, Ellen walked out onto the floor, dressed as elegantly as ever and carrying a microphone in her hand.

"Ok, well... welcome to the Santa Fe Swingtacular!" she announced, excitedly. And Myrick didn't note even a hint of trepidation in her voice, as if Ellen had done this so many times that it was essentially old hat to step in last minute and run a show. "Get ready for an *amazing* weekend. And we're going to kick it off right with my favorite part of all... the Routine Divisions! Afterward, we'll open up the floor again to everyone for social dancing the rest of the evening. And don't forget that tonight's social is themed for Halloween. I'm hoping to see some spooky good costumes. In the morning, we'll start off with the Strictly Swing Divisions and then move into Jack & Jills for the afternoon. So get ready for an exciting weekend… and *very* little sleep. Alright, our first showcase routine of the weekend… Alexander Kozlov and Natasha Levin!"

Ellen stepped away from the dance floor, the lights dimmed once again and then the backdrop was lit up with a purple-hued ambient light, setting the mood for the performance. Myrick could see that a row of people had lined the entire exterior of the floor, sitting Indian-style, and trying to get as close a glimpse of the routine as possible. There was a perceptible air of excitement in the room. On cue, Alexander and Natasha stepped out of the shadow of the curtains. The two then hurried out onto the floor, stopping almost dead center, looking away from each other and allowing the silence to create a moment of anticipation.

As soon as the first beat of the music hit, Alexander and Natasha turned their heads in dramatic fashion and stared into each other's eyes. They then immediately went into a choreographed routine. It was brilliantly orchestrated. Alexander was strong and strapping, whereas Natasha was thin and graceful and Alexander easily twirled her around, with moves that plunged her so close to the ground at times that her head was only inches from the floor as she was quickly dipped toward it. Myrick imagined that the practices for the performance must've been grueling and he understood Natasha had to place an immeasurable amount of trust in Alexander to pull off such risky maneuvers. The performance, however, went off without a hitch as far as Myrick could tell, and the audience burst into applause at the end of it; the two competitors displaying huge smiles of joy as they bowed before the audience and then made their way off the floor.

"That was absolutely brilliant," Jayde simply remarked, her eyes still on Alexander and Natasha as she spoke. "I really hope that when I make it to the pro ranks, they're still around to mentor me. I could learn so much from Natasha."

Next up were Deion and Isabelle, who made a stunning pair in their green and gold costumes. Whereas Alexander and Natasha's performance was fast paced and full of acrobatic flair, this one was markedly different. Deion and Isabelle may not have been as flashy, but their dance was no less intriguing, at least to Myrick. Their style was as flirty as their song choice, and it had a sultriness to it that was unmistakable. While Natasha had been shown off as the focus in her dance with Alexander, Myrick picked up that Deion was the star this time around, and his entire interaction and movements conveyed a storyline as if he was possessing Isabelle, waving his free hand over her eyes mysteriously while he dipped her down low to the floor then snatched her up in dramatic fashion, as if bringing her to life once again.

"She's cheating her footwork," Jayde suddenly spoke, not looking at Myrick, but clearly intending for him to hear her comment.

"Looks impressive to me," Myrick noted.

"They'll give her high marks... they won't want to disappoint Deion... but this is anything but impressive."

"How exactly do you decide the winner in something like this when all these people are so talented?"

"It's no different than a lot of things in life that have a subjective element of judging - ice skating, beauty pageants, high dive competitions, etcetera. The judges each have tablets and are scoring them on various factors: timing, connection, musicality. Later on, they'll get together privately to see how their marks and tallies add up. Then, we'll all eventually get a group text or see a post on social media at some point tonight that scores have been posted, and we'll all race back down to the ballroom to see who won. It's probably the most interesting part of the night... or at least has the most intrigue. If you place high, it makes the whole rest of the weekend way more enjoyable. You don't, and it can make you wish you could just go home and sulk."

"And you don't think this performance deserves to score well," Myrick had turned his attention to Jayde as he spoke, trying to size her up, curious at the hint of jealousy he'd picked up in her voice, and relatively certain that she hadn't received the same level of favoritism as Isabelle.

"No, I think she's just coasting. *Annnddd,* I'm pretty sure she's drunk. Probably downed a few too many drinks before the routine to calm her nerves. It doesn't matter though, Deion's an incredible dancer. He'll carry the performance for them. All she has to do is just follow his lead," Jayde's eyes hadn't left the dance floor for the entire time she'd spoken, clearly studying every second of the routine, and evidently aware of technical mistakes being made that Myrick would never have noticed.

In fact, Myrick turned his attention back to Deion and Isabelle as well, curious to see if he could spot the same things that were clearly vexing Jayde. He couldn't though. Sure, he could tell the routine wasn't as impressive overall. It had a sultry flair to it, and the song was slow and graceful, not lending itself to outlandish moves. But Myrick did still enjoy it nonetheless, as it almost had a theatrical performance feel to it; two dancers gliding around in stirring fashion, portraying an air of romance that the audience too seemed to be eating up.

"You see that?" Jayde pointed out, while watching; and Myrick was certain this time that it was only a rhetorical question. "She's still cheating her footwork. That was an *entire* eight count without a single triple-step. She's just walking. So frustrating to watch."

Myrick didn't interrupt her train of thought, as he really had nothing to add, she was talking about dance terms that meant nothing to him. But what did mean something to him, and what did fall within his expertise, was the change in her demeanor and what it meant in his investigation. Jayde evidently had a love-hate relationship with the people she competed amongst, and she wasn't good at hiding those conflicting emotions.

The rest of the routines continued on throughout the night, and it was an opportunity not only for Myrick to get more familiar with the pros that he'd interviewed in Colorado Springs, but also to pick Jayde's brain regarding each of them. And she was an open book, having an opinion and compelling take on just about everyone they watched compete. In fact, interestingly, Myrick noted that she'd make a fantastic detective, herself, and that she might even turn out to be a huge asset to his investigation.

It was close to 8:30 when the final routine of the competition took place, and from the shadows emerged a couple decked out in all black attire; and as he learned more about them, he began to wonder if these two might just be the most likely suspects in his investigation yet. Their names, Jayde explained, were Sacha Arnaud and Victoria Monroe. As always, they both had interesting backstories according to Jayde, but Sacha's was particularly intriguing to Myrick. Jayde told him about how Sacha was one of the top pros, but that things had turned and that he'd been blackballed by his contemporaries. Unlike Deion's routine, where Jayde was certain he'd get high scores, Jayde insisted Sacha and Victoria would not.

Again, Myrick watched to see if he could find the flaws or anything to distinguish how one routine stood out from another's, but to his untrained eye, they all seemed faultlessly performed. After a good minute or so of observing in silence, Myrick ventured to ask Jayde's opinion.

"What do you think of this one?"

"Pretty impressive so far," Jayde insisted, and Myrick could tell she respected the performance. "Sacha may be a first class jerk… but he's nailing it."

"And what about his partner?"

"Also good."

"But you think Sacha's is better?"

"I respect his *skill*," Jayde emphasized, "But I think Victoria's making a mistake teaming up with him. She'd be better off with just about anyone else. She's either incredibly naive… or she's playing his game also… which would be too bad because I've always thought Victoria was a genuinely good person. Beware the innocent seeming ones, right?" Jayde shrugged her shoulders in resignation.

"Interesting," Myrick returned, appreciating that there was far more going on than just a simple exhibition of skill. "What was it that he did that caused him to be blackballed?"

"There's rumors that he had an affair," Jayde paused, then glanced over at Myrick, a slight wry smile on her face, as if knowing her next words would have an impact, "with Natasha. And I know it's true because I caught them together. I've just never told anyone... until now."

But if Jayde had expected a perceptible reaction from Myrick, she was about to be disappointed. Myrick betrayed very little astonishment, instead simply pulling out his little notebook and recording the important detail in the same tedious fashion as he did all the others. Emotion, it seemed, played very little role in the way Myrick processed facts.

"Seems this whole environment lends itself to complicated relationship dynamics," he commented, once he was done writing in his notepad.

"You have no idea. Imagine what it's like to have your whole life judged by the same people you also have to spend an entire weekend hanging out with. Sacha not only has to compete and let these same people tell him what they think of his performance, but he's also got to stick around all weekend for social dancing, private lessons, workshops... that's why I respect him so much. You have to be incredibly tough to fight through all that. But then again, he has no choice. This is his career. This is how he pays the bills."

"So pros don't have other jobs outside dance?"

"Oh sure, some do. But being a pro is more about what happens behind the scenes than people realize. There's hours and hours of practice each day, which is exhausting both physically and mentally. Then there's the private lessons late into the night. Between studio time and travel, there isn't much time for a second career. At least not one that would really pay much," Jayde explained, then revealed one more interesting fact. "I've sort of lucked out though. I'm a bartender at a club and so I can just hit the dance floor right after my shift is over to get some practice in. The manager is a decent guy and he lets some of my friends stick around so we can use the dance floor to work on routines."

"Seems like a long night. You must not get much sleep."

"I'm a night owl... and an insomniac. I'm pretty sure a lot of the people in this room are."

Myrick finished up watching the routine by Sacha and Victoria. It appeared as flawless as all the others had to him, but he did particularly enjoy the unflappable appearance of Sacha, understanding now the backstory, and how clinical the performance was. It seemed to Myrick that Sacha even glanced over at the judges once or twice, as if to dare them not to score him well. The melodramatic aspects of it were almost more enjoyable than the routine itself. Once it had ended and the song had faded out, the two dancers did as the others, taking their bows in front of an appreciative audience and then summarily making their way off the floor.

As the lights faded up once again, Ellen was back out in front of the crowd, an electric smile visible on her face. She was literally beaming with how impressively the convention had kicked off, and appeared a bit relieved that the only significant hiccup had (at least so far) been the failure of her emcee to show. Ellen explained that competitions would continue in the morning, and that the newcomers would be going first, followed by Novice, Intermediate, Advanced, Masters and All-Star, in that order. The floor was then turned over to social dancing for the rest of the night, and the excitement in the air was palpable.

"You want to dance?" Jayde suddenly turned to Myrick.

Very little ever fazed Myrick, even the unexpected. Over two decades of police work, he'd engaged in life and death shootouts with suspects; chased down carjackers and armed robbers; and gone toe-to-toe with some of society's worst and most dangerous. But none of those things intimidated Myrick quite like the thought of walking out onto the dance floor did, and so he politely (and quickly) declined. In turn, Jayde shrugged her shoulders, as if to indicate it was his loss; and without putting up any further argument, she got up from the table and walked toward the crowd.

Almost immediately, Myrick caught sight as another attendee hurried over to Jayde, spoke a few words and then led her out into the crowd of people. He continued watching for a minute as they quickly got to dancing, and Myrick could tell that Jayde was indeed an accomplished dancer, maybe just as good as the pros had been, her movements fluid, rhythmic and impressively styled. Seeing this only made Myrick even more grateful he'd turned down the request, as he had no desire to make a fool out of himself. He also remembered the wise words of Ox, and how important it was to stay on task, which he was absolutely determined to do. Only it wouldn't be long until he found out how impossible that was going to be and the temptations that lay ahead.

CHAPTER NINE
Accentuate the "1"s

It took an eternity for Ellen to finally reach the table in the back of the ballroom where Myrick was sitting. All the while, he watched in fascination as Ellen was bombarded by the conference's attendees who all wanted a word with her as she pushed her way over to him. He waited patiently and had barely gotten in a "hello" when she was cornered by another dancer who had "an emergency" and needed to know if it was possible to still register for the Novice competition despite missing the deadline. Ellen calmly answered the girl's question, and it was impressive to see how adeptly she solved everyone's problems. No doubt, she was great at her job.

Given the circumstances, Ellen insisted Myrick follow her and then she led them back to a side hospitality room, where only the pros were allowed to enter. Once inside there, Myrick could see it was relatively empty at the moment, as the professionals were either social dancing or back in their rooms changing out of the costumes worn in the night's earlier performances. Only one other person was in the room, Sacha Arnaud's partner in the routine - Victoria Monroe. She was stunning with long strawberry-blonde hair, fair features... and azure blue eyes, which were the complete opposite end of the color spectrum from her hair color and thus stood out even more. Ellen went over to Victoria, said a few words to her and then Victoria turned to leave the room. As she did, she passed right by Myrick, offering a smile in his direction, and he got a whiff of her perfume, which was a textured fusion of floral and woody, and which lent itself to a certain mysteriousness. Myrick allowed his eyes to linger on Victoria even as she stepped through the doorway and out of the room.

"Finally," Ellen offered up in exhaustion, oblivious to the fact that Myrick's attention was not yet entirely on her. But in her defense, this was also the first opportunity for peace that Ellen had had, and she practically slumped into a nearby chair, just grateful for the brief moment of calm.

"You're quite in demand," Myrick noted as he finally took a seat in a chair as well. The sound of the music coming from the ballroom was muted by the walls, but could still be faintly heard, and the relaxed environment was a nice contrast to the boisterous nature of things taking place next door to them.

Ellen paused to collect herself before she spoke, and there were a few seconds of quiet contemplation. "Sometimes even *I* wonder why I do this," Ellen chuckled a bit as she spoke, but it was the laugh of a woman teetering on the edge of madness. She then continued, "I feel like a bride on her wedding day... that's caught up in a perpetual loop. I put so much hard work getting things prepared for these conferences. More goes into making them happen than people could ever understand... and then when the big day arrives, it all passes in a whirlwind of excitement. It's hard to just stop and savor the best moments.

And it seems as though I blink and then the weekend is over, all in a blur."

"Then why do you do it?"

"I don't know. Maybe I'm some sort of sadist or something. Or maybe if I'm being honest," Ellen's tone changed a bit and betrayed the truthful reflection in her words, "maybe I just crave the attention. I competed for years. The adulation and celebrity status is hard to move on from. So when it's gone... when you're past your prime and a new, younger group starts to come in... it's hard to give all that up completely. I filled that void by becoming a host of these events, I guess."

"I'm sure a lot of these people are very grateful for what you do," Myrick offered up, believing what he was saying, as he could see that the attendees were all having a great time.

"That's what I keep telling myself," Ellen laughed back. She then sat upright a little more and leaned forward to indicate a change in the conversation. "So, um, I should tell you, I'm a bit surprised to see you here."

"I'm sorry, ma'am. I did try calling. Your voicemail is full."

"Oh, yes... I get so slammed right before the conferences. I can't keep up with all the calls and last minute needs of everyone. Even my emcee ducked out on me... Which I'm not happy about, *at all*."

"I heard that happened. But the show must go on, right."

"Exactly." Ellen paused, now considering how it might have seemed rude that she'd not returned the detective's calls. "I apologize about not reaching back out to you. What is it that I can do to help?"

"I still haven't had an opportunity to interview two primary suspects: Alexander Kozlov and Natasha Levin, and I have some followup for some of the others present in Colorado Springs, especially Sacha Arnaud. I could use some help coordinating that."

"Of course," Ellen responded, then had another thought. "Where are you staying? I wish I'd have seen your calls, I could've gotten you a room comped here for the weekend."

"I booked a motel off site, just a couple of miles away. It's a bit seedy but beats sleeping in Ol' Blue," Myrick mused to himself, aware that Ellen wouldn't understand the jest. "I'm good."

"No, that won't do. I'm going to get you a room here tonight. My dancers booked out this whole hotel. We bring them in a small fortune of business. The hotel can comp me a room in return. I'm pretty sure there's one or two still available... we had a couple of attendees back out last minute, as usual."

Myrick thought about protesting, but then also remembered the troubled state of the motel he'd dropped his stuff off at, including the half-eaten sandwich and beer can he'd found still sitting on the bedside table, and knew instantly he'd made a mistake going with a budget inn. Besides, it would also assist his investigation to stay as close as possible to the action. And so, he finally accepted Ellen's offer, grateful once again for her hospitality.

"I also came here for another reason," Myrick then revealed. "It's been something of a hindrance not being familiar with the ins and outs of what actually goes on at these events. I could use your help showing me around and explaining things."

"You know I would, but you just got a small taste of how busy I am. The minute I walk out of this room, they'll be hounding me with more requests and emergencies. It won't be long until the pros are back and they need me to figure out scheduling issues, and booking side rooms for private lessons, and issues with music or costumes or whatever. It never ends."

"I understand. I really didn't comprehend just how busy you'd be."

"But I do have an idea. I can get you someone to assist. Someone who isn't quite as overwhelmed as me."

"That'd be great."

"I saw you were sitting with Jayde. And I'm sure you've figured out that she knows this setting better than anyone. She's a volunteer this weekend. I've got her scheduled to assist with late check-ins and comp registrations tomorrow. The way it works is you volunteer and you get a free pass to the entire weekend. But it means she has to put in a good eight to ten hours of volunteer work as well. I'll bet she'd be thrilled if I relieved her of that responsibility. She could then help with whatever you need investigation wise."

"That's really kind of you."

"I don't mind at all, Detective," Ellen smiled, and there was a bit of a flirtatious air to her words. "I'm also going to call over to the hotel manager now to get you that room."

Myrick wasn't the most perceptive when it came to women. He had been with Riley since high school and had never dated anyone other than her, and quite literally only had eyes for his wife. So without her, he was wholly unaware of the clues that women sometimes offered in their choice of words or mannerisms to exhibit interest. Plus the entire concept of dating had changed radically over the decades and very little about the rushed nature of it appealed to him anyway. So Ellen's subtle hints were hopelessly lost on him as well; and Myrick simply thanked her again, while standing up from his chair to indicate he understood how busy she was and that he didn't want to take up too much of her time.

"I did have one more question though, the girl who was just in here... Ms. Monroe... this is the pro room, right? But I don't remember her being one of the judges at the Colorado Springs event or at least not on the video you showed me."

"Oh, Victoria... yes, she was at Colorado Springs also," Ellen explained. "But she wasn't scheduled to judge that particular competition. We rotate so the pros get some down time also. She was backstage with me. I needed help going over the schedule and the night's announcements. She's good with those types of things... a big help to me. It was only the two of us back there, I believe."

"Just making sure not to overlook any important details. If you don't mind, let's set it up for me to interview her along with Kozlov, Levin and Arnaud tomorrow morning. I'd appreciate it."

"Of course, Detective."

"I guess I'll head back over to my motel to grab my belongings and check out," Myrick said, clearly relieved and grateful for the favor.

"I understand," Ellen returned, now standing and smiling to indicate she understood that Myrick also needed to leave so that he could get back to business. "And again, if you need me for anything, I'm here."

"I appreciate it," Myrick nodded, tipping his tweed cap to show his appreciation. He then ran his fingers through the hair along the back of his head three times in apparent contemplation, before finally turning to leave the room.

Yet, as he opened the door, he almost ran straight into Sacha. The two made brief eye contact and it appeared the man was in a bit of a hurry and there was a perceptible fire in his gaze. Myrick stepped aside to let him pass. As he did, Sacha made no attempt to apologize for his hurried state. Myrick then watched as the visibly disconcerted man walked over to Ellen, wanting to talk about something urgent with her. Myrick took his cue and without saying more continued to make his way out of the room, closing the door behind him as he did, but also catching a whispered, although heated, word or two between Sacha and Ellen in the process; and learning that there was apparently a bit of trouble with Natasha.

The loud music from outside, though, ultimately drowned out Myrick's ability to make out anymore of the conversation than he already had, and so he was resigned to letting things play out however they may. In the meantime, he could see that he was standing on the fringes of the dance floor and the multitude of people all having a good time on it. Myrick felt it best to make his way out of the ballroom and so he pushed through, although as he did so he was approached a couple of times from women requesting dances, which he politely declined, a quizzical look on his face each time it happened.

Exiting the ballroom, Myrick made his way past the litany of vendor booths, admiring the dresses and jewelry and other items for sale. There were plenty of dancers milling about as well, and it was evident that despite the increasingly late hour, there'd been an uptick in the amount of people decked out in costumes for the Halloween-themed portion; and things were actually starting to come even more alive, as if the best part of the night was still to come. Myrick took it all in, more fascinated than ever by his new surroundings and then headed out into the large foyer of the hotel where things were a bit more subdued.

Myrick was almost past the check-in desk, when he noticed an argument taking place over by the elevators. Alexander and Deion were both there, and it appeared they were in the midst of a tense disagreement. Deion was doing the majority of the talking, evidently lecturing Alexander. In turn, Alexander clearly wanted nothing to do with whatever Deion was saying, his arms crossed and a stern look pasted on his face. A split second later and the elevator door opened. Myrick watched as Alexander and Deion disappeared inside it, and their muddled voices were faded out as the elevator's doors closed.

The last thing Myrick heard was Deion say something to the effect of: "You shouldn't have let her get under your skin, man. That was your first mistake." Or at least that's what it *sounded* to Myrick like had been said, he was too far away to be certain. Regardless, as far as Myrick was concerned, this was yet another quintessential example of the tension that existed at these conferences. He guessed (rightly) that these events were a perfect storm of excitement, unpredictability and emotions, making each one an interesting weekend, and Myrick found himself on-edge wondering what unexpected developments would come next.

Turning to make his way out of the lobby through the sliding doors, Myrick was immediately hit with a burst of cool nighttime air, and cloudy vapors even appeared from his breath as he exhaled. The dingy motel was only a mile or so away, and it was tempting to walk and just enjoy the nighttime scenery of downtown Santa Fe and its pueblo-style architecture, most of which was stunningly lit up with lights. Myrick, though, didn't want to delay even a moment longer than necessary, unable to shake the feeling that if he lingered for too long, he'd miss out on something important. Although, what he would soon come to find out is that by the time he returned, regardless of whether he hurried or not, he would indeed come back to find circumstances had completely changed - and not for the better.

CHAPTER TEN
Master the Basics

It only took Myrick about thirty minutes to go to the motel, cancel his reservation, grab his bag and return to the site of the conference, but before he'd even gotten to the hotel's parking lot, he caught a glimpse of the flashing red and white lights of the rescue ambulance parked outside the entrance. Pulling up to the curb quickly, he arrived just in time to see a medic rolling a patient in an upright gurney and into the back of the ambulance. Immediately, Myrick recognized the face of the woman lying in the gurney - it was Natasha.

There was a second medic standing nearby, apparently filling out medical forms. Myrick walked over to her, displayed his badge and then began asking a few questions.

"What's Colorado Springs PD doing here?" The medic asked, her long hair in a ponytail, and tucked underneath a cap that had a medical cross on it and read, "SFFR".

"Following up on a string of homicides, including two from my jurisdiction," Myrick explained, flipping the recessed badge wallet closed as he spoke, "and just hoping there's not another victim to add to the case."

"Oh no, it's nothing like that," the medic returned. "She's just a Code 2 response."

Myrick was familiar with the term and understood that the situation had already been deemed "an acute but non time-critical" transport by EMS.

"Most likely a case of food poisoning," the medic continued. "She'll be fine."

"You're taking her in?"

"It's precautionary only. She's been throwing up a little bit of blood, and it scared her. She asked to be transported... and there are slight signs of hematemesis so we're going to have the hospital run a few tests on her."

"She say anything?"

"No, she's actually not saying much. Just seemed scared by the sudden onset of the vomiting. The boyfriend actually did all the talking. Told us that they'd just competed and afterward wanted to get drinks, but he got distracted talking with another competitor named Sacha Arnaud. Apparently, that upset Ms. Levin and so she actually snatched a drink out of Mr. Arnaud's hand, quickly downed it, then insisted it was time to go. The boyfriend admitted they'd argued all the way to the elevators, but he said he'd never laid a hand on her... and she doesn't have any visible marks or bruises on her body. Didn't seem like it was cause for too much concern, and we agreed with him, but she requested the transport," the medic shrugged her shoulders as she explained.

Myrick considered asking if he could have a few words with Natasha, but then heard the discernible sounds of her gagging once again and knew immediately this wasn't the time or place to interrupt the treatment she was receiving in the back of the ambulance.

"You mind giving her this and asking her to contact me when she's discharged from the hospital?"

"Of course," the medic took a smallish white card from Myrick that had the Colorado Springs PD insignia, his name and cell number on it.

Seconds later and the initial medic Myrick had seen rolling the gurney popped his head out of the back of the ambulance and called out to his colleague who was still talking with Myrick, "Let's get moving, Brooks!"

"10-4," she confirmed, turning and walking over to the front of the ambulance, opening the driver's side door and getting behind the wheel of the vehicle. As the ambulance sped off, sirens and horns now activated, Myrick watched for a brief moment then turned his attention back toward the hotel and the small crowd of onlookers that had gathered by the entrance. Alexander was present, concern evident on his face. Standing a few feet away from him was Deion, who had his arm around a visibly affected Ellen to comfort her.

As the ambulance disappeared from sight, the crowd slowly began to disburse, their murmuring voices drifting into the distance as they went back inside the hotel to gossip and theorize about what had happened. Myrick decided to head inside also, planning to ask Alexander a few questions. Before he could get to him, though, Jayde appeared from out of nowhere.

"So do you respond to danger or does danger just follow you?" Jayde asked of Myrick.

"Maybe a little of both," Myrick pondered the significance of the question.

"I'm really worried about, Natasha," Jayde then elaborated, and her words had a level of genuine worry in them. "I'm glad they're taking her to the hospital. With everything going on, it's better that they take her situation serious."

Myrick smiled at Jayde, respecting how much she seemed to care for her friend and contemporary. "I'm sure she'll be fine."

"I don't know. I don't like any of this," Jayde returned, less convinced. After a somber pause, she turned her gaze back to Myrick, changing the subject, "Ellen mentioned to me that you might need my help this weekend. I'd hoped she meant with the investigation… but she said it was solely limited to the dance side of things."

Myrick still wanted to get to Alexander, but his conversation with Jayde seemed well-timed also, and he could tell that she was going to be far more helpful than just with showing him the dance ropes.

"Yes, it seems more apparent with every twist and turn just how out of my element I am here."

"It'll become more familiar eventually. You'll see. Soon, you'll be one of us," Jayde winked as she spoke, betraying the dark burgundy eyeliner under her lids that perfectly (and frightfully) matched the slayer-type shirt she wore as a Halloween costume.

"Did you see anything?" Myrick ventured to ask, not yet convinced Natasha hadn't been the latest victim of a crime.

"Not really. But the rumor mill has already started up, no surprise there."

"Many times there's a hint of truth buried in rumors. Where there's smoke, there's fire."

"Then you should talk with Sacha because he's the one yelling 'smoke' the loudest."

"Good idea," Myrick concurred, walking inside the hotel, glancing around as he moved through the lobby, studying the faces of everyone around him as he did. Ellen was visibly upset and seemed to be peppering Alexander with questions, wanting the full scoop about what had happened. Myrick imagined she was doing a better job than he could ever do getting answers from him and so he let Ellen do her thing; instead trusting Jayde's intuition that Sacha was the one to talk to at the moment.

As he turned a narrow corridor, there was a charmingly furnished sitting area, conceptualized with earth-toned color combinations and rustic artwork. Sitting alone in a soothingly deep blue hued chair was a singular individual - Sacha Arnaud; and he seemed to be alone and struggling with his thoughts. Nearby was a glass enclosed fireplace that had been secured at the base with a cylindrical shaped, lime-washed lower wall, and the flickering of its flames gave the space a warm, inviting feel as if it was beckoning Myrick to come over. Deciding to do so, he took a few steps in the direction of the sitting room only to realize he was being followed. Jayde was still trailing close by, apparently convinced she was part of the investigative team.

"I appreciate your help," Myrick stopped and turned to speak to her, "I really do. But let me play detective alone during this part."

"You sure?" Jayde questioned, then offered a reason for him to reconsider. "Sacha's not much of a talker. You're going to make him uncomfortable. It might help if I was there to take some of the edge off, give him a familiar face in the room. Someone he can trust."

Myrick considered the point, and agreed there was a measure of wisdom in it. Witnesses tended to clam up pretty quick when the potential for getting dragged into the legal system arose. Society had changed in the two-plus decades Myrick had been doing police work and he understood that people had changed with it, less trusting and willing to talk than they used to be.

"Fair enough," Myrick relented. "Just get introductions going and let me take it from there."

Jayde grinned, a look of youthful vigor in her expression. She then gave Myrick a nod and side glance as if to indicate to Myrick that something had happened, and he turned to see that Sacha had gotten up from his chair and was walking away in the direction of the ballroom. He had his dance shoes in his hand.

"Hey, Sacha," Jayde called over to the man with a face as interesting as the room they were currently in. Hearing his name, he then glanced over at her, a searing expression in his eyes like those of a wolf. "This is Detective Myrick. You got a minute to talk with him?"

"I know who he is. We talked in Colorado Springs already," Sacha returned, a bleak tone to his voice. He stopped walking, his voice even less inviting than before, "Hello, detective. Not sure there's much more I can tell you than I already have. But is there something I can do for you?"

"It looked like you and Ellen were having a heated discussion earlier. You want to tell me what you told her... what it is Alexander did or said that had you all upset?"

"Not really," Sacha answered, he then indicated with his eyes that he was going to continue on in the direction of the ballroom, although as he did, he still kept talking so Myrick and Jayde followed. "Alexander and I just don't see eye-to-eye, especially when it comes to scheduling matters."

"You're telling me that what had you that angry was solely over a scheduling issue. I find that hard to believe." Myrick knew that Sacha was holding something back.

"Well, that's all it was. You can choose to believe me or not." Sacha stopped once more this time only a few yards away from the entrance to the ballroom. "So, unless there's more you wanted to know, I actually came here to have some fun this weekend. I think we could all use a little of that after the nightmare that was Colorado Springs, don't you think?" He then glanced over at Jayde and spoke again, "You want to follow me inside for a dance?"

Jayde shook her head immediately, clearly caught off guard by the strangeness of his request. "Now's not the time, Sacha," she answered back quickly, a hint of confusion in her voice. "He's only here to help," she insisted.

"Then I'm sure you can tell him everything he needs to know about me… you know all my dirty secrets. Just remember though, two can play that game," Sacha cryptically replied.

"That's not what this is about," Jayde went to protest, but her voice trailed off as Sacha continued over to the ballroom door, walking past Jayde as if she wasn't even there.

Myrick's stare stayed on Sacha as he went over to a group of people huddled about just outside the entrance to the ballroom. He then whispered something in the ear of one of the girls that got her attention. Taking his hand, she followed Sacha through the door and into the ballroom. In turn, Myrick and Jayde walked over, peering inside just in time to see the two were already out on the dance floor and had begun dancing to a slow paced song, their movements deliberate, sensual and dramatic.

"I'm sorry, that wasn't how I expected things would go down," Jayde offered up, her voice apologetic.

"I thought you were going to be some sort of asset to me," Myrick returned, although not in a condescending but more so amused fashion.

"Not sure what to say. I'm not wrong often."

Myrick's cheeks rose in a smile, now enjoying the company of his new friend and appreciative of someone to bounce theories off. "So, Ellen suggested you help me," Myrick changed the subject to something he felt less certain about, "with dance? Hmmmm. I guess the noble thing to do then is to let you tag along on the investigation. You teach me a thing or two about this unique environment… I'll show you a little about what it takes to be a detective. Deal?"

"That's the deal." Jayde offered back a wide grin, already certain of her next move. She then took Myrick's hand, determined to get him out on the dance floor.

"Um, what're you doing?" he asked.

"You want to understand dance, right? Well, there's only one way to do that."

"I want you to *tell* me about it."

"That's a little like someone trying to explain how to paint… or play an instrument… or even become a detective. Sure, we could try that… but you might as well read an instructional book if that's solely your goal. To really understand it, you have to experience it for yourself… you're going to have to let me actually teach you what to do, music playing and all. Trust me, I got this. I know what I'm doing."

Myrick didn't like this idea… in the slightest. And he attempted to stand his ground, hopeful he was going to win the battle. Meanwhile, Jayde had other ideas, and was equally stubborn in her persistence.

"Come on," she pushed. "There's literally no one who's watching right now. This is the perfect time to get out there." And as she was talking, Jayde was slyly pulling Myrick forward and toward the dance floor. "Let me at least show you a move or two. You might even gain a little street cred with Sacha in the process."

Continuing to nudge Myrick along, Jayde had him on the edge of the dance floor before he even understood what had happened. The music was infectious and Jayde was already swaying to the beat, as if she could start dancing at any second. She then moved to the side of Myrick and pointed down at her feet.

"Watch me," she instructed. She then took two steps in place, "One, two…" she spoke as she did so. Then she took three more faster-paced steps, explaining, "three-and-four." Finally, she did the exact same thing, taking three more fast steps and stating, "five-and-six." Jayde then stopped, looked over at Myrick and added, matter-of-factly, "That's it. That's West Coast Swing. And I know you can totally do that."

Myrick returned a very doubtful look, not convinced in the slightest that West Coast Swing was as simple as Jayde had made it seem; and he was wise to the fact that years of practice had given her the gift of making dance look like an easy thing.

"Just try," she persisted, and then she spoke again to reinforce the simplicity of the steps, "one... two," she began marching in two steps. "Three-and-four... five-and-six," she called out rhythmically to the movement of her feet. "The first two steps are called 'walking steps'... and the last four counts are all done to a 'triple-step' timing. At least give it a shot for me."

Again, Jayde started her cadence, and as if in a trance, Myrick felt himself follow along.

"One... two," Jayde continued, and Myrick marched in place like a soldier plodding along.

It took everything in Jayde not to smile, aware of how cute and awkward Myrick's footwork appeared, and not wanting to dissuade him. "Three-and-four... five-and-six," she kept time perfectly with the music; Myrick shuffling his footwork on the triple-steps, not really distinguishing between them, but also making an admirable attempt.

"There you go," Jayde encouraged him, and she was a bit impressed that he'd gotten the gist of the triple-step down so quickly. "Now, try with me," Jayde moved in front of Myrick, took his left hand in her right, and then stepped with him to the music, calling it out in perfect timing to the music. There was a smoothness to her every movement, like a billow of willowy smoke through breezy air. And there was a contrasting Frankenstein-ish appearance to Myrick's efforts, which *fortunately* he couldn't see in himself. Still, it was a start, and Myrick was having more fun than he expected; wisely guessing that he was only doing as well as he was because Jayde was there guiding him along.

Emboldened by the circumstances and lost in the moment a bit, Myrick swayed his head from side to side, apparently picking up the beat of the music. Unfortunately, just as he did, his tweed cap went flying off in front of him. Myrick was too slow to react... but incredibly Jayde wasn't. Without even breaking stride, she reached out with her free hand and snatched the cap out of the air before it hit the ground. Still clearly in perfect step with the rhythm, she playfully tossed the cap onto her own head, chuckled a bit and continued their dance, as if a simple thing for her to do. Finally, as the music started to fade out, Jayde stopped calling out the cadence, handed Myrick back his hat with a slight curtsy and then led him off the dance floor.

"I feel like I'm ready for the big time," Myrick sized up his performance in jest.

"Um, don't get ahead of yourself there, Chief. You're not quite ready for the 'wild' just yet," the left edge of her mouth rising to a beguiling, half-smile as she spoke. "We'll get you there *eventually*, though. Just keep working on those steps. Maybe head up to your room, put on some music and try to follow the beat. Keep it that simple."

Myrick glanced down at his watch. He could see it was getting late, and he'd yet to even check into his room. He wanted to be up bright and early and ready for the interviews to continue, and which Ellen had set up for him to begin at 8:00 sharp. Alexander was first up and Myrick had plenty of things to ask, especially given the night's latest drama. Meanwhile, he was hoping that Natasha would also be back and over her stomach bug, and able to provide some answers as well.

Turning to walk out of the room, Myrick thanked Jayde for the dancing tips. He agreed that she'd been right that there was something to her logic, although he stressed to her, part in jest and part serious, to *never* do that to him again. Jayde agreed that a private lesson was the answer next time around. Meanwhile, Myrick could also see in her eyes that she'd lost interest in their conversation and was ready to be off to dance with someone else. No doubt, music ran through Jayde's veins and he imagined that she could groove to it all night long if given the chance.

More people had also ventured out onto the dance floor by this point, evidently following Sacha's lead, aware that he wouldn't be out dancing if there was really anything seriously wrong with Natasha or to be overly concerned about. Drama wasn't exactly out of the ordinary at these events, and most of the attendees had learned to roll with it, chalking it up to part of the experience. In fact, some of the wildest and most unpredictable moments didn't take place until it got much later, when the dancers had drunk themselves into a stupor, and were in search of a bit of mischief. It was then that a chandelier or two would get broken, or someone would even fall headfirst into the pool. The antics were always on full display as the moon rose higher in the sky. And this night would be no exception.

CHAPTER ELEVEN
Become a Member of the Breakfast Club

Myrick was up before dawn, and given the fact that it was five o'clock and the sun wasn't out yet, he surmised that he would be the only one from the dance convention already awake. He'd come to imagine them all to be pixies, hearing them roaming the halls full of laughter and mischief late into the night, and it only emphasized even more so just how out of place he was in this setting. Glancing around the room, he could see there was no coffeemaker, and so he resigned himself to the fact he'd have to go downstairs and hope the hotel had a complimentary coffee station set up.

The pajamas Myrick wore were mismatched. He had on an old, tattered t-shirt that had the nickname of a tactical unit he'd been a member of almost a decade ago: "The Gatekeepers". His sweatpants were a bright green accentuated with elves on them, which was a Christmas present and had become Myrick's favorite to sleep in, although he wouldn't want to be caught dead in them in public. Still, Myrick was desperate for some caffeine and not thinking entirely straight, and so he'd felt confident that the risk was worth it and that he could pull off his covert mission downstairs without being spotted.

Walking barefoot down the narrow hotel room corridor, it was eerily quiet, and Myrick could tell that his prediction had been right, as he saw and heard no one the entire walk to the elevator. He then pressed the button to go down and was grateful when the elevator doors soon opened and he stepped inside to see that he was the only one on it. The elevator then took him down to the equally empty lobby area. Myrick and his elf-green sweatpants took a determined step forward and out into the open space in search of the coffee machine. As soon as he found it, he realized he'd made a terrible error in judgment; there was already someone there pouring a cup - Jayde.

Quickly, Myrick realized the degree of his predicament. He was a trained detective and his expert instincts had already kicked in, and so in that split second he came up with an intricate plan; he was going to do a 180, duck back into the elevator and return to his room to change, not making this mistake *ever* again. Despite the brilliance in his plan, it was already too late; Jayde had turned around, the steam from her cup of coffee drifting whimsically into the air, and as she took a sip her eyes spotted Myrick on the other side of the room. Staring up from her coffee cup, Myrick could see the edges of Jayde's mouth inch upward into a smirk. There was no walking away now.

Now Jayde was walking over to Myrick, her feet gliding across the floor as she was evidently wearing her suede-soled dance shoes still; and so he did the same, hoping that he could keep the conversation brief and mitigate any conversation over his attire and weary, coffee-deprived state. That was the hope, but it wasn't likely to pan out that way. Jayde looked as lively as she did a good five hours earlier when he'd left her in the ballroom.

"That's a cute get-up," Jayde remarked, a sly expression of appreciation on her face.

"Oh, yeah," Myrick glanced down at his ratty t-shirt, Christmas sweatpants and bare feet, as if only now noticing what he was wearing. "I probably should've at least thrown something else on before coming down here."

"No, I get it... it's like a grunge thing, but with a Christmas flare. I like it," Jayde's eyebrows rose in amusement as she spoke.

Myrick didn't try to respond. He realized that the best he could do in this moment was to simply acknowledge the comical nature of the awkward situation, and hope that Jayde didn't linger on it for too long. Fortunately, she was the one to change the topic.

"Coffee's not bad," Jayde remarked, taking yet another sip of the drink in her hand, which was a dark black, devoid of any cream or sugar. "You'd think they'd put out some almond milk though for those of us who are nondairy."

Myrick nodded his (somewhat) understanding, then glanced over Jayde's shoulder as if to assess his best path to get around her and over to the coffee station. He was about to walk over to it, when another thought ran through his groggy, slightly-embarrassed head. "What exactly are you doing up this hour?"

"Oh, I'm with the Breakfast Club."

"Huh?" Myrick responded, clearly not understanding.

"It's sort of a badge of honor. Dancing goes on all night. Usually around two or three o'clock it starts to thin out. And then at some point even the DJ calls it a night. That usually happens around five or six," Jayde looked down at her cellphone as she spoke, checking the time. "So basically about now. Anyway, the few that make it to the end are called the Breakfast Club. We usually take a quick group picture of all of us looking exhausted or passed out on the dance floor or whatever. They then post it on social media. It's cool. I think this is like the tenth time I've made it to the end. But I also don't sleep much... or really at all."

Myrick was about to respond when suddenly they heard a shrieking yell in the distance, which echoed through the lobby of the hotel. Myrick looked over at Jayde and the two quickly made eye contact as if both astonished at what they'd just heard. A split second later and the two sleuths, one expert and one amateur, hurried through the expansive foyer and down the hallway toward the ballroom where they'd heard the scream come from.

Almost as soon as they entered the ballroom, they ran straight into a woman who was rushing out of the same ballroom door, a look of panic on her face. She collided straight into Myrick, coming almost face to face with him, instantly making eye contact and he could see how traumatized she was.

"Are you okay?" Myrick immediately asked, his hand was on her shoulder and he could feel that she was shaking. He also recognized her as the girl who'd been in the pro room earlier - Victoria Monroe.

"We need help..." Victoria's words were hurried and scattered, "Sacha's hurt!" The frightened woman glanced back toward the back door that led into the hospitality side room, and now Myrick could see two other panicked individuals coming toward them from that same area, appearing just as spooked as Victoria.

"Watch her!" Myrick directed over to Jayde, simultaneously heading quickly over to the back room.

"Um, ok," Jayde barely got the words out, as she observed Myrick hurry over to the two other individuals, who Jayde recognized were Jonathan and Deion.

"He's in there, Detective!" Myrick heard Jonathan call out and then point to the hospitality room.

"What happened?" Myrick asked as he hurried past them.

Myrick was already through the doorway and could see a body slumped over on a table, as Jonathan responded, "Sacha's been stabbed by someone!"

Walking over to the table, Myrick could see that it was indeed Sacha Arnaud and that the long handle of a blade was sticking out of his back, having been buried deep into it. There were also blood stains circling Sacha's shirt, evidencing what appeared to be his only wound, and proof that the one stab had been a mortal one.

"Is he dead?" a voice stammered from behind Myrick and Myrick turned to see it was the girl who Sacha had asked to dance earlier.

Without saying a word, Myrick turned back to Sacha's body, and placed two fingers to his neck, confirming what he already knew, that Sacha had no pulse and was long gone.

"Has anyone called the police?"

"I called Ellen," Deion offered. "She's not answering."

Myrick found it odd that Deion had called Ellen and not 911, and so quickly followed up, "Well, make a call to police now. We'll want them here as soon as possible to investigate."

"Aren't you the police?" Jonathan ventured to ask.

"Yes, but this isn't my jurisdiction. We need the Sheriff's Office here ASAP."

While Myrick knew that the Santa Fe SO would be taking over the investigation, the fact that they hadn't arrived yet at least gave him a first glance opportunity to survey the scene and search for undisturbed clues. The knife had a finger-grip type handle that was stuck into Sacha in such a way that appeared as though it must have been a downward blow onto his back. It made Myrick curious as to how anyone had even gotten the drop on him, undetected.

"Who was the last to see him?" Myrick pressed for answers, his voice all business.

"I was," the girl who'd been dancing with him returned, hesitation in her voice. "But I didn't do this," she immediately insisted. "We'd had a few drinks and then he started acting all tired. And then I noticed he'd leaned back in the chair and closed his eyes and had nodded off. So I left him in here maybe thirty minutes ago. Deion had asked me for a dance."

"That right?" Myrick asked of Deion.

"It is," Deion answered quickly. "Denise and I were out there for a good thirty minutes or so. Neither of us saw Sacha come out of the room. Finally DJ calls last song. When it ended, we gathered for a quick picture to post. And then someone asked if Sacha was going to be in it. Victoria went to check, and found him just like this, knife sticking out of his back. We all came running in when we heard her scream."

"Did anyone move him?"

Myrick looked around at the five people in the room: Deion, Denise, and Jonathan, as well as Jayde and Victoria who'd also caught up with them. He could see them all shaking their heads that he hadn't been touched by anyone. Myrick then had another thought.

"So just the five of you made it to this Breakfast Class."

"Breakfast Club," Jayde corrected.

"Just the five of you, right?"

Again, he watched as the five present nodded this time their agreement with his statement.

"And what about the DJ?"

"Well sure, she was here too," Jonathan offered up the obvious.

"And who was that?"

"Vince normally DJs, but I'm pretty certain it was Nicole up there starting around 2:00 or so. She usually takes over the late night shift. I think I remember her boyfriend being there with her at some point too," Jonathan added.

"Is the boyfriend a dancer?"

"No," Jonathan continued. "I'd never even seen him before this weekend."

"And where is Nicole now?"

"Good question," Deion chimed in. I haven't seen her since she queued up that last song. She wasn't there when it ended. By the time the song faded out, she was long gone. I just assumed she was off with her boyfriend or something."

"She'll show up eventually," Jayde chimed in, a hint of investigator in her tone. "We can ask her a few questions then."

"*I*," Myrick emphasized, having no desire for an assistant in his investigation.

"Meant to say *you* can ask her questions."

Myrick glanced around the room at the gradually dwindling number of potential suspects. Deion was acting surprisingly calm for a man who'd now witnessed multiple murders. Victoria was sitting at a chair nearby, hysterical and white as a ghost. She hadn't even been a potential suspect of his until now, but Myrick was far from counting her out. He'd met his fair share of criminals that were also fantastic actors. Jonathan seemed appropriately composed and concerned about the situation, which (given the cast of characters) actually stood out as a bit odd. Denise was a new player in this, but Myrick was also aware that she hadn't been at the Colorado Springs event and she didn't appear on any of the paperwork given to him regarding the attendees there. Nicole Whitlock, the DJ, was nowhere to be found. And then, of course, there was Jayde. While helpful to his investigation, she'd had just as much opportunity to kill Sacha as any of the others in the Breakfast Club.

There was no indication of Alexander being around, though. And, once again, it did appear that Ellen could be crossed off the list as a suspect. No one had mentioned her presence anywhere near the dance floor for hours and it would've been extremely difficult for her to slip by undetected. Although just as he'd eliminated her as a suspect, Myrick received some peculiar news.

"Just got someone to answer Ellen's phone," Deion interrupted. "Only it wasn't Ellen. It was her roommate, Val. Val says that Ellen never returned to her room last night and hasn't heard from her in a while."

"But none of you saw her in the dance room?" Myrick pressed.

"No, but it was a lot busier around 2:30-3:00 so it's possible she was down here about then," Deion answered. "Although we'd have definitely seen her in the last couple of hours. It's really just been us in here and a few other stragglers that eventually called it a night also. I want to say the last to leave was Kendall probably about an hour ago. She wanted to rest up for comps."

Myrick glanced around for more clues. He noted the position of the body... that there were no signs of a struggle... and that the room itself was relatively undisturbed. Sacha's clothing, other than the blood stain on his back, was orderly. Sacha was wearing a white pair of sneakers, his dance shoes packed away in a cloth bag, which Myrick guessed was a sign that Sacha was already done dancing for the night when he was murdered.

A few minutes later and Myrick could hear voices coming from the ballroom and increasing in loudness, and he correctly guessed that the Sheriff's Office had arrived. Proceeding outside of the doorway, Myrick spotted two detectives and beckoned them inside the hospitality room. He then stepped aside to talk to them privately, displaying his badge and filling them in on what had happened and the prior murders that he'd already been investigating. There were two detectives present from the SFSO, and both of them appeared sharply dressed and on top of things immediately.

"Thank you, Detective," the female, and apparent lead, SFSO investigator answered back. Her hair was tied neatly back in a ponytail and her expression was as stern as her voice. "We can take it from here."

"Of course," Myrick replied, aware that this was not his turf and he certainly wasn't going to step on any toes, knowing that if he let the sheriff's office do their job, they'd be far more willing to share information with him along the way.

Handing the female detective his card, she did the same and Myrick could see that her name was Detective Kiara Bradley and that she was a Lieutenant in Homicide. Myrick then stepped outside the room, leaving them to do their job. Jayde followed behind, knowing that eventually she'd be summoned to answer questions but fortunately not at the present moment.

She turned to Myrick. "I'm going to head up to my room and get some shut eye. The sun'll be up soon and that's when I sleep. Otherwise, I might burn to a crisp, vampire-style," Jayde's cheeks edged up in jest, but there was no smile accompanying it, just an air of exhaustion.

"Good idea," Myrick answered. "I do appreciate your assistance so far. It's turned out to be invaluable. Just don't forget that I'm the detective here."

"Understood. Sorry about that. I admit, I get excited to help. Maybe a little *too* much," Jayde shrugged her shoulders. "You should probably go change by the way," she noted, wryly. "I think those two will take you far more seriously if you were dressed more detective-like and not so Father Christmas."

Taking the hint, Myrick agreed it was time for both of them to retire, for Jayde to get some much needed rest and for Myrick to find something else to wear. Jayde sat down at a nearby table where she'd left her sneakers, and so Myrick waited patiently while she changed out of her dance shoes. Once done, the two walked out together and Myrick noticed how Jayde was picking some debris out of the bottoms of the suede soles, which had a nappy texture, and he could see why dancers hated walking around anywhere other than the dance floor in them, as they seemed to gather up everything they touched. Yet again, another *quirky* aspect of dance that Myrick would've never understood had he not immersed himself entirely into it.

There'd already been enough excitement for one day - Natasha's emergency transport to the hospital and now Sacha's death. Myrick found himself hoping that this would be the last surprise development of the weekend. Only, he would soon realize that far worse things were still to come, and that even his own life was about to be put in danger, as he came to understand just how far off the trail of the real killer he truly was. This was a culprit unlike anyone he'd ever had to match wits with before, and he'd have to start thinking very differently if he was going to turn things in his favor.

CHAPTER TWELVE
Learn the Predictable Patterns of Phrases

The restaurant was relatively empty at the moment and the breakfast crowd had long since cleared out. Most were completely unaware of the death that had occurred in the ballroom, which had been sealed off with no explanation and the morning's dance competitions cancelled summarily. This, of course, only got the rumor mill circulating more out of control, and Myrick had overheard quite a few farfetched assumptions from patrons at the various tables nearby throughout the morning.

Myrick was a deliberate person and so he took his time eating his avocado omelet, three slices of bacon and heavily-jellied toast; finally getting to savor a good cup of coffee as well. For awhile he'd surveyed the people around him, most of whom he was certain were there for the swing conference. And he'd listened in hopes of gleaning a few bits of potential information from the rampant gossip taking place. Ultimately, he came to the conclusion it was nothing more than speculation though; especially the assumption that Ellen was being investigated for a violation of labor laws and overworking her volunteers.

So Myrick eventually turned his attention to his normal routine and one of his most simple pleasures - coffee and reading the Bible. Myrick had read the book inside and out several times, yet always caught something new and interesting each time he studied it, as if it had more hidden meanings than any one human could decipher alone. He particularly appreciated that aspect of the Bible; he was a sleuth and savored a book that required introspection. And the Bible definitely challenged him on many levels. It also surprisingly gave him insight into why things happened the way they did, even those that were dark and often uncomfortable to broach.

The Good Book was presently turned to Judges, Chapter 16, and Myrick had been studying the story of Sampson, who he found to be one of the most fascinating individuals of the Bible. He was fixated on the fact that one of Sampson's most admirable qualities - his trust and loyalty - could be used against him as well, and how masterfully Delilah had manipulated her lover.

"Seduce him, and see where his great strength lies," it was recorded in Judges that the lords of the Philistines directed of Delilah, "and by what means we may overpower him, that we may bind him to humble him." While studying the passage, Myrick mused that this was likely a similar downfall of more than one cop as well, having gotten involved with the wrong lover. Watching this happen over and over only made him miss Riley even more. She was one in a million, and Myrick was certain he'd never meet another like her.

Then Myrick read about how Delilah pressed Sampson to help her conquer him, literally asking, "Please tell me where your great strength lies, and how you might be bound, that one could subdue you." It seemed highly unlikely that any man would be foolish enough to divulge such information, but then it was also entirely true that men had done far more ridiculous things, giving away government secrets and throwing away fortunes, all to ensure the affection of an enticing woman. And so when Sampson made his reply, Myrick was appreciative of how easily the mistake could be made in a moment of romantic bliss: "My hair has never been cut, for I was dedicated to God as a Nazarite from birth. If my head were shaved, my strength would leave me and I would become weak as anyone else."

And there it was, Sampson, the mightiest of men, was felled by his own words. Myrick found himself grateful that the flaws of those who followed God were included in the Bible so that others could learn from mistakes made, aware that even God's most devoted followers were vulnerable to the seduction of lies. Yet, Myrick had read this passage before and that particular principle wasn't a novel concept to him. This time around, however, Myrick had a strange new sense of things and found himself wondering if there was a more applicable purpose to the story in his present circumstances as well. Several new people had come into his life and perhaps not all had the most noble of intent. The most dangerous person oftentimes was the friend who got close enough to stab you in the back. Myrick had a gut feeling that he was being cautioned of that particular danger and he'd learned long ago to listen out for God's warnings, including the auspiciously timed ones.

"There you are Detective!" a troubled voice broke the silence, and Myrick looked up from his reading just in time to catch Ellen's panicked approach. "I've been looking for you all morning."

Myrick didn't speak, but intuitively pulled a seat out from underneath the table and Ellen took the cue to sit down, although still as flustered as before. She appeared a bit disheveled, especially for a woman whose appearance seemed rather perfect most other times. Myrick noticed that her blouse was slightly wrinkled, as if she'd slept in it.

"I know you must've heard," Ellen continued, even as she was sitting into the chair, her voice proceeding a mile a minute. "Sacha's been found dead!"

"Yes, I did know that," said Myrick casually. "I guess the better question is where were you all last night? Mr. Mitchell said he was trying to call you and that you weren't in your room."

"Like I'd mentioned before, I had to take over all of the emcee duties when Justin backed out last minute... I'd even booked a room for him. With all the comps and all the changes and everything that had fallen on my plate, I figured I'd set up things in his room and use it as a sort of triage spot to get things done, uninterrupted. My roommate, Valerie... she was hosting a party in our suite. I just needed a quiet space to work. I was so exhausted and eventually I ended up passing out in bed. It wasn't until I woke up this morning that I found out what happened."

"And your phone?"

"I slipped out of my gown and into more comfortable clothes down in the ballroom's changing area, and Val was already heading upstairs so she offered to take it to the room for me. Then later I realized I didn't have my phone. I looked everywhere. It wasn't until this morning that Val told me it was in the bag of clothes I had given her and that she'd mistakenly taken it with her."

Myrick found Ellen's story rather peculiar and unlikely, and he jotted down all his thoughts in his notepad. He also wasn't surprised to hear she had come up with answers for where she'd been, she'd had plenty of time to do so. Given the situation, he studied the posturing of her body and the inflections in her voice very closely, hoping to gain more insight into whether she was telling the truth, but spotted nothing definitive either way.

"I hurried straight down to the ballroom as soon as I heard what had happened," Ellen continued, unnerved by the fact that Myrick wasn't speaking but only writing down thoughts. Sometimes the best skill of a detective was just staying quiet and letting a potential suspect talk, and Myrick had mastered that talent, giving Ellen time and opportunity to tell him all she knew, true or not. "I ran into an officer down there. She said she was from the sheriff's office... hit me with a ton of questions almost immediately."

Taking a sip of his coffee, Myrick appeared unaffected by the flustered state of Ellen, making no effort to assuage her concerns. He did, however, feel a little bit bad that she'd been blindsided by the appearance of Lieutenant Bradley and her team, as he was certain that Bradley had been as curt and to the point with Ellen as she'd been with Myrick earlier. Myrick guessed the Lieutenant was quite good at her job and that she probably had come to her own conclusions about Ellen and her reasons for disappearing.

"I'd like to talk with Alexander this morning. Could you get him down here for me?"

"I would but he's not back from the hospital yet. Natasha took a turn for the worse shortly after her arrival. They had to admit her. Alexander wanted to make sure she was okay. I'm guessing he stayed there overnight."

"That's information you probably should've shared with me." Myrick was caught off guard by the surprise development.

"He and Natasha were scheduled to judge the comps this morning. It was part of my panic last night. Without them, I had to figure out how to reconfigure the scoring minus two judges. It's just been a mess. I know I should've told you, but honestly I've been in survival mode ever since that development."

The Bible was still sitting out on the table, turned to the passages on Sampson, and Myrick picked it up in his hands, carefully dog-eared the page he was on, and then began to get up from the table.

"Where are you going?" Ellen pressed, still in a state of disbelief and practically fumbling her words.

"To the hospital," Myrick explained, soberly. "I think it's time I had a talk with Alexander."

"I'll come with you," Ellen returned, pushing herself up from the table as well as she spoke.

"No, please stay here… at least for now. This is Santa Fe SO's jurisdiction. This is their investigation. Last thing I want to do is pull a *key* witness away from a scene," Myrick emphasized his words as he spoke. "The first 48 hours subsequent to a murder are critical… and they can also be the most unpredictable. My guess is that Lieutenant Bradley is going to have plenty more questions for you, especially since you're in charge."

"I understand," Ellen answered, defeat evident in her voice.

Myrick picked up on her subdued response, and so he suddenly felt a level of regret about the tenor of his words. He decided to tone it down some, considering the possibility that she *might* actually be more innocent than she initially seemed, no matter how contrived her earlier explanation had come off.

"Just explain everything to them like you did just now to me." There was a hint of compassion in his voice as Myrick spoke. "They'll understand. But right now, we're trying to track down a serial killer... and so the most important thing you can do is be open and honest."

"I will. I have been."

"Let's hope so," Myrick answered, sincerely. He then turned to walk away from the table, noticing as he did that Ellen had sat back down into the chair, still in a state of shock.

Before leaving the hotel, Myrick decided it would be a good idea to make one final detour over to the ballroom and find out the latest on the investigation into Sacha Arnaud's death. He'd made it a point to keep his distance, careful not to overstep his bounds, but also aware that there'd been plenty of times he'd worked with detectives from other jurisdictions on serial homicides, and as long as the chain of command was respected, it tended to be a win-win for everyone involved. Fortunately, he'd already dug up several clues from his own investigation so far and he was certain Lieutenant Bradley would appreciate knowing what he'd uncovered up to this point.

"Looks like you decided to fight crime in different attire I see," Bradley smirked when she spotted Myrick, who was now wearing dress slacks, a white collared shirt and a cardigan sweater.

"Yes, well, I try to keep my suspects on their toes. Choice of attire can be disarming and helpful at times."

"I'm sure it can, Detective Christmas."

"It's Detective Myrick."

"I know," Bradley offered a half-smile in return, then completely turned her attention to business. "Follow me, I'll give you a quick rundown of what we've found out so far. And meanwhile, you can tell me more about the previous murders. I believe there've been four others to date... and which appear connected to this newest one."

Myrick took a deep breath. "I'm certain the same killer is responsible for all of them. Although, I don't think the last one in Colorado Springs had been planned out... a young woman by the name of Jill McKenna... who I believe had valuable information to provide. I'm relatively certain her murder was committed in desperation. And of course that's where the most mistakes are made. I've pieced together a lot from her death."

Myrick then explained more of his reasoning to Bradley, who in turn took everything in, practically hanging on his every word and impressed with how he'd processed things so far. She could tell he was going to be very helpful in her own investigation, and so she was happy to fill him in on everything she'd learned as well, hoping that they could bounce ideas off each other and solve the murders before the killer struck again.

Pushing underneath the crime scene tape, Myrick stepped inside the side room to see that Sacha's body was no longer present at the scene. The ME had taken him away in a body bag and an autopsy had already been ordered, as Bradley wanted to be sure that the stabbing wasn't simply a cover up for something else and which might be the real culprit in his death.

It was certainly plausible, given the late hour of the night, that he'd been so tired that he'd closed his eyes to nap and that the killer had seized on that particular instance to strike with the blade. It was also entirely possible that the perpetrator had covertly slipped a drug or poison into Sacha's drink and that had incapacitated him. Regardless, toxicology would inevitably provide answers to all those questions.

Bradley explained that the knife had a nine inch steel blade and that it came from an Alpine-style, washed-rind cheese block set that had been placed in the hospitality area for the pros to cut into and snack on. It was also a wise choice for a murder weapon as it likely had the fingerprints of almost all of the murder suspects on it already, given they'd been cutting cheese plates throughout the evening. Bradley explained though, despite the apparent futility of it, that the knife had been properly preserved and sent to forensics for analysis also. More importantly, at least to Myrick at the moment, she was able to give a definitive answer as to how the knife had been used, explaining that it had come down on Sacha's back from above and straight down into his back while he lay, unaware, on the table.

His tragic death, which occurred while he was apparently either asleep or sedated, certainly explained why no one had heard screams or a struggle, and how the murder had been carried out so covertly. The perpetrator had not only thought this particular crime out quite thoroughly, but also had the foresight to know when it was best timed to carry it out, undetected. While Sacha's death left many clues as to *how* it was executed, there were few indicators as to *who* committed the heinous crime - or at least none that Bradley had picked up on.

In turn, Myrick gave Bradley an important rundown on the process he'd used to narrow his suspect list so far, and those that were still on it: notably, Deion Mitchell, Jayde Ch'en, Ellen Cromwel, Victoria Monroe, Jonathan Scott, Kendall Callaway and Claire Callaway. There was also the potential to add the DJ Nicole Whitlock, who still hadn't been tracked down, as a possible malefactor. Finally, he emphasized that Alexander was an original (and prime) suspect of his, but might no longer be if proven he'd stayed overnight at the hospital.

Once he'd shared *almost* all he knew, Myrick took what he'd learned from this latest crime scene and decided that it was time to let Bradley get back to work, uninterrupted. He then walked out of the ballroom, which was teeming with police now, and back toward the lobby of the hotel. Interestingly, he caught a quick glimpse of Ellen sitting at the same restaurant table as when he left her earlier, still apparently despondent over events, only this time being consoled by someone who appeared from a distance to be Jayde.

Myrick found it a bit odd to find Jayde still awake, especially after her speech about being up all night and wanting to finally get some needed rest. But, while her attire was changed slightly - which Myrick surmised she'd gone up to the room at some point to do - she still had on her signature all-black, goth attire that matched her distinctly jet-black hair. And given his particular angle of view that was really all Myrick could see of her at the moment.

Although, he was surprised by Jayde's presence at the table, he was grateful to see that someone was at least tending to Ellen. *If* Ellen was telling the truth... and *if* she wasn't involved in the killings... this was clearly about as tragic a circumstance as one person in charge of an event could face. Ellen seemed to treat and consider the dancers around her to be family, and so to lose so many people she cared about in such a devastating manner would send anyone into a fit of despondency.

Purposefully slipping through the lobby unnoticed and not wanting to be spotted by Jayde, who would no doubt insist on coming with him, Myrick successfully made it out of the exit doors and into the early morning air. It was dreary outside, with a bit of misty rain. The cold chill remained as well, and Myrick wondered if the region wasn't in for a rare snow flurry in the future. And while any snowfall would be quite a surprise to the residents of the area, Myrick was in for a shock of his own once he got to the hospital to interview Alexander and Natasha.

CHAPTER THIRTEEN
Stay In Your Slot

"I'm sorry, who did you say you were here to see?" the woman at the hospital's reception desk asked, her attention only partially on Myrick as there were several emergencies all taking place at once. However, when she saw Myrick pull out his shiny five-point badge, he suddenly had all of her attention.

"I'm Detective Evann Myrick... Colorado Springs PD. I need to speak with one of your patients."

"What's a detective from Colorado Springs doing in *my* hospital?" the woman asked, not entirely convinced his badge alone was going to get him the information he sought.

The look on the front desk coordinator's face only added emphasis to the stern nature of her tone, and Myrick knew that whether he got in to see Natasha was going to be entirely at her discretion. The mark of a good cop though was more about people skills than anything, and Myrick was adept at building trust, sizing up what was most important to a person. And what this receptionist clearly wanted to know most was whether a detective... from another jurisdiction... thought he could just march his way into *her* hospital. Deference was going to be key to what happened next or else she'd have him drowning in red tape and hospital protocols.

"We've had a string of homicides around the country. Appears to be the same culprit every time," Myrick started off, divulging way more information than he should, but also knowing he needed the receptionist on his side and trusting his good intentions. "There was another one last night; a young man. I believe that one of your patients has information that could really aid our investigation. She might even be the key to solving the entire case. I drove all the way down here, only because time is of the essence. I'm in the business of saving lives. I know you and your hospital are too. And I just need a few minutes talking with her."

"What's her name?" the receptionist asked, narrowing her eyes as if somewhat considering his request, but also toying with Myrick a little.

"Natasha... Natasha Levin."

"Interesting timing. I just had another individual ask to see her."

"Was it a younger guy with a distinct Russian accent?" Myrick threw out, guessing she was talking about Alexander. "Little taller than me. Goes by the name Alexander Kozlov."

"Yes, that was him. Interesting character. Looked like he hadn't slept in days. But Ms. Levin indicated during her initial admission that Mr. Kozlov was family and that she wanted him placed on the visitation list. I verified it all when he arrived earlier this morning."

"You mean he wasn't here all night?" Myrick asked the next logical question.

"Well, he might have tried, but we've limited visitor hours ever since the pandemic. Quite frankly, it's only been just recently that we started letting family members come inside the hospital. Presently, we're limited to one visitor per patient and only during certain times of the day. If I let you in, that'd be two... and a violation of the rules."

"Technically, I'm a first responder so wouldn't qualify as a visitor," Myrick added, not wanting to sound like he was questioning her decision-making, but more so to give her some ammunition in case she did decide to help.

Again, the receptionist looked Myrick over, not certain if she trusted him. Finally, she glanced over at the computer screen one more time, read the documentation on it and then paused once more to consider what she wanted to do with the information she now had.

"Room 213... ICU. First set of elevators on the left. Take it up to second floor and they'll direct you at the check-in desk where to go from there."

"Did you say ICU?" Myrick didn't want to push his luck, but was also caught off guard that Natasha, who had only a slight stomach bug, would have been transferred to an Intensive Care Unit.

"Yes, that's right," the receptionist took a glimpse over at the computer screen one more time to reconfirm what she already knew to be correct. "She was moved there earlier this morning. That's really all I can tell you though."

"You've been a great help. I really appreciate it."

Myrick turned quickly to head over to the elevators, all the while the receptionist watching out the corner of her eye, as if still wondering if she did the right thing trusting the detective.

The elevator doors opened almost as soon as he got to them, and he stepped inside quickly before the receptionist could change her mind. He then pushed the button to the second floor, which lit up with a whitish hue.

A few seconds later and the door opened again to a rather empty hallway, and Myrick stepped out, following a series of signs that explained in red lettering where the ICU was located. There was a solid interior door up ahead with an access control system, and so Myrick pressed a button on the intercom and waited for a response over the speaker.

"Nursing station. Who are you here to see?"

"Natasha Levin. Room 213." Myrick held up his badge so that it was in view of the dome security camera mounted above.

The door buzzed open, and Myrick turned the handle to walk through it. On the other side of a bend, he could see the nursing station and a woman dressed in ceil blue scrubs standing behind it. She was thumbing through a patient's file, and only slightly acknowledged Myrick's approach.

"You're here to see Ms. Levin," the nurse spoke without looking up from her file. "Did they explain to you downstairs how she's doing?"

"No, actually they didn't."

The nurse quickly peered up from her file, her attention now on Myrick as she took off her reading glasses, which were as aged as her face. Myrick guessed he was speaking to a senior nurse. She then spoke, "Ms. Levin isn't going to be able to assist in your investigation, Detective."

"Why not?"

"She's unresponsive," the nurse revealed. "She's in a comatose state."

Myrick was shocked by the news, and immediately pressed for more information. "Less than twenty-four hours ago, she was fine."

"She was. But not anymore. Whatever happened to her, hit her hard. Her fever spiked to 106. She couldn't keep anything down, not even water so a decision was made to move her to the ICU where we hooked her up to an IV and began external cooling. But things escalated quickly and she suffered rapid onset of Hyperpyrexia and severe mental status decline. The coma is actually acting to regulate her temperature at the moment and reduce brain swelling. Unfortunately, we may not know for some time if she's suffered neurological damage as a result."

"Can I at least see her?"

"Of course, Detective. There's already someone in there with her now. I believe it's her boyfriend."

"Was he here with her last night?" Myrick asked, wondering if perhaps the downstairs receptionist hadn't been present during the graveyard shift and wasn't aware that an exception had been made for Alexander to stay overnight.

"No, I believe he arrived only a few hours before you," she explained, glancing down at the watch on her wrist as if to be certain.

"You sure?"

"I am. I'm at the end of a twelve hour shift as the head nurse on this floor. No one comes on it without me knowing first. He wasn't here. Although that's no surprise, he couldn't have gotten on the floor overnight. We're short staffed... in the middle of a pandemic. Some sacrifices had to be made... and that happens to be visitor hours unfortunately. He couldn't have come into the ICU much earlier than he already did."

Myrick had gotten enough information from the nurse and so he thanked her and then headed to where she indicated Room 213 would be. Slowly pushing the door open, Myrick peered inside the dark room and spotted a hospital bed with Natasha lying on it, rather motionless, in the spacious 20-by-25 foot room. On the other side of the bed was Alexander, leaning over Natasha, looking spent and disheveled.

"Alexander Kozlov?" Myrick spoke in a whispered voice. "Detective Evann Myrick. We met briefly at the hotel. I'm here just to ask you a few questions."

Alexander looked up for the first time. His eyes were tired and sunken, and he appeared nothing like the exuberant dancer Myrick had watched perform in front of an audience only a short time earlier. There was an eerie quiet as the two made eye contact from across the room, and even Myrick wasn't certain what would happen next, as the man almost seemed a bit crazed.

"I did this," Alexander finally spoke, his words trailing off as if he was only partially aware of where he was and who he was talking to. "This is my fault."

"Why, Alexander?" Myrick asked, his voice purposely muted and devoid of judgment. "Why do you believe that?"

"Because I fought with her," Alexander admitted.

"There was violence."

"No," Alexander had briefly looked away, but as soon as he heard the detective's accusation, his attention was immediately back on him. "I'd never hit Natasha."

"Then this isn't your fault," Myrick explained, although he doubted Alexander was telling the entire truth, already aware that Alexander had hit Natasha in the past.

"But I insisted she come this weekend. She was tired. She didn't want to compete anymore. I told her that this was our livelihood and she was being unreasonable. And then we argued. And we argued some more. And then I forced her to go out on the dance floor, but now I see she had nothing left to give. So you see, this *is* my fault."

"There's a rumor going around that Sacha Arnaud caught you yelling at Natasha. Is that true?"

Alexander hung his head in shame, already feeling more guilt than the detective's words could add. He didn't speak, but his actions and the nodding of his head told Myrick all he needed to know.

"Sacha's dead," Myrick revealed. "He was stabbed this morning. Where were you, Alexander? I know you weren't here."

The tension in the room was palpable, and Alexander's eyes morphed from sorrow to anger in a flash. He slowly looked up and glared right at Myrick, evidencing that there was still life left in him. And Myrick wondered if perhaps he hadn't made a critical mistake leaving his firearm in Ol' Blue, as he hadn't wanted to cause any commotion going through hospital security. Instinctively, Myrick patted along the side of his hip where the gun would've been, but now all he felt was the leather of his thick belt.

"You think I killed him, don't you?"

"I don't think anything, Alexander. I just want you to help me solve his death. That's the only reason I'm here."

"The man was a bastard. He liked to collect and hold secrets over all of us. Any number of people could've killed him."

"But you had more reason to hate him than most. I was told about the concerns you had about him and Natasha," Myrick returned, knowing that he was risking his own safety in doing so, but also picking up that Alexander wanted to talk. He seemed almost desperate to confess his anger to someone.

"Yes, I did believe that. But I didn't kill him... even if I wanted to."

"Then where were you last night?"

"I drove up here when the hospital told me that Natasha wasn't doing well. I'd thought she'd be okay. She obviously was not," Alexander glanced down at her weakened state as he spoke and a tear rolled down his pale cheek. "They wouldn't let me in. I called Ellen. She didn't answer her phone. I left a message that I wasn't going to leave the hospital until I knew Natasha was going to be fine. So I slept in my car... or if you can even call what I did sleep... and then as soon as they would let me inside, I came in. And this is how I found her. I can't even believe my eyes. They say she's doing very poorly. Her condition is not good."

Myrick studied Alexander's expression, not saying a word himself at the moment. The skeptical look in Myrick's eyes told Alexander everything he needed to know.

"I know what you're thinking," Alexander spoke again. "If not me, who would do this? And that's a good question. Natasha was loved by everyone. So only a scorned lover could be guilty of harming her. And to a degree this is indeed my fault. I should've seen how much she needed me and not been so hard on her. But if whoever killed Sacha… if he hurt Natasha too. It was not me, Detective. And I don't know who to tell you, other than Sacha, that I think would've harmed her."

"Let's hope Natasha pulls through then… and gets a chance to tell us herself."

After a few tense seconds of silence, a physician entered the room, interrupting the conversation. She had a pleasant demeanor and smiled over at both Myrick and Alexander. Meanwhile, as she made her way toward Natasha's bedside, Myrick glanced over to see that Alexander was following her with his eyes, a soulless, lost look about him. The doctor gently took Natasha's hand, simultaneously scanning the array of monitors all tracking Natasha's vital signs. The steady beat of the heart monitor was haunting as it cut through the otherwise silent room.

"You'll be alright, sweetheart. The surgical team will take good care of you," the doctor spoke as if Natasha was awake to hear what she said.

"Surgical team?" Alexander belted out.

"Yes, she's going to have to be wheeled down to pre-op soon. The quantitative results of her bloodwork revealed a toxin - Paraquat - in her system, which explains her gradual loss of kidney function. The medical team has recommended a partial nephrectomy to remove the affected region and restore functionality. At least we know now what caused her symptoms and can start treating her."

"So she's been poisoned… is that what you're saying?"

The doctor didn't attempt to answer Alexander's question. She could see the intense anger welling up in his eyes and she wasn't in a position to speculate how the toxin got into

Natasha's system. She was only there to treat the problem now that it clearly existed. Once the patient was stabilized, then there would be time and opportunity to speculate on how the toxin may have actually gotten into her.

"I think we need to let the medical team do their job right now," Myrick interrupted, seeing the uncomfortable position the doctor was in. "Let's give them that chance, Alexander."

Alexander was staring in disbelief at Myrick as he spoke, but then his eyes slowly moved back over to the physician, sizing her up, almost as if to make sure she knew that there would be hell to pay if *anything* happened to Natasha during surgery. The visibly intimidated doctor, in turn, looked away and back toward Natasha, hurrying up the last of her tasks, then picking up a chart from along the bedside and making a few notes in it.

"We'll be taking her back in about five minutes," the physician explained, talking mostly in the direction of Myrick, not wanting to risk eye contact with Alexander again. "I promise we're going to take good care of her."

"We know you will," Myrick returned, believing that the doctor was caring and that her team would do an excellent job, but more so to give finality to the conversation and an opportunity for the doctor to step out of the room, simultaneously providing Myrick a few more critical minutes alone with Alexander.

There was an anxious silence that persisted, and Myrick got the feeling that Alexander was teetering on the edge of reasoning. The tension was only amplified as Alexander finally did speak again, his words haunting in their pain: "I should've listened to Claire. She was right all along."

"Right about what?" Myrick pressed.

"That Sacha was bad news. She's the one that figured it out. She's the one that had cared enough to warn me. Competing on the professional circuit is hard enough on couples. Natasha and I had once been so happy, and Claire knew something had changed. She told us to take some time away from dance. Away from the pressures... and influences. Natasha was listening. I wasn't... I was wrong."

Myrick had learned enough from the brief conversation with Alexander. The man was becoming more despondent with each painfully uttered word, and any good detective understood when it was time to take a step back. *This* was that time in Myrick's wise estimation.

Turning to walk out of the hospital room, he could see that a team of doctors had gathered in the hallway. The physician from earlier was there also and Myrick saw that she had passed over Natasha's medical chart and notes to the team to review and staff, pre-op. He caught a few of their words as he passed by, and he could tell that Natasha's prognosis was far worse than the doctor had let on in front of Alexander. Myrick would follow up with the hospital in a few hours to find out how the surgery had gone and when the earliest would be that he could speak with Natasha. She'd obviously be the best source of information *if* she recovered.

Until then, Myrick had another - arguably far more important - suspect to interview. He was going to return to the hotel and track down Claire Callaway. Alexander's last words had been revealing, and Myrick got the impression that Claire was playing more than the role of friend when she meddled in Alexander and Natasha's affairs. Myrick had enough experience to know that oftentimes the most dangerous person in the room was also the one who liked to pull the puppet-strings behind the scenes. And Myrick was about to find out just how manipulative Claire really could be, especially when it came to protecting her legacy.

CHAPTER FOURTEEN
Recognize Pauses & Take Time to Breathe

The last person Myrick saw when he left the hotel on the way to the hospital was Jayde, sitting with Ellen; and upon his return a good four hours later, the first person he spotted was Jayde yet again, this time sitting on a stool outside the lobby coffee shop - alone. Myrick wasn't in a particularly talkative mood, he wanted to track down Claire Callaway and ask her a few more questions. Unfortunately, as he was hurriedly skirting the edge of the lobby to make his way to the elevators, Jayde caught sight of him and waved a hand up in the air lightly, and Myrick knew he needed to at least walk over and *briefly* acknowledge her presence.

"Where've you been?" Jayde scolded in her usually abrupt manner, ignoring any formalities. She was wearing dark shades, which might appear odd for most while indoors, but seemed to work with Jayde's persona.

"I went to the hospital. Natasha's not doing well."

Myrick noticed that Jayde's expression immediately changed, as if deeply affected by the news, and it was almost as if Jayde was realizing one of her worst fears had come to fruition. Of course, it didn't help Myrick get a good read on the situation since Jayde had on the sunglasses and looked like she'd just woken up from an all-night bender, which in some ways was actually accurate.

"Was Alexander there?"

"He was."

"And did you ask him about his argument with Sacha?"

"I did," Myrick suddenly felt a little like the roles had been reversed and *he* was a witness being questioned. Still, he continued with the short and to the point dialogue, aware that he had very little time for it and needed to be elsewhere.

"Hopefully he was truthful with you about it. Natasha's a good person. I looked up to her. Did he admit abusing her?"

"Not in so many words, but to a degree yes."

"There's no middle ground in abuse. That's like saying you sort of got pregnant. You either did or you didn't."

Myrick caught a hint of offense in Jayde's tone, and wisely changed the subject, aware of the large cup of black coffee sitting on the table in front of Jayde and how desperately she needed the caffeine intake.

"You aren't entirely awake yet are you?" Myrick asked, eyes narrowed.

"No, I really am not. There's no amount of pain meds and coffee that will dull this pounding headache." Jayde rubbed her forehead with one hand, while taking a sip out of the coffee cup with the other.

"You seemed to be doing a lot better earlier when I saw you talking to Ellen."

"Huh?" a flash of confusion suddenly appeared on Jayde's face.

"In the restaurant this morning. I saw you talking to Ellen. It was nice of you to try to console her. She was taking all this incredibly hard."

"I don't know what you're talking about," Jayde returned surprisingly. "That wasn't me."

"Then who was it?"

Jayde shrugged her shoulders, equally confused. "Maybe you're the one who needs to get some sleep? But me? I was in bed all morning. I crashed right after you and I left the ballroom. There's a reason I have this massive cup of coffee... although I'm not sure if it's even enough to do the trick."

"Must've been a case of mistaken identity," Myrick shrugged his shoulders in resignation, aware that he could always find out from Ellen who she'd been talking to and believing that Jayde was telling the truth that it wasn't her. "Very well then, I've got to track down a few more for interviews. I'm going to see if I can find Ms. Callaway and her daughter. Hopefully they haven't disappeared to dinner somewhere in downtown Santa Fe."

"You know, I'm starting to worry about you, Detective. You seem to be behind the eight ball sometimes. A lot has happened since you've been gone."

"Oh really," Myrick was amused by the unsolicited assistance of his self-appointed junior detective. "I assume you're about to fill me in on what I've missed then?"

"You're more fortunate than I think you realize to have me around," Jayde smirked slightly, taking yet another big gulp out of the coffee cup, suddenly coming a bit more alive, more so from the excitement of the case than the caffeine itself.

"Detective Bradley shut down the rest of the conference. It's over."

"No surprise there. I'd actually expected Ellen to go ahead and do that."

"It wasn't Ellen's call. She wanted to keep going. We're all stuck here until our Sunday flights leave anyway. She thought it was better for the dance community to push forward."

"Questionable logic, but perhaps she's not thinking straight, given all that has happened."

"Yeah, I get the feeling Ellen is on the verge of a breakdown. She's checked out, if you ask me." Jayde spun her finger around in a circle along the side of her forehead in a looney bin fashion, her eyebrows raised knowingly. "Anyway, Bradley stepped in and shut it down so, um, that's that. Which is obviously a good thing… and it's nice to have a voice of reason around. Bradley instructed everyone not to leave the hotel. We're pretty much confined within these walls until we leave for our flights. Although I get the feeling Bradley may even make some of us stick around beyond that. Maybe even me," Jayde offered, not seeming entirely upset at that prospect, as she clearly appeared to want to solve the mystery as much as anyone.

"That was certainly the right call. Also makes it a little easier for me to track everyone down. You know what room Ms. Callaway is in?"

"Nope."

"So much for being a crack detective," Myrick joked.

"I can't do everything for you."

"No, I guess not."

Myrick took the cue and decided to head over to the front desk, planning to get the information he needed from there.

Leaving Jayde to her coffee, she did make him promise to let her know if he learned anything new *or exciting*, which Myrick did agree to do - although solely to placate her.

After getting the information he needed, Myrick made his way up to the top floor, where Claire's suite-sized room was located. He knocked on the door and Claire soon answered, peeking her head just enough through the door so that she could carefully see outside, almost as if she was nervous about being the next victim. But once she recognized it was Myrick, she let him in, her expression somber.

Claire's suite was quite nice with an expansive living room area that had a large pull-out couch (which Myrick noted had already been made into a bed) and even a kitchen area. As he entered the space, he could see a closed door over to the side and surmised that it led into a separate bedroom. Since the pull-out couch had been opened up and the sheets messy, Myrick suspected that Claire was sleeping on the couch and that Kendall was likely using the separate bedroom.

"Is your daughter here also?" Myrick asked, and Claire nodded that she was, placing her index finger to her lips to indicate that she wanted them to keep their voices low.

"She was up all night dancing," Claire whispered. "We're pretty much on completely different sleep schedules at this point. I don't mind it though; gives me time to enjoy some peace and quiet, maybe watch a few of the old dance videos." Claire pointed over to a laptop that was sitting table-side at a makeshift work station, and Myrick could see that there was a dance performance video paused on it.

"That you?"

"Yes... and Warren... back when he liked to compete. We were quite the team. I was just reminiscing on the good ol' days. Things were a lot simpler then."

"Most things were," Myrick agreed, and it suddenly dawned on him that he might have more in common with Claire than he'd originally suspected. He then quickly considered how that commonality could be used to his advantage. "Detective work used to be different back then too; it was built more on gut instinct and taking risks. Nowadays, we're all under a microscope 24/7... things are done strictly by the book to avoid second guessing... and the skills we brought to the table seem entirely lost on the younger generations. A lot of the seasoned cops end up feeling *very* under-appreciated, as if time and change have left us behind," Myrick gave purposeful emphasis to his words.

"Sadly, dance has become much the same. Back in the day, we found ways to look out for each other... and when you paid your dues, it actually meant something. Sure, there was money and maybe some fame in it, but not like today... there's a lot more competition for a piece of the pie... and the instant celebrity status that social media brings."

"I imagine it makes it even harder on you... wanting the best for your daughter... and remembering how it was back then... and probably should *still* be. I have a hard time fathoming how I'd feel if I had a child trying to make it as a detective in today's world. The anti-police sentiment... the politics within the Department... it really makes you wonder sometimes."

There was a lowball cocktail glass sitting by the laptop on the table and it had a distinctively dark liquor in it. Claire picked up the glass and took a generous sip of the rich alcohol inside. After savoring the drink for a moment, she went to speak again, a smoky scent of whiskey on her breath. Interestingly, however, Myrick was about to find out that the alcohol had apparently numbed not only her senses but also her interest in commiserating with the detective.

"You and I could probably talk all night and take a drive down memory lane, but I know you didn't come for that, detective... so what *exactly* did you come here for? Detective Bradley told us she's lead now and has interviews set up for both Kendall and me early tomorrow morning. Is there something pressing that it can't wait until then?"

"No, I suppose not," Myrick was admittedly caught off guard by the change in both the subject and Claire's demeanor. It was hard to argue with her reasoning as well, and he had no intention of creating a situation where she suddenly decided to clam up. *Bradley would not be happy if that happened*, and it could easily offset the good will he'd carefully established between the two investigative agencies up to this point. Myrick was going to have to toe a cautious line with his next questions, which he hadn't come entirely prepared to do.

"I just left the hospital. I went to get an update on Natasha." Myrick strategically decided to reveal a small amount of information, more so to gauge Claire's reaction than anything.

"How is she? I'd have expected her back by now," Claire responded, but with an almost obligatory tone, as if it was the respectable reply to such a conversation.

"She's actually not doing well at all. She's having surgery as we speak."

Unlike before, Claire's tone changed noticeably and her reply betrayed some level of concern, although it was difficult to be certain if it was genuine or feigned. "Surgery? I can't believe it. They said she just had a bit of food poisoning."

"Apparently it was more than that. We'll know more after the procedure, I'm certain. Alexander's there with her now. I'm expecting he'll update me when she gets out of surgery and they tell him more about what her long term prognosis is."

"Alexander's a good man. I'm not surprised he's by her side during all this."

"But you don't always agree with his decision-making do you?"

"I beg your pardon."

Myrick leaned in a little more as he spoke, careful not to be *too* confrontational, although this was typically the point in an interrogation where he'd do so and go for the jugular. Instead his response was deliberately measured, "Well, I believe you were trying to be a good friend and warn him that he and Natasha should take some time off."

"You mean because of Natasha's burnout."

"Yes, exactly. Her burnout. That must be a real concern in competitive dance."

"It is, quite frankly. I did think it would be best for Natasha to take some time off."

"And it had nothing to do with the fact that Kendall and Natasha were competing against each other?" Myrick pressed, knowing he might be going too far with his questioning, but caught up in the moment and willing to press his luck - to a degree.

Claire's reaction proved his concern right, and she became instantly defensive. "Kendall doesn't need my help to make it as a pro. She'll get there on her own," Claire paused to reflect for a moment, and her voice turned condescending. "Let me guess, your little detective friend - Jayde - told you that, didn't she? I'll bet she said the same thing about Jill as well."

Hearing Claire's response, Myrick suddenly had a new rabbit hole worth delving into. And while he had no intent to get into an argument with her, he did want to get a better sense for what she believed *and knew*. "Jayde did mention something to that effect, although maybe not quite in those exact words. But I do get the feeling that Jayde has the right intentions."

"I know she may come off that way. But the girl has serious issues. She imagines situations that aren't real... thinks that everyone is out to get her. We've all judged her performances, myself included. But you can't give her *any* honest critique whatsoever. She takes it all personally, like there's a conspiracy to drive her out of dance. I've even wondered if she's got some psychological issues - unaddressed insecurities that a professional could help her with. I'm not saying Jayde's a bad person... please don't misunderstand me. I really like her and she's a gifted dancer. There's just some demons she's dealing with that make you wonder about her mental state."

In his time as a detective - especially working homicides - Myrick had become something of a psychologist himself. It was an inevitable fact of the job, especially when dealing with so many types of troubled personalities and attempting to get down to the truth in their convoluted stories. Myrick had learned to recognize character traits and what they signified in various individuals. This one he knew all too well. It was both a dangerous quality to have... and incredibly effective when it came to manipulation. Claire was a master at gaslighting. She was going to influence Myrick, turning his attention away from her and Kendall and back toward an easy target - Jayde... who wasn't even there to defend herself.

The equally interesting part was that, despite his read on Claire's ulterior motives, there was a hint of truth to her words, regardless. He'd placed a good bit of trust in Jayde, and wondered if perhaps that might've been a mistake. There was a great saying in life, "Trust but verify"; and it was a creed that Myrick had lived by. Given the circumstances, it was probably best at this point to at least do a little digging and find out more about Jayde, as even though Claire was clearly using a deflection technique to turn any attention away from her or her daughter, there was some logic in what she was saying as well. Still, Myrick wasn't there at the moment to deal with Jayde; he was trying to size Claire up, and he'd done so - rather brilliantly. Now it was just a matter of making sure to ease her concerns so that Claire remained cooperative, willing to share information with Bradley as well.

"I do see your point. It's interesting that Jayde was the one to put the thought in my mind. I appreciate the warning about her."

"It's important to know *all* the facts."

"Indeed... Well, then I intend to follow up on your suggestions. Thank you for your time, Ms. Callaway," Myrick stood up from his chair, placing his notebook back in his coat as he did so, knocking his knuckles against the work station desk his customary three times and then turning to leave.

"Of course, Detective," Claire replied, a sense of calm returning to her voice and demeanor, and Myrick was glad to see that he'd ended things on a good note, accomplishing exactly what he needed to without hindering the investigation being undertaken by Bradley and her team. "Please let me know if there's anything else you need from me," Claire whispered a little lower now that they were walking closer to the side room, and where she'd alerted Myrick that Kendall was sleeping.

As he reached for the handle of the door, he slowly opened it, not wanting to make too much noise, intending to respect Claire's wishes that they keep things quiet for her daughter. Only Myrick would learn soon that Kendall wasn't asleep at all, and never had been. The lies were piling up, but Myrick had learned with time, those same deceptive ways came back to haunt the people that told them, including Kendall's elaborate one now.

CHAPTER FIFTEEN
Never Back Lead, Unless You Have To

"I figured there'd come a point when you'd start prying deeper into my life," Jayde answered, responding to Myrick's rather obvious line of detective-like questions.

"Well, I do have a job to do."

"And I *am* a suspect also."

"Sort of," Myrick replied, but with a caveat. "You weren't even there when Yves Lavigne's death occurred in Sacramento."

"Kind of hard to commit murder from 150-plus miles away."

"Very true."

"Still, you've got a job to do. I'll answer anything you want. Just do me one favor."

"And what's that exactly?"

"We're stuck here and I'm going stir crazy," Jayde took another puff from her cigarette, which emitted a minty aroma, and Myrick captured a glimpse of the nervous energy Jayde had been holding back as her hand jittered ever so slightly. "I came here thinking I was going to be competing. That's my outlet.

Let's at least turn this into a dance lesson. Trust me, you could use it. And then I'll be a captive audience for all your questions. Win-win, right?"

Myrick didn't think Jayde's suggestion was a win for him *by any measure*. He also had sized up Jayde enough to know that she really didn't care much for authority figures, and so she could easily ignore his questions - or worse toy with her responses - just to get a rise out of Myrick and prove her point. It put him in a real predicament. The last thing he wanted to do was engage in a dance lesson. It was, however, pretty evident at this point that the more he'd experienced it first hand, the more that knowledge had paid off in his investigation; and that was something to consider, enough so to even sway the pendulum just slightly in favor of acquiescing to Jayde's request.

"That's fine I guess, but the ballroom is closed," Myrick decided to point out the obvious, lest Jayde had forgotten that important detail.

"I know, but Ellen has a whole area blocked off on the second floor for private lessons. We can use some of that space."

Myrick's broad shoulders sank a bit as his surefire way out was summarily shutdown. Before he could reconsider, Jayde began heading down the hallway, expecting Myrick to follow which he begrudgingly did. The two then made their way up to the second floor; meanwhile, Jayde led him over toward a set of double doors, with the name *The Blue Lotus Room* emblazoned in gold letters above the threshold.

"Here's where we can practice," Jayde explained, while reaching for the door handle, pulling it open and then peering inside.

While she'd expected the room to be empty, she quickly realized that she wasn't the only one who'd decided to steal away to the second floor and get some practice in. There was music playing inside the room, and a sole occupant - Victoria Monroe. She was working on body isolations, her two feet planted firmly to the floor and her knees slightly bent, as she tried to remain grounded while the top of her body (from the waist up to the head) moved from side to side in fluid motion.

"You okay if we come in?" Jayde called over to Victoria, who had just noticed them standing in the doorway.

"Of course," Victoria replied, reaching for her cellphone and cutting off the music that was playing through the bluetooth-enabled speaker system. She then quickly skipped over to Jayde, giving her a long hug, revealing a bond between the two dancers and a shared sadness over the loss of some of their friends. "You okay?" Victoria asked as she released Jayde from the embrace.

"I will be. More shocked than anything else right now. It all feels so surreal."

"No surprise that the two of us would try to find solace in dance with all this going on. It's been the answer to every other stressful thing in our lives... and the only thing really that makes sense in this crazy world."

"So true."

"Well, I'm here too if you need me."

Myrick listened to the two contemporaries talk and he suddenly realized that there was an underlying respect and camaraderie between them, which actually surprised him a bit, as all he'd seen so far was the competitive side of things, and the contentious feelings that pervaded as a result. He wondered if perhaps he had prejudged them unfairly, not exactly understanding the complex relationship dynamics involved. And quite frankly he was impressed that the two were both possessed of a fierce drive to succeed, and yet could somehow forge a bond of friendship away from competition.

Suddenly, glancing over Jayde's shoulder, it seemed as though Victoria noticed Myrick for the first time, and she almost appeared embarrassed to have not yet acknowledged his presence. She waved at him, her face had a radiant nature about it, and Myrick couldn't help but notice how quickly her smile lit up the room.

"You scared off by us dancers yet?" Victoria quipped, aware of just how different things could feel for an outsider, let alone one that happened upon West Coast Swing in the midst of a string of murders.

"Maybe a little. I certainly didn't expect it to have a life or death element to it."

"Don't listen to him," Jayde cut into the conversation. "He's going to be fine. In fact, I was just going to give him a quick lesson on footwork."

"Oh wow, okay. You're full of surprises, Detective." Victoria squinted her eyes slightly, as if trying to get a better read on him. And, as she did, a sort of male bravado welled up in Myrick that he hadn't expected, almost wanting to prove to Victoria that he was *indeed* as mysterious as she apparently believed.

"Enough of the chit-chat," Jayde interjected. "Can you turn the music back on?"

"Of course." Victoria swiped at her phone and the music sprang back to life. It had a very definitive beat to it, and Jayde seemed happy with the choice of song.

"Watch me," Jayde directed as she stepped rhythmically to the music. "One-two," she counted as she took two steps back to demonstrate the lead's footwork. "Three-and-four..." She tripled-stepped in place, collecting her balance and weight. "Five..." She took a bold step forward as if to emphasize that particular number and beat. Then finally she added, "-and-six." Jayde finished the second part of the triple step so that her feet were collected underneath her, as if anchoring in place.

Jayde continued repeating that exact same pattern over and over, each time to the six beats in the music and hitting the up and down notes just perfectly. Myrick was no fool and he understood very well that she was making it look far easier than it would be for him; but what he could definitely sense (much to his own credit) was how precisely her footwork matched up to the music itself.

When the song finished, Jayde indicated for Victoria to play the exact same song again, this time insisting that Myrick give it a try, which he reluctantly did. As expected, he clumsily attempted to copy the footwork, confirming his suspicions that Jayde had made it appear simpler than it actually was. There was very little emphasis on keeping timing, but he did notice out of the corner of his eye that Victoria had a smile on her face, evidently seeing something about him that Myrick himself did not.

"Not bad," Jayde offered, as Myrick stopped his steps halfway through the song, almost overwhelmed by that basic exercise alone.

"I'm impressed," Victoria added.

Myrick noted that Victoria, in particular, seemed genuine in her praise, and he almost hoped that she wasn't doing it solely to placate him. He was even more grateful to know that not only had he pulled off this small feat *but also* that it was mercifully over. Instead, though, a new challenge presented itself, and Myrick was hit with both a sense of school boy exhilaration and primal fear as soon as he heard Victoria's next suggestion.

"Why don't you try it with me?" Victoria offered, stepping towards him and taking his hand in hers before he could even process what was happening.

"That's actually a great idea. I can watch his steps and see how it's coming along," Jayde agreed, a studious look on her face; and Myrick realized that she was definitely in her element.

Nervously, Myrick took both of Victoria's hands in his, and it took everything in her not to laugh at how awkwardly he did so. But she impressively kept her composure, placing Myrick's left hand in her right. She then crept a little closer toward him so that there wasn't a gaping sea of distance between her and her dance partner, knowing that it would be impossible for him to lead her if they didn't establish some sort of connection.

"Okay, a couple of ground rules before we start," Jayde began. "You don't arm lead in dance," Jayde explained, and then jerked her arm back to exhibit - in over exaggerated fashion - what *not* to do. She could see that Myrick got the hint. "You lead with the body. If you take a step back, Victoria will follow. If you take a step forward, she'll feel that as well. No need to push and pull." Jayde paused to make sure that what she was saying had sunk in and Myrick nodded, obligingly, that he understood, beads of sweat forming on his forehead as his nerves went into overload. "Also, don't look down at your feet."

"Keep your eyes on me," Victoria added, and she looked right into Myrick's eyes as she did so, which only added to her allure.

As Jayde continued, Myrick's gaze stayed on Victoria, and she flashed a smile once more, evidence of how happy she was to see that he'd taken the advice to heart.

"Okay, I'm going to start the music and count you in. When you hear me say 'one' that's your cue to take your first step back. Just don't stop. Keep your feet moving. Everyone makes mistakes. Worst thing you can do is stop."

Hearing every word Jayde spoke, Myrick was quite certain he wasn't going to be able to do *any* of the things she said. There was at least a 99.9 percent chance he was going to freeze up, and then (since he wasn't allowed to look at his feet) he'd be captive to the disappointment as it manifest in Victoria's expression. He was certain this would be the most humbling moment of his life.

Jayde gave Myrick the side-eye as if to be certain he was ready to go. She noticed Victoria giving her the "okay" sign that she had it all under control, and so Jayde went ahead and fired up the song once more. The same distinct cadence played out within the music. Jayde demonstrated with her finger moving up and down, accentuating where the high and low beats hit. She then began to count in the music, eventually reaching the "one" and indicating for Myrick to start dancing. Instead, Myrick's feet remained firmly planted in place, and they felt like dead weight, as if they were suddenly heavier than concrete blocks.

The tension was palpable, and Jayde realized the situation was on the verge of going south fast. She'd seen her fair share of new dancers try a style of dance, struggle and then decide they never wanted to do it again. This, too, would have been one of those times as well, except Victoria had already decided she wasn't going to let that happen.

Her eyes stayed on Myrick, determined to give him confidence. It worked as he stared, in return, into her soft blue eyes and got lost in them just long enough so that Victoria could back lead the dance. When the "one" in the music came around again, she gently guided Myrick backwards and he instinctively took the cue. Her movements were so subtle that Myrick wasn't certain if he wasn't actually the one who had led it. Somehow, Myrick found himself hitting the one and two beats almost right on time. His triple step was sloppy, but still he remained moving. Now, he was on his second triple step and anchoring in place.

Had Myrick looked down at his feet, he would've seen just how awkward he looked. He was marching backwards and forwards, almost like a toy soldier. Still, he was on beat and what he was doing *could* pass for dancing and that (in itself) was a small miracle. More incredibly, he was having fun. He'd carried the beat all the way to the midpoint of the song, and Victoria could see that he now had it pretty down so she decided to have a little fun of her own, adding some flair with her movements - sometimes angling her body as she stepped into him; sometimes getting a bit more grounded and lowering herself into her hips more on her anchor steps. Her movements were a mixture of beauty and seduction, and Myrick was in awe of her.

He also had a hunch what was happening. Victoria was making him look good. She was so expert in her craft that she was able to not only back lead him, but do so without him really understanding how it was all happening. It was easy for Myrick to fool himself into believing he was the lead on the dance, and he was having so much fun that he decided to just go with it. Almost before he knew it, the song reached its dramatic conclusion, and Victoria slyly pulled off a dip into his arms on the final beat as it faded out.

Jayde clapped once the song was over, and Victoria smiled deeply at Myrick, and it was clear that the two women were both genuinely impressed with his effort. They were acutely aware that *all* new dancers had to push through that original anxiety, especially those that didn't start dancing until late in life, and so Myrick's determination alone had made a real impact. Myrick was even a bit surprised with himself, trying hard to contain his sense of self pride.

"I felt kind of stiff out there," Myrick pointed out, correctly. Maybe I should do more with the upper half of my body?" Myrick allowed his chest to cave in then extended it back out in exaggerated fashion so that his neck and head tilted back and finally forward again, in what appeared to be a sort of wave-like body roll motion - but really just looked like he was on the verge of throwing up.

"Um," Jayde cut back immediately, seeing what Myrick was trying to do, "please *never* do that again."

Jayde had a serious look in her eye, but then the edge of her mouth edged up into a smirk, and the three of them got a chuckle at Myrick's expense. Impressively, he didn't take the remark seriously, which strangely had the added effect of making him feel more a part of their group.

"Understood," Myrick laughed, although he noted to himself that *he really never was going to do that again.*

"So are you ready for more lessons?" Victoria chimed in, eagerly.

"Nope," there was a distinct certainty in Myrick's reply, as he was smart enough to quit while he was ahead.

Jayde could tell by Myrick's expression and reaction that he'd gotten enough of a taste of the exhilaration in dance that he'd try again later, and that was really all she wanted to create in him anyway. She could always pick up where they'd left off and build on that foundation. The original euphoria of finding out he'd actually enjoyed it would be enough to carry Myrick forward as she taught him more and more along the way. Jayde was a fantastic instructor and she had an innate ability to get the most out of her students; now apparently Myrick also.

Only, it was also pretty clear that it may not have worked out quite as well without Victoria there, and even Jayde picked up on the chemistry between the two. She was definitely going to have to follow up on that once Victoria and she were alone and could talk. For now though, it would be Myrick who suddenly had all the questions, and he was ready to return to his more comfortable role playing police detective.

"Alright, I upheld my end of the bargain. Now, it's your turn."

Jayde glanced over at Victoria, as if to indicate with a change in her expression that she'd prefer to talk with Myrick alone. Victoria took the cue, this time hugging both Jayde and Myrick, lingering a bit longer on her hug with Myrick, and then picked up her things to exit the dance room. As the door closed behind her, Jayde and Myrick were left alone to talk.

"She likes you," Jayde began instantly, breaking the silence.

"Nice try, but this isn't about me. It's time for you to start being more forthcoming about yourself. No more deflecting."

"Dang, you're good."

"We'll see. I'd like to find out if my read on you is what I think it is."

"And what is that?"

"Well, you didn't come from a privileged background like, say, Kendall Callaway has."

"That's for sure."

"And you've had to fight your way up the ladder in dance. You don't seem to have any quit in you... which I'm willing to bet is reflective of how you were raised."

"Both my parents were military. You wouldn't believe the high standards they had... or how hard they pushed me to excel," Jayde explained, a bit surprised that she was revealing those facts, as she rarely divulged much information about herself. She was a private person and didn't like people prying into her past. Myrick, though, had a way about him, and somehow had gotten her talking; and Jayde found it strangely cathartic opening up to him about some of the obstacles she'd overcome.

"Being a military brat can be tough on a kid."

"Then throw in that neither of my parents understood why I was drawn to dance. They wanted me in ROTC or sports... really anything other than the creative arts. My mom was a Special Forces Weapons Sergeant, and she'd suffered severe PTSD after returning from overseas. She didn't talk much... I don't think she ever spoke of her time in combat. She was an expert in the use of weapons and eventually took a civilian job as a firearms instructor. I used to go with her to assist, sort of as a support system to her as well. It just wasn't easy for her to function in society. I learned a lot during that time... mostly that I didn't want to follow in my mom's footsteps. I think that really hurt her, although she never said so in as many words."

Myrick found it interesting that Jayde spoke about her mom in the *past tense*, and there was a deep sadness in her voice, but before Myrick could find out more, Jayde changed the direction of the conversation to the other profound role model in her life - her father. Interesting, by the change in her tone, it seemed as though he represented more pleasant times.

"And, then my dad was a Recon Marine, and... incredibly..." Jayde continued, almost chuckling a bit at the memory, "he built an entire Marine-grade obstacle course on our thirty acre property in Fernley, Nevada for us to practice drills on. That's actually how the two of us would bond. We'd spend hours and hours out there, but..." Jayde's voice noticeably changed, the sadness returning, "even that came to an end. My dad got called back up to duty. I was left to take care of my mom. Then her PTSD got worse. I also found out that - despite all the sacrifices she'd made - my mom was nothing more than a statistic to the system. Getting aid from the military was next to impossible. Eventually I couldn't take it anymore and moved out."

"I know that had to be a tough decision, but we all have to forge our own paths in life eventually," Myrick purposely threw out a response he knew Jayde would agree with, and sure enough she did. "You can't live in your parents' shadow forever."

"Sometimes I worry I waited too long though… missed my opportunity to make it in dance. It's a small window… you can age out pretty quickly. I don't even think people know… or care how difficult it has been to get to where I have so far."

"I certainly do, that's for sure. Especially after trying to do just the basics."

"At least someone appreciates me," Jayde joked as she replied, although Myrick sensed that her comment hid a layer of truth to it.

"So, let me see if I understand then. Without a support system… and in the face of adversity… you pushed through to make a career in dance. You must've felt at least a little frustrated to learn about all the favoritism and politics in competition."

"Who wouldn't be?"

"Good point. But I guess you probably can see my point as well… there's certainly reason to believe you *might* harbor a degree of resentment toward some of the other dancers."

For a split second, Myrick sensed a change in Jayde, and she seemed genuinely taken aback, offended by his comment. She'd been a huge help so far; more than he dared to admit. And judging by not only her answer, but the tone in her voice, he could see that she felt slightly betrayed by the insinuation he was making.

"You could believe that about me, I guess. But if you really knew me… really understood what I was about… you'd know that wasn't my game. Dance is my family. It's literally all I have. There's plenty of room for me… Kendall… whoever, to make it to the top together."

Jayde's answers confirmed many of his suspicions. She'd lived a hard life; yet she'd also come out on the other end a stronger person for it. Not wanting to lose her trust, he then decided to do something he rarely did, he was going to let her in on the details of his plan to uncover the murderer. He was even *relatively* certain he was making the right decision in doing so.

"I've got a hunch that solving the case runs through surveillance of the Callaways. The two have their fair share of fascinating secrets. Fortunately, I noticed when I was in Claire Callaway's suite earlier that she kept the blinds drawn, and as I stood near the window, I had a clear line of sight from her room down to the pool area. It would reason then, that if I select a concealed location to stake myself out on the pool deck, I'd be able to get a view into that suite."

"Why would you believe the Callaways did the murders?"

"I didn't say that exactly… just that I believe this is the next move I need to make, especially if events transpire the way I expect they will tonight."

"You're talking in riddles. Can't you tell me more?" There was frustration in Jayde's voice.

"Well, I can't give away all my secrets. But let's just say that our suspect has left enough clues that I can piece together who the next likely target would be. Now, all that's left is to catch the perpetrator in the act."

Jayde's eyebrows rose in fascination with Myrick's theory. She was truly impressed with his instincts and she believed he was on the verge of finally solving the crimes. The only thing really throwing her off at that point was why he hadn't already moved forward toward an arrest, although she expected that must mean he didn't quite have the evidence yet to prove his reasoning in a court of law.

While Jayde had proven a worthy instructor in the practice room earlier, Myrick was now teaching her a thing or two about what it took to be a top notch detective as well. Jayde, meanwhile, was grateful for his trust, and figured she'd take it to heart, honing her own skills at reading people, which was a useful skill in all things, even dance. Only Myrick hadn't revealed all his tricks quite yet, and there was still one in particular that he was keeping close to his vest, waiting for just the right time to unveil it. That is, if he ever got the chance, as things had changed markedly and he'd grown too close to dance himself, now becoming a potential mark for a killer on the loose, and who might be desperate to send a message.

CHAPTER SIXTEEN
Treat Dance As An Intimate Conversation

The elevator's doors up ahead had opened, and Myrick was about to hurry over to catch it, when he noticed Victoria out of the corner of his eye. She was sitting at the restaurant bar, alone. She was also one of the few people left that Myrick hadn't really gotten to know, and this appeared to be the perfect opportunity to interview her in a less confrontational setting.

It was getting late and the sun was just starting to set. Soon, Myrick would need to head over to the storage shed by the pool area, but he also knew he still had some time to kill. Making his way over to the bar, there was a neon sign just above the open entry way to it that read: "La Última Oportunidad Cantina" and Myrick mused at the appropriateness of the name, as it certainly had an air of finality to it.

"Hey there, Detective," Victoria nodded as she caught a glimpse of Myrick. She was wearing yoga-style dance pants and a tank top that accentuated her alluring figure, and her light coppery red hair, which matched the color of the bittersweet martini she was sipping on, was tied back in neat braided twists.

"You mind if I have a few words with you?" Myrick asked, and he could see instantly that Victoria seemed a bit disappointed, recognizing instantly that this was less of a social encounter and more of a business one.

"Of course. Take a seat," Victoria patted her sultry hand on the distressed wood stool next to her. "Let's talk."

Myrick obliged, sitting down at a corrugated iron bar that had a stone base and a rustic flair. Behind the lengthy bar, was a restaurant section with seating tucked along the side walls. Myrick and Victoria were relatively alone at the moment, which was how the two of them preferred it to be, although for distinctly different reasons.

"What can I get for you, sir?" the bartender asked as he inched over to the counter.

"Café del tiempo," Myrick decided, preferring something with a kick of espresso in it.

"You're not going to indulge in a cocktail with me, Detective?" Victoria pressed, a pouty hint to her words.

"I really can't. I'm technically on duty," Myrick explained.

"Couldn't you bend the rules a little? I highly doubt anyone would know if you had a drink. It's been quite a stressful weekend already."

"*I'd* know I bent the rules. And a cop really has to judge himself by how he lives up to his own principles. It's a high standard."

"Seems impossible."

"Sometimes feels impossible too."

Victoria took a deliberate sip of her martini, as if to emphasize that there were no rules binding her from enjoying the intoxicating beverage at the moment, and Myrick almost allowed himself to smile a bit, knowing that she was teasing him. He had absolutely come there for business, but he was also human too and he was no fool to the attraction between the two of them. Unfortunately (or perhaps fortunately), Myrick was there solely to follow up on his case and to ask Victoria a few questions about the homicides, and so that is exactly where his focus was directed.

"How well did you know Jill?" Myrick began.

"Pretty well," Victoria answered back through narrowed eyes as she sized up the conversation's change of subject. Still she intended to prove herself as an honest source of information to the detective, so she continued, "Jill and I started about the same time. She and I were driven to succeed. We actually disliked each other originally, I think it's fair to say. But that pushed us both, and we probably never would've become what we did if not for the fierce rivalry between us. By the time we got older, and closed in on the pro ranks, we'd formed a mutual respect for each other. She was a fantastic dancer, and her determination and hard work were so inspiring to me. Nothing was going to stop her from getting to the top."

"I would assume her blunt nature rubbed you the wrong way from time to time."

"It did. She definitely had a way with words. She got under my skin at times. She got under *everyone's* skin at one point or another. If anyone tells you they never had a run in with Jill, you can almost be certain they're lying."

There was a tear in Victoria's eye as she spoke, and she took a larger than before swig of her martini, almost finishing off the last of it as she wiped a bit of liquor from her lips. Myrick could tell that Victoria was struggling as she reminisced on the past, although he was also relatively sure that talking about Jill wasn't the sole reason for her sadness.

"Tell me about you. My guess is it wasn't easy for you to reach the top either."

"It wasn't. But for different reasons, I guess. I was actually already running my own dance studio and making good money when I decided to start competing in West Coast Swing. I was trained in classical dance, but then I met my future husband... well, my future *ex*-husband, at a charity dance event. We were randomly paired up and told to choreograph a dance. He was skilled in several types, but insisted that his favorite was West Coast Swing. I'd dabbled in it. When you run a dance studio, you have to be familiar with all types of dance. But we did mostly ballroom so I wasn't nearly as skilled at it as him. Anyway, long story short, he and I had amazing chemistry on the dance floor. He swept me off my feet... and I followed him into the West Coast Swing realm. We competed for years together."

"Seems like a fairy tale of sorts."

"That's how it always appeared to people from the outside as well. Which only made it so much more painful when it didn't work out. Other dancers treated us like celebrities. We had an image to maintain. I can't tell you how many young up-and-coming competitors told me that I was their inspiration and how they loved watching Mike and me dance. But behind the scenes, it was horrible. He didn't love me anymore. Maybe never even really did. We stuck it out for as long as we could, traveling and competing. All the while, I kept up appearances, a perfect smile of contentment always pasted on my face."

"Sometimes the worst of hells is the one people suffer in silence." Myrick offered, his words sincere.

"I'm okay with it, actually. Funny how when you go through something like that, it can end up one of two ways - you can give up or it can make you stronger. I feel like a whole new person on the back end of what happened. And I know you might not understand... but I feel like I found God in the midst of it... or really *He* found me. Because with all the hurt, I shouldn't have had the confidence to dance again. I shouldn't have been brave... or crazy enough... or whatever you want to call it, to walk back out there. I used to perform to please others... my husband... the judges... but now I just dance for me. And I'm grateful to God for the chance to do that while keeping things in perspective."

Victoria kept her eyes on Myrick, studying his facial features, imagining that he was about to dismiss her heartfelt words, which took more courage to voice than he could understand. Instead, though, Myrick's mouth widened a bit and his stare tightened, and there was an evident look of understanding in his eyes.

"When my wife passed away... Riley... I felt like I'd lost all hope as well," Myrick explained. "But it helped knowing that I wasn't the only one who'd gone through suffering... and I started to realize that a lot of good people push through unimaginably hard times, sometimes suffering all alone... and I decided I could at least relate to that pain... and that I could make a difference just by being there for someone in their darkest time. I think that's what God needs me for... and it's defined not only who I am but what I feel like my purpose in life is..."

"I see it the same way. I chose a hard career path, but it's what I was meant to do. Dance life is a constant struggle. It's also where you meet and become friends with some of the best people. Most wear their heart on their sleeves and put themselves out there for crowds and judges to all say whether they're good enough or not. If you're a couple, no matter how much you love each other, the pressures of competing in dance can weigh incredibly on you. Divorce... breakups... they hit almost all of us. I can be a true friend in those circumstances now. I've been there myself. And while I wouldn't wish what I've been through on my worst enemy... at least I can understand and relate when someone else is in a similar spot and needs to talk... and know it will *eventually* be alright."

Victoria stopped talking and simply smiled at Myrick, grateful that the detective, who was on duty, still found time to show a little compassion within his work. She also could sense the profound sadness in him, and understood that her loss, while having some similarities, also had significant differences. Myrick hadn't revealed how long ago he'd lost his wife... or the circumstances of it... but Victoria could tell that he wasn't entirely healed yet either.

"You know we all have our war stories," Victoria decided to change the subject, knowing that it would help distract Myrick if she gave him some information about one of his suspects. "Has anyone told you about Deion's background? He hasn't had it easy either."

"I've heard bits and pieces. He seems particularly unaffected by Jill's death, which gives me concern."

"I think he's hurting more than he lets on. We all have our defense mechanisms. Deion and Jill still competed together, but they'd grown distant long ago. What made them work originally is what also broke them apart. Jill was serious about everything. Deion was as laid back as they come, never letting on that *anything* phased him. Win or lose, he was always even-keeled... and still the life of the party. I think Jill wished he'd take things more seriously... but if you pay attention to how much he's achieved, it's pretty clear he works just as hard as all the rest of us behind the scenes."

Myrick was listening to Victoria. He was curious about Deion, and this latest insight was intriguing. But he didn't have his entire attention on Victoria at the moment. Instead, another couple had caught his attention.

On the far end of the restaurant, at a table tucked into a corner booth, was a young man and woman. Their location in the restaurant was darkened a bit, and it was difficult to make out their faces, but Myrick already had a suspicion who they were and it definitely added a level of intrigue to his theories of the case.

Watching out of the corner of his eye, he noticed how the young man and woman interacted and could tell that the two were in a relationship. Although by the hushed way they whispered to each other and the booth they'd chosen in the otherwise empty restaurant, it was equally clear to Myrick that they didn't want to be seen. Myrick could understand why. He imagined Claire would be quite upset if she knew that Kendall was not asleep like she'd thought... and that instead Kendall had slipped out of the room through her side door undetected... and that she'd done so to meet covertly with Jonathan.

"Where was Deion when Sacha was murdered?" Myrick asked, no longer paying attention to the couple at the side table, as he knew he'd have a chance to follow up on that later.

"Last I remember, he was talking with Jayde. I remember because he kept stealing bites of cheese off her plate. Both Jayde and I thought it was funny. Then she said something about wanting to go grab a coffee from the lobby. She handed the cheese plate to Deion and told him he could finish it off. Then no more than fifteen or so minutes later, I found Sacha... stabbed. He was my friend. Sure, he could be a *prima donna...* we all have our issues.... I definitely have mine. I'm quite the head case when it comes to relationships. I'm sure you've interviewed enough people who have expressed an opinion about my bad behavior after the breakup with my ex."

"I was told you've learned some hard life lessons... just like all of us eventually do."

"No doubt you've heard plenty of sad tales like mine. Probably much worse."

"I have, actually." Myrick was intrigued that Victoria was being so forthright with him. "Although, many times, they only tell me these things after they've hit rock bottom and done something they truly regretted. Sounds like you got a fresh start... a new lease on life." There was an incredible empathy in Myrick's tone as he spoke, and Victoria appreciated that she wasn't being judged.

"That's what I tell myself. And I am happier now. *Much* happier actually. I'm back to myself. Still, it hurts. We run into each other from time to time at events. We're lucky that there are enough West Coast Swing conferences around the circuit that we can kind of stick to our own favorites and avoid each other, but every once in a while our paths cross. And, believe it or not, there have even been times we've had to dance together again in front of everyone at a randomly-paired pro show. It just happens. It's almost surreal the unique things that could only happen in this profession."

"Smartest thing I did was follow Ellen Cromwel's advice. I wouldn't have been able to solve this case if I hadn't listened to her... she was right that I needed to immerse myself in this environment... that was the only way I was going to truly appreciate its quirks and idiosyncrasies... things are far different than I imagined."

Victoria was quick, and she picked up on the exactness of Myrick's words. "So you've actually solved it, you think?" she noted.

"I'm getting close," Myrick's reply evinced that he was quite impressed she'd picked up on that fact. "Still some things that don't add up though."

"Does that include me? Is that why you're interviewing me?" Victoria had a determined look in her eye as she turned the conversation around, now assuming the role of interrogator.

"Unfortunately, you're a suspect, just like everyone else. I can't be certain of my conclusion until I tie up all the loose ends."

Again, Myrick could tell that his response had disappointed Victoria. She didn't like hearing that she was still viewed as a suspect, although it did at least appear that she respected his truthfulness, even if Myrick himself somewhat regretted the need for it in that moment.

"Well, hopefully you'll be able to eliminate me from your list soon. I have nothing to hide. And then you can solve your case..." Victoria paused a minute pondering her next words. "And then maybe you can actually have that drink with me."

"I'd like that," Myrick found himself replying back, quicker and more readily than even he'd expected. It was nice to have an attraction to someone; he hadn't felt that in years. And it was even more enticing to understand the reciprocal nature of it. Myrick had almost forgotten how that sensation felt, and what a simple conversation over drinks at a bar could do to him. It was a wonderful feeling, no matter how unlikely it was to develop into anything more, especially under the current circumstances.

"Well, I've got to go," Myrick suddenly shifted gears, knowing there was a bigger issue to attend to and that he'd miss out on if he didn't get moving soon.

"Until next time," Victoria returned, clinking her martini glass off of the double-walled glass coffee mug that the bartender had slipped in front of Myrick.

"Agreed... until next time," Myrick smiled as he spoke. He then placed a twenty on the bar, intending to cover the tab for both his drink and Victoria's entirely-consumed martini.

Victoria noticed the gesture and her eyes softened in appreciation. She could tell Myrick was a man of few words, but there was a quiet confidence - a mysteriousness - about him, and she found herself intrigued, hoping that she'd eventually get the chance to know him more.

That, however, was a thing entirely out of Victoria's control. Myrick's determination to solve the case was about to throw him into the heart of the danger. If his instincts were wrong... if he'd guessed incorrectly... it was likely to cost him his life. For all her allure, his next drink with Victoria was the last thing that he needed to be concerned with at the moment. The only thought on his mind had to remain catching a killer... and one that was *already* plotting to get rid of him.

CHAPTER SEVENTEEN
Emphasize Weight Transfers

The hotel was shaped a bit like a horseshoe with a pool deck tucked into the center of it. The pool itself had closed at ten o'clock and it was now nearing midnight so there was no one else roaming the area as Myrick made his way amidst the various lounge chairs. High above was a full moon, and there were dark lines of nimbus clouds partially obscuring it from view. The clouds grew darker and more ominous in the distance, and Myrick could see that a storm was moving in fast and would likely be hitting soon. Walking along the edge of the pool, he peered across to the other side of the hotel, where he knew Claire's top floor suite was located. There was a light on inside the hotel room and the thinner of the two curtains, a sheer layered one, had been drawn shut, so that Myrick could only make out the silhouettes of anyone inside the room.

But that wasn't the only reason Myrick had come to the first floor pool area. He had a hunch and so he decided to survey the area some more. There were numerous deck and reclining chairs on all sides of the rectangle-shaped pool. The light on the far end of it, reflecting across the water, gave it an ethereal glow.

The setting was serene as Myrick walked from one end of the pool to the other. On the far side was a Mexican-themed bar with turquoise outdoor seating that Myrick had seen serving food and beverages during the day. He glanced around the restaurant area, finally finding a plain-white side building that he'd noticed earlier, having spotted it when he'd looked down from the window in Claire's suite.

Myrick guessed that the two-story hut likely was used for the storage of the hotel's pool and maintenance supplies. It was winter and the air was cool, and although the pool was open there were very few daring enough to take a dip in it. The pool wouldn't require quite as much up-keep as it needed during the summer months. Walking over to the front of the storage hut, Myrick spotted the door's handle, noticing what appeared to be damage to the lock of the door, as if it had been pried open at some point.

Judging by the fresh shards of splintered wood on the ground, Myrick guessed that the door had been jimmied open within the last twenty-four hours. Anything longer than that and the debris would've already been blown away by the cool breeze. Cautiously, Myrick went to try the handle. The door creaked as it slowly opened, and Myrick took a guarded step inside the darkened room, which was lit at the moment only by the rays of moonlight.

Fumbling around with his hand, Myrick eventually located the light switch and went to turn it on. He flicked it but nothing happened. He tried again, still nothing. The power to the building had apparently been lost. Myrick wondered if perhaps someone hadn't cut it. Aware of the danger, Myrick still pushed forward, this time aided by a handheld flashlight. He'd also pulled out his firearm, training both the weapon and the light in front of him as he made his way further into the space.

The room was a cluttered mess, and Myrick almost tripped as he navigated through it, despite having the flashlight to guide his way. There were a myriad of pool supplies, old life preservers, tarps, CPR training manikins and various other dingy items scattered in disorganized fashion, as if they'd simply been tossed into the building and relegated to their various spots over time. Up ahead, the flashlight illuminated what appeared to be a set of wooden steps that led up to the second floor of the storage room, and which was where Myrick had wanted to go, giving him a better vantage point of Claire's hotel room.

As soon as he'd ascended the steps, he could see moonlight piercing into the room through a second story window. Myrick had spotted the window from the outside of the building, and figured it would give him a concealed but unobstructed opportunity to watch the drama he predicted was about to unfold. The window was a bit grimy and so Myrick used the sleeve of his jacket to wipe it off. Doing so had helped some, but there was still a layer of smudged film on the pane of the glass. Myrick didn't mind, he only needed just enough line of sight so that he could survey any action that took place inside Claire's room.

Fifteen or so minutes passed as Myrick waited patiently, and eventually a few raindrops pelted against the outside of the glass. They were large droplets and pounded against the window sporadically, but each hit was forceful; and Myrick could tell that the approaching storm was going to be a formidable one. There were Bigtooth maple tree growing all along the outside of the hotel, and Myrick watched as their stunning red and orange leaves swayed violently in the breeze, as if they were the ones under a sudden attack. The wildness of them was so entrancing that Myrick almost missed what he'd came there actually suspecting to observe.

Up to that point, there hadn't been any movement in Claire's hotel room, but suddenly two dark figures came into view. Myrick could make out very little from this distance, so he pulled out a small pair of binoculars from his jacket pocket. The sheer curtain was drawn just enough so that there was no way for Myrick to see who the two figures were, but he knew it had to be both Claire and Kendall; and based on the body posturing and the tenseness of their movements, he guessed an argument had ensued, likely as Claire had uncovered that Kendall had snuck out and was now confronting her about where she'd been.

The volatile encounter was predictable, and Myrick had a gut feeling that Kendall even wanted to be caught by her mother. They were finally going to have it out, but were also doing Myrick a slight additional favor in the moment, creating an opportunity for him to prove if his predictions about the killer were correct. Admittedly, he was chancing another death by taking such a risky tactic with the investigation. On the other hand, he also knew he didn't have nearly enough proof at this point to make a conviction stick and so the risk had become necessary in his estimation.

Myrick continued to watch through the binoculars, ready to abandon his location if things got out of hand. Finally, and as he'd expected, the argument ended and one of the figures darted back out of the door he'd seen her enter through earlier. The other figure, he was certain was Claire, disappeared from view as well. Just as quickly as he'd gotten a bead on his two suspects, they were out of sight again; and as Myrick remained in the room still observing from a distance, neither of them returned.

A good thirty more minutes passed. The storm was now almost on top of the hotel. Myrick watched as a mixture of darkness and beauty enveloped the sky above. The wind howled as it traversed the pool and brushed along the side of the building. Then the rain started to come down hard. And suddenly, Myrick heard the door to the downstairs exit slam shut.

It was time to go. Myrick had lingered longer than he knew he should, and he had a gut feeling things were about to get hairy. The trek across the long pool deck to the dry confines of the hotel was going to be nearly impossible to negotiate without ending up soaked by the torrential downpour… but then again, that was the *least* of his concerns at the moment.

The stairs creaked noticeably as Myrick made his way down them. He held the flashlight tightly in his hand and turned it toward the depths below as he descended the steps, which was necessary as the ambient light from above was gone; the moon having been completely blocked by the ominous clouds. Just a step from the bottom, and Myrick heard a noise coming from the back of the room. The circular glow from his flashlight lit up the 40-by-30 foot space. As he crossed around one of the pillars that held up the makeshift hut, he felt something brush along his shoulder. Myrick glanced over, wondering if his mind was playing tricks on him. A split second later and he realized it wasn't just his imagination, there was a hand dangling down toward his back.

Immediately, Myrick spun around, his flashlight dancing across the beams of the open ceiling, revealing an arm… a body… and then a girl's face hanging down from the rafters above. Myrick knew instantly who it was... it was the DJ... Nicole Whitlock... and she'd been murdered. Her body hidden in the rafters of the storage room, but the sheer power of the storm had apparently shaken her loose.

Myrick took a step back to get a better look at the deceased girl and to size up how she'd gotten there, when his foot caught the edge of a box, sending him reeling backwards. In that exact moment, there was a flash and a bang sound, as if a gun had been fired amidst the darkness. Myrick's body fell hard to the ground; simultaneously, his flashlight went flying through the air until it clanked along the concrete floor and finally came rolling to a stop a few feet away. Lying still in the darkness, careful not to move, Myrick wasn't sure if he'd been shot already. His right side hurt, but that was likely from hitting the floor violently and completely unprotected.

From where it came to rest, the beam of light from his flashlight cut through a small sliver of the room, and just for a second, Myrick thought he caught the sight of movement. Seizing on his opportunity, and as his eyes tried to adjust to the darkness, Myrick slid his hand along his side, feeling for the holster of his firearm. As he carefully slid the gun out, he turned his eyes slightly to the side, noticing a large wooden crate only a few feet away, perhaps giving him some cover if he could get to it.

Myrick knew that if his eyes were adjusting to the darkness, so were the killer's. It was just a matter of time until he was spotted sprawled out on the ground amidst the clutter of pool supplies, and the killer was likely to start shooting again at any second. Myrick was going to have to do something.

He had a general idea of where the gunfire had come from based on the movement he'd spotted, and so he decided to let off a few shots in that general direction, not expecting to hit his attacker but just to buy himself enough time and cover to pull himself up off the floor and sneak behind the wooden crate. Pulling the trigger, the flash from his gun lit up the room spectacularly. Myrick kept firing his weapon in the same general direction, even as he was already rolling over and darting for cover.

There was return fire, as the killer got a drop on him and began unloading shots that ricocheted all around the crate, splintering the wood along the top of it. Myrick had been in several firefights before and he'd been trained his whole career on how to deal with life and death situations, and so he reflexively slid low to the ground and stole from one concealed spot to the next, apparently unseen. Meanwhile, the continued shots allowed him to triangulate where his assailant was currently positioned.

The gunfire stopped almost as suddenly as it had begun, and Myrick seized on his opportunity, peering around the beam of wood he'd bladed himself behind, and searching for even the barest hint of movement. Sure enough, the attacker did move, but far faster and deftly than he'd expected. The killer literally leapt cat-like over a nearby stack of storage bins. Myrick didn't even try to fire, knowing his shots would be wasted and that he didn't have a good line of sight.

Almost instantly, it dawned on him exactly where the attacker was heading, no longer trying to shoot Myrick, but instead making a break for the exit door and hoping to pull off a daring escape. Turning all his attention toward the closed door,

Myrick trained his firearm at it, ready to open fire. A split second later though, and Myrick found out he'd guessed wrong. He heard more movement, this time hurried steps along aged boards and turned to see that the killer was darting up the steps to the second floor. This time, Myrick didn't wait for a precise line of sight, instead firing two rounds that hit just along the steps and only inches away from the feet of the swift assailant.

Myrick knew he'd missed, but he wasn't giving up the chase. The killer was now cornered on the second floor. Myrick stole quickly over to the side of the steps, glancing up from a concealed location, careful not to become an easy target in the process. He was just coming up with a plan on how to make it up to the top level without taking a bullet, himself, when he heard the smashing sound of glass breaking. Myrick knew he had no choice now; he couldn't hesitate there any longer.

Racing up the stairs, he got to the top so that he could just see onto the floor of the second level and trained his gun forward, wisely preparing himself for an ambush. When none came, he pushed up a little higher so that his eyes got a better sense of the situation above. There was rain and wind blowing in from the now-open window, shattered glass scattered all along the edges, as if someone had kicked it outward. Myrick's eyes darted from side to side, yet he saw no one in the empty room, coming to the conclusion that his attacker must've dared a jump.

As he got to the window and glanced quickly down, the assailant was nowhere in sight. The rain was pummeling the water of the pool, and Myrick guessed it was a good six feet from the base of the maintenance hut to the edge of the pool. Very few could make that leap successfully, but somehow his agile suspect apparently had.

Turning back to the stairs and then quickly descending them, Myrick kicked open the door to the outside, swinging his firearm in front of him as if expecting someone to spring out at him from around the corner. After a few tense seconds, Myrick realized the killer had abandoned the attack completely and was making a run for it. Out of the corner of his eye, he caught sight of a figure scurrying along the far end of the hotel property, which was protected by a fence about five feet high. In pursuit, he rushed through the rain, which hammered against his face and obscured his vision, then finally reached the location of the fence line where he'd seen the figure making an escape. It was too late though, the attacker was clearly gone and there was no visible trail to follow thanks to the downpour.

Running his hands through his soggy hair, Myrick turned and proceeded back toward the glass door that led back into the hotel, and into the dry covered entranceway. Once inside, he fumbled around in his pockets until he found his cellphone, pulled it out and tried his best to dry his wet hands on his shirt so that he could begin dialing. Finally, he got the number punched in and waited for a voice on the other end.

"Myrick?" a familiar voice answered, evidently recognizing the name and number of the caller.

"I located Nicole Whitlock's body, Lieutenant," Myrick immediately explained. "Her throat was slit. How quickly can you get down here?"

"Give me fifteen." Bradley instructed.

"And one more thing," Myrick continued. "The killer wasn't done yet. There was another intended victim."

"Who was that?"

"Me," Myrick said, matter-of-factly. "Just as I suspected would happen."

CHAPTER EIGHTEEN
Add a Touch of Flair to Your Footwork

"How did she get up there?" Bradley pondered aloud, glancing up at the open rafters of the hut's ceiling and noting where Nicole Whitlock's body had been found. There were still visible blood stains on the timber ceiling joists.

"It couldn't have been easy to pull off. But whoever did this was only trying to buy some time before the body was ultimately found. This isn't the best or easiest place to stash a homicide victim," Myrick returned.

"No, but if you're in a rush and trying to hide one, it'd serve its purpose for long enough. Keep in mind, our suspect will be boarding a plane out of Santa Fe soon," Bradley glanced down at her watch as she spoke, "most likely in less than 24 hours. And at this point, we don't have probable cause to detain anyone. We're going to have to let them all scatter to their various hometowns if we don't catch a break in the investigation quick."

"We will. The perpetrator isn't done striking just yet."

"I don't know if I agree. That's quite an assumption. Best thing to do right now would be to lay low. Get out of town as quickly as possible without calling attention to yourself."

"That's not how our suspect thinks, though."

Bradley glanced over at Myrick, not trying to hide the quizzical look on her face as she attempted to size him up. He was quite an odd individual, keeping most of his thoughts to himself. But the level of confidence in his words was unmistakable and it strangely made Bradley believe that he was correct in his assessment of things.

"You do understand that you're a victim of an Attempted Murder now also? You're going to have to fill out some reports for us, including a Use of Force Report. Also," Bradley hesitated at this last part, "I'm going to have to ask you to take a step back while we conduct the rest of the investigation here. You can remain on the hotel property, of course. But I need you to let us handle things, at least until we've either made an arrest or the last of our suspects has boarded a plane back home."

"I understand. I expected as much," Myrick conceded, relatively certain that there wasn't anything more he could do at this point anyway. He was convinced that the next move would have to come from the killer, and that all law enforcement could do at this point was wait and see what would happen from here.

"I have interviews set up early morning with all our suspects. I'll make sure to fill you in on everything I learn. Deion Mitchell's flight leaves the earliest - 12:30 - so I've got him first in the lineup."

"Good. I think you'll gather a lot from his conversation. He's holding back on what he knows."

"Detective's intuition?"

"Sort of," Myrick replied cryptically.

Nicole's body had been removed from the scene by medics, and now an evidence technician crew was combing the storage building for additional clues. They had brought out florescent light devices that were used to scour the floors, walls and ceilings for signs of blood, DNA and other forensic matter. Traces of blood were located from the entry door to the hut all the way over to the back of it where Nicole's body had been found, as if perhaps she'd been dragged along that area.

The sole penetrating wound on her body was a deep horizontal cut along the neckline across the front and both sides of the throat, evidently severing both carotid arteries. There were no other signs of injury or struggle, giving an indication that this had been a surprise attack, and the acute nature of the cut ensured that the victim was rendered unconscious within 5-15 seconds, unable to fight back or cry for help. Meanwhile, as lead detective, Bradley made the call for Nicole to be taken for an autopsy to confirm that conclusion.

The last known individual to have seen Nicole before her disappearance was her boyfriend. As such, Bradley had tracked him down already and had interviewed him just hours earlier. Based on what she'd learned from him, Nicole's death was going to come as quite a shock.

"The boyfriend told me they were together that night, up until about five a.m.," Bradley explained, taking the opportunity to fill Myrick in on what she'd learned. "He says Ms. Whitlock announced last song, queued one up on the playlist and then they snuck away to be alone. But he works the opening shift at a coffee shop, and eventually had to leave... that part of the story *does* add up... I checked and his employer says he did show that day right at six. Last thing the boyfriend says is he said goodbye to Ms. Whitlock and she mentioned going on a hunt for food. She said she hadn't eaten anything and wanted to see if any of the hotel restaurants were open yet."

"They wouldn't be that early," Myrick noted.

"I expected the same. And I believe the boy's story. He didn't kill her."

"No, he didn't. This wasn't a crime of passion. These are all cold, calculated murders. Our suspect chose each of them for a reason."

"We have a hotel full of dancers and just need to get them through today and keep them safe until we can get them on their flights. I'm going to have officers set up throughout the hotel. There won't be anymore attacks."

"I believe you're right. Although, I don't think this is the last of the surprises."

"We'll see. Regardless, I'm going to do everything in my power to prevent additional casualties. In the meantime, I really do hope you're okay, Detective. Please go talk with medical and fill out those reports. Leave everything else to me for now."

"Thanks, Lieutenant. I'm glad you and your team are on this. Let me know if I'm needed for anything. If you do, you know where to find me."

"In your hotel room," Bradley completed Myrick's sentence with a stern voice.

"Exactly," Myrick agreed, making certain she knew he was respecting both her crime scene and her authority over it. He then turned and left the storage building, leaving Bradley and her team to continue to scour it for clues.

The storm had passed, but there was still a light sprinkle of misty rain coming down, the last remnants of it. The wind had died down as well, and there was a soothing calm in the air. Myrick appreciated the setting as it afforded him more of an opportunity to think in peace.

As he walked along the pool deck once more, he glanced up at the window of Claire Callaway's suite to see the two figures from earlier were apparently back in the room. This time, there appeared to be no theatrics or arguing occurring. Myrick noted this fact, and then turned his attention back toward the door that led into the hotel. Once inside, he walked through the empty hallway and out toward the exit where two EMT trucks and a slew of patrol cars were waiting, all with lights activated so that they lit up the area in an array of color.

As instructed, Myrick went over to an EMT and allowed him to conduct a medical workup. The EMT checked Myrick's vitals and asked a slew of questions, treating him with the same compassion and concern he'd give any victim of a shooting. After checking out, Myrick answered a few questions for a detective who he'd met earlier and who was Bradley's *number two* on the investigation - Rashon West. He also filled out the Use of Force Report, noting that he'd returned fire and the reasons for doing so.

The entire time, however, Myrick found himself surveying the exterior of the hotel. He'd done as Bradley requested, but that wasn't his only reason for proceeding outside so quickly. Myrick was certain the killer would have to return to the hotel, although somehow undetected. He glanced around to see where camera placements were located, and what entry points might be possible. The most notable area, he surmised, would be the expansive conference center. It was possible with so many doors that one might have been left ajar. Plus, it was pitch dark, and if a door had to be jimmied open, that'd be the most concealed spot to try and pull it off, especially partially assisted by the concealment the storm provided as well. If so, perhaps the assailant could get back inside through that area, unnoticed.

Myrick could only hope that if that was the entry point, the killer didn't run into any hapless victim along the way, as things had turned desperate, and violence would likely ensue. Fortunately, with the assistance of Bradley's team, they could lock down the hotel and limit any potential casualties. While Myrick was filling out the last of the forms, he saw that detectives had received their orders from Bradley and were mobilizing in different directions as if to more secure the area.

There wasn't anything left for Myrick to do at the moment, and so he thanked the officers for their work and then proceeded back into the hotel and up to his fourth floor room. Entering into it, he'd realized how dark it was and that he hadn't left any lights on earlier, as it'd been daytime the last time he was in the room. Reaching toward the light switch, Myrick changed his mind at the last second and decided to leave the lights off. He moved toward the window, pulling the blinds open and then looking out from his darkened room and out toward what parts of the hotel were within his view from that concealed spot.

From his vantage point, Myrick was on the same side of the hotel as Claire Callaway's room and so he couldn't see that particular area of the hotel at all. The rooms had no balconies, and so Myrick's only option was to glance out at the areas that were on the other side of the horseshoe-shaped hotel. It was nearing 2:00 in the morning, but Myrick wasn't surprised by how many lights he could see were now illuminated. The dancers that had attended the conference were mostly night owls, as Jayde had explained, and were also quarantined to their various rooms. They no doubt had seen all the police cars and heard the commotion and gunshots, and were likely huddled in their various spaces trying to figure out what had happened. Myrick could only imagine how confused and worried they all were.

And they had reason to be, in Myrick's estimation. The killer wasn't done yet. At least it aided him tremendously to know that Bradley was doing her best to secure the hotel. Meanwhile, Myrick planned to wisely use the time to fill in the gaps necessary to solve the crime.

There was still one problem that nagged at him and which ran contrary to his theory, and Myrick knew it couldn't be ignored. So, after thirty minutes of contemplation in the darkness, he wasn't entirely surprised when he saw his phone light up. He expected to see Bradley's number on there, and that there had been a new development. Instead, it was an entirely different caller; it was Ellen. And Myrick knew that meant trouble.

As soon as he picked up, Ellen went to explaining the situation through hurried breaths. Jayde had been the latest attack victim. She'd been found unconscious and badly injured in one of the dance practice rooms. Myrick then wisely asked the next logically question - *who had located her?* Ellen then explained it was Jonathan... that he'd immediately called her and that she was racing down to the practice room herself, only stopping so that she could make the panicked call to Myrick.

"On my way now also!" Myrick immediately explained to Ellen. "Make sure to inform Bradley also," he insisted.

"That was my next call!" Ellen answered back and then she hung up so that she could fill Bradley in on the stunning development.

Throwing his herringbone jacket back on, Myrick raced out of the room. He knew Bradley wouldn't be happy with him. He'd disobeyed her orders already, but that was the least of his concerns. He was determined to be the first to get to Jayde... who he correctly assumed was just fortunate to still be alive.

*****

As soon as he came bolting into the practice room, Myrick immediately spotted Jayde leaning against the far wall. Ellen was in a panicked state, doing her best to tend to a visible gash along Jayde's forehead. Meanwhile, staring blankly from a few feet away was Jonathan, awkwardly keeping his distance, as if he wasn't sure what to do to help.

"Myrick," Jayde spoke weakly, "you're here."

"I am," Myrick returned, hurrying quickly over to her, and immediately sizing up the extent of her injuries. Jayde's arm was crooked and appeared badly broken, and Myrick could tell that she was in serious pain. "What happened to you?" he pressed, deep concern evident in his voice.

"I was attacked," Jayde continued, her voice incredibly frail, and Myrick was already checking her vital signs, at least confirming that her injuries were external only. "It all happened so quickly. I came in here to practice, reached for the light and then someone grabbed me from behind."

"You're lucky to be alive. Can you tell us anything about who did this to you?"

"No. All I remember is my arm being twisted up into my back and then I heard it snap. I cried out in pain and I guess the person who did this wanted to shut me up so I was slammed into the wall." Jayde indicated with her eyes over to a side wall that Myrick could see had a visible break in it about head level. "That must've knocked me out cold. When I came to, I was lying on the floor. I called out and was just lucky Jonathan heard me and came running in to help."

As Jayde was explaining, Myrick noticing that several other officers had already entered the room, followed shortly thereafter by Detective Bradley. "You're going to be okay," Myrick reassured Jayde. In the same breath, he glanced over at Bradley, aware that he needed to step aside immediately to let her do her job.

Jayde's eyes met Myrick's one last time, as if to be certain he wouldn't leave her. Myrick smiled back reassuringly, which told Jayde everything she needed to know. A medic came on scene and made a beeline over to her, so that he had her complete attention, peppering her with questions to gauge the extent of her injuries and start providing treatment.

Meanwhile, Bradley made her way over to Myrick, intending to get as much information from him as she could about what'd happened. There was a stern, unfriendly expression on her face as she spoke.

"I thought I asked you to stay put," she began.

"That was always my intent, but then I got Ms. Cromwel's call," Myrick answered. "Someone needed to get down here. There was no time to waste."

"Hmmm, maybe so," Bradley conceded, although her tone betrayed that she wasn't entirely convinced by Myrick's explanation, remembering their earlier conversation where he'd intimated that the killer likely had one more surprise still in store for them. "Is this how you found her?" Bradley glanced over at Jonathan who was standing only a few feet away, his eyes methodically turning in Bradley's direction as he realized she was speaking to him, a troubled expression painted on his face.

"Yes... I mean I helped lean her up against the wall..." Jonathan's words were strangely detached as he then lifted his hands, turning them up so that his palms were now showing. There were smears of red blood on both of them. "That's how I got this," he tried desperately to explain.

"What were you even doing in this area of the hotel? I shut things down. Everyone was to be confined to their rooms until I gave word otherwise," Bradley practically barked back in return, and there was a level of shock in her voice that her order hadn't been completely followed.

"I didn't... wasn't aware of that," Jonathan stammered, "I was in the editing room. That's what I always do. I hole myself up in there for hours on end so that I can get work done. I had no idea... I swear... I didn't know this place was on lockdown. I just had heard Jayde cry out. That's why I came running to help her."

Bradley struggled to believe Jonathan's story, but she had no discernible proof that he was lying either. She was also confused as to how any attacker could have gotten past the officers whom she'd stationed at all points along the building.

"This shouldn't have been possible regardless," Bradley wasn't talking to Jonathan anymore, but instead voicing her thoughts toward Myrick. "I've got my people teaming all over this place."

"Hard to say how long ago this happened, though," Myrick answered back. "She says she was knocked unconscious. This might have all gone down before your team even arrived. If the assailant was just entering the hotel through the conference center doors and decided to hide out in the practice room, that'd explain why Jayde was attacked."

"Maybe," Bradley considered, not entirely persuaded. "I do agree that injury to her arm couldn't have been self-inflicted though."

"No, it couldn't have been," Myrick looked over at Jayde's arm. Medics were placing it inside a brace that extended all the way up, as if the break was an entire one and difficult to even stabilize.

Myrick watched as Jayde winced in pain, while the medics rolled up the sleeves of her light blue shirt, so that the brace could be secured all the way up to her biceps.

"I sort of blame myself for this," Myrick spoke with sympathy in his voice. "I could've prevented this from happening if I'd have acted faster."

"You can't blame yourself, Detective," Bradley answered, changing from the disappointed tone she'd had earlier to one of understanding and compassion. She'd been there many times herself. It was a hazard of the job, and one of the hardest to overcome. The detectives that cared… the ones who put the most into the job… those were the ones who suffered along with their victims, thinking it was somehow their fault for not putting an end to all the evil in the world. "She'll be okay. Medics are taking good care of her."

Myrick smiled over at Bradley, knowing where her concern was placed and appreciating her words. "I guess I should turn this room over to you now."

"You have any more predictions that I need to know about before you go?" Bradley pressed, sincerely wondering if he did.

"No," said Myrick. "I don't think the perpetrator would dare strike again at this point. Too many mistakes have been made already. That's what happens when desperation sets in. I doubt we'll hear about any further attacks before the dancers all board their respective flights and leave."

There was a quizzical expression on Bradley's face as she took in Myrick's words, not having expected to hear that response at all. She had her own theories about who the killer was; and had come to the conclusion that she needed to expect the unexpected at every turn in the investigation; and so she was entirely puzzled why Myrick was *now* so certain that this was the last of the attacks.

"You want to tell me why you feel so strongly that way?"

"Not yet," Myrick paused for a moment before continuing. "Not here. Let's just see how your interviews go. I have a feeling they're going to be very telling."

"Starting with Deion Mitchell's?" Bradley clarified, as if wanting to gauge Myrick's reaction again.

"Yes, starting with Mr. Mitchell's."

Myrick turned to walk out of the room, only to be interrupted by Bradley one last time.

"I'd like you to be there for them," she added, as Myrick was only a few steps away from her. "10:00 sharp. At the station."

"Then I'll be there," Myrick called back, still walking away as he did.

Leaving the practice room, Myrick decided to take the long way back to the elevators. He knew from earlier that the corridor wound around so that it passed the conference room doors and then circled back over to the lobby area. It was a longer walk than necessary, but one that Myrick was certain would prove fruitful.

Sure enough, not far from the entrance to the conference center, he spotted the thick wet footprints in the carpeted floor, much like he'd expected to see from someone who'd been soaked by a storm outside. The footprints then stopped, as if whoever had made them didn't want to continue leaving a trace and there was a larger smear of water as if perhaps someone had sat down momentarily to remove their water-soaked shoes.

Myrick surmised that the killer had made a wise decision doing so, but in his estimation that decision had been made too late in the game. Still walking, Myrick glanced around at the various vendor booths that were still up. He imagined the vendors had been cleared out of the area before they'd even been given a chance to entirely pack their things. Bradley was going to have to eventually let them back in to do so, although their continued presence at the moment did add a new and fascinating clue to his investigation... and he was intrigued by what it meant.

CHAPTER NINETEEN
Study the Techniques of the Pros

Myrick hadn't slept well. It wasn't getting shot at that had him so shaken; he'd had plenty of near death experiences in his career. Myrick knew where he was going eventually and who would be waiting for him there, and so he didn't fear death. It was the painfulness of memories that sometimes got the best of him... and the loneliness that inevitably ensued. Riley had never talked to him about his cases, Myrick had a hard and fast rule about that, mostly because he knew how all-consuming they could be. But Riley didn't need to talk to him to know when Myrick was hurting. Oftentimes, on the worst of days, Myrick would just lie in her arms and she'd run her fingers through his thick hair, a perfect distraction from all the things he'd seen and the pressures he bore for others, and the two would eventually drift off to sleep together. Now, that sentimental respite was no longer an option, and so it tormented him, regardless of how secure he felt in other aspects of his life.

The rings around his eyes had grown darker, if that was even possible, as Myrick pulled himself out of bed, readying for the most important phase of his case. He needed to be sharp... and he needed to be clear-thinking. Yet right now he was succeeding at neither. Coffee, like always, was just going to have to be the solution. Fortunately, as he pushed his way out of the hotel room door one final time, his only bag all packed, he saw that the kitchen was still serving breakfast and so he headed over to it, hoping to get a quick meal in before heading over to the police station.

There was an exterior seating area at the restaurant and, even from a distance, Myrick noticed several familiar faces sitting at one of the tables. Ellen Cromwel was there. So were many of the other main suspects: Kendall, Claire, Deion, Jonathan, Jayde and Victoria. Myrick couldn't help but muse at the surreal nature of the scene. Six potential victims all sitting and talking pleasantly, yet unknowingly, with the person who planned to likely kill them all if given the chance. Fortunately, Myrick wasn't going to let that happen. The killer's days were numbered, even if that person didn't know it yet.

Myrick approached the surreal scene, coming up to the table with Jayde facing away from him, so that she was actually the last to notice his approach. Ellen spotted Myrick first, and there was almost relief on her face as she beckoned him over. She wasn't the first face, however, that Myrick caught sight of, as he made eye contact with Victoria, whose mouth inched northward in a curt smile upon seeing him.

"Good morning, everyone," Myrick began. Still standing behind and just to the side of Jayde as he spoke.

"Good morning, Detective Myrick," Ellen answered. She motioned to a seat next to her at the circular table. "There's a spot right here if you'd like to come eat breakfast with us."

"It looks like you're just now finishing up. I didn't mean to intrude."

"Not at all. Several of us will be heading out soon and we may not see each other again for a while… and so we figured we'd catch a quick breakfast beforehand. Deion's flight is early and my understanding is he's supposed to be at the police station by 10:00 so we were about to finish up."

"I heard about that. I'll be heading that way too."

"We've all got interviews set up," Ellen continued explaining. "I believe they're organized to accommodate our flight schedules. I'll honestly just be grateful to be home."

"I'm sure you'll *all* be," Myrick emphasized, wanting the killer to hear his words and feel a sense of security that Myrick wasn't on the verge of solving the case, although one key perplexing detail was definitely still nagging at him.

"We'll miss seeing you, Detective," Victoria chimed in, sincerity in her voice. "Perhaps not under these circumstances," she then quickly emphasized. "But still it was very nice getting to know you."

"There won't be too many more dance events for a while," Ellen noted, and Myrick wasn't surprised to hear her words. "I think we've all suffered so much that it's best to cancel the upcoming ones. We need to heal. But I hope once we do start up again, you'll come to a few of them. I heard you're quite a natural at it. Victoria told me all about getting to practice West Coast with you," Ellen winked over at Victoria, knowing already about the fondness between the two. "And of course Jayde had mentioned that she believes you'll be ready for competitions in no time." Ellen smiled, wryly, hoping that Myrick had gotten hooked on it like most inevitably did. "I wish she was here to tell you that herself." Ellen added, a bit disappointed.

Myrick was instantly confused, almost immediately glancing to his right and over Jayde's shoulder, wondering if perhaps he hadn't heard Ellen correctly. Only, it wasn't Jayde sitting there. The girl turning to face him resembled Jayde. She had jet black hair; fair-skinned features accentuated by dark makeup; and wore an all black ensemble, which in all respects matched Jayde's goth appearance. The only notable differences were the slightly rounder face and the blonde roots that barely showed in the girl's hair, revealing that she'd dyed it... and of course, the fact that Myrick could now see and tell that she did not have a broken arm.

"I don't think we've met before," Myrick suddenly noted, his attention on the girl in the chair immediately next to him. "I'm Detective Evann Myrick."

"Oh, hello," the girl replied, rather reserved. "I'd heard all about you."

"I'm sorry, Detective," Ellen chimed in. "I'd thought you'd already met."

Myrick turned his attention briefly to Ellen but then his gaze returned to the girl next to him even as Ellen was speaking, amazed at the eerie resemblance between her and Jayde.

"This is Amber," Ellen continued. "We're sort of celebrating her rise in the rankings. She just made it into the Intermediate Level."

"I figured I'd never get there," Amber responded, contritely. "Seems like I spent an eternity in Novice."

"Which just makes it even sweeter now that you have," Ellen answered back in a motherly tone, evidently proud of Amber's accomplishments.

Myrick couldn't help but notice that the table felt a bit like a family - if, admittedly, a dysfunctional one - but still a group of friends closer than most. Ellen acted as the matriarch of it, and she seemed to genuinely cherish the role. She had the time and resources to set up events, which resembled in many ways family gatherings, and she was the central force in bringing them all together. But, like most families, there were also moments of discord and betrayal, and a particular one was taking place right before his eyes, even if not everyone at the table was yet aware of the extent of it.

Myrick glanced over at Jonathan who was conspicuously sitting farthest away from Kendall, still engaged in the charade and apparently blissfully unaware that the ruse between him and Kendall would be coming to an end soon. While Claire hadn't figured everything out *yet*, she had learned enough, already confronting Kendall about where she'd been that night. She also had her sources poking around to find out if anyone had seen anything… and it was only a matter of time until someone fessed up having spotted Kendall and Jonathan together.

"You know," Myrick began, speaking in the direction of Amber, "I apologize but I honestly mistook you for Jayde."

"Oh, no worries. I get that all the time."

"I can understand why. The two of you are practically twins."

Myrick could see that Amber took his words as a compliment, almost blushing at the comparison. He also caught a glimpse of some of the reactions of the others around the table, which were equally telling, including Deion's who rolled his eyes and seemed to visibly slight the comment. Myrick realized that he needed to follow up with Deion about that, if given the chance by Bradley to ask a few questions of his own during the interview.

"I'm no Jayde," Amber noted with a bit of a laugh, although it was clear she certainly aspired to be a "Jayde" herself. Myrick guessed that she'd even changed her hair color to mimic her idol.

"Well, I hate to have to cut this short," Deion chimed in, looking down at his watch as he spoke. "But I need to be getting on the road. If this interview takes too long, I'm going to miss my flight."

Deion stood up from the table, placing his napkin on the spot in front of him. Myrick watched, intently, sizing up his suspect, but also knowing that he'd get another chance in just less than an hour to ask a few more questions and see if he couldn't confirm many of his suspicions. Myrick then watched as Deion left the restaurant, disappearing from view. Ellen then hijacked the conversation once more.

"We probably do all need to get going," Ellen admitted. "I know I've got so much packing to do. I'm sure we've all been a bit shell-shocked over these past couple of days... and it's been hard to get my act in order... and so I'm going to pull myself together so that I can get out of here on time as well."

As Ellen beckoned the waiter over once more, Myrick took one last glance around the table. Claire seemed perturbed, and was doing a terrible job concealing her feelings - her arms crossed and her body language reflecting that she wasn't pleased with her daughter's deceptive conduct. Kendall, in turn, seemed rather contented, more so than Myrick had seen her in all their encounters so far, and Myrick guessed that she was basking in the fact that she'd so boldly stood up for herself for once.

Jonathan, however, had a contrasting befuddled expression painted on his face, his head tilted slightly as he tried to size up the curious behavior of both Claire and Kendall. Victoria was her usual pleasant self, and Myrick was hopeful he'd get a little more alone time with her to talk, and not just in an interview setting at a police station.

Meanwhile, Amber was an intriguing new suspect in the whole matter; an absolute wild card. Myrick was practically kicking himself for not having figured her out earlier. Arguably, the most fascinating aspect of the case had been there right before his eyes the whole time, and Myrick had completely missed it. *Evidently my investigative skills aren't as honed as they used to be*, Myrick mused to himself. Nonetheless, there was still time for Amber to be interviewed, and so Myrick intended to make a call to Bradley as soon as he could, recommending she interview this newest suspect also, which Myrick was certain that Bradley would agree to do.

Myrick directed his attention to Amber. "Do you mind if I ask what time your flight leaves?"

"I got a late flight out," Amber answered. "It doesn't leave till nine tonight. I wanted to get in as much time as I could this weekend, especially since I hadn't been to a dance event since the Sacramento one."

"And that was the conference that Yves overdosed at," Ellen added, somberly. "Otherwise we would've already gotten to celebrate you making it into Intermediate. Hard to believe it's only been a couple of months that Yves has been gone… and all the tragedy we've been through since then. I'm sorry the best we could do was a breakfast celebration… but I promise all your hard work has been noticed."

"It's okay, I'm just happy to be sitting at the adult table finally," Amber jested, although Myrick picked up on a bit of lingering embarrassment in it, as if Amber had been waiting for this moment for quite a while.

"You were at the Sacramento event?" Myrick asked curiously.

"Yes, but it wasn't long after scores were posted that we found out about Yves. My emotions were all over the place."

"She actually had some of the highest marks from the judges," Kendall explained, proud of Amber. "I think most had you placed first overall."

"All but Trisha," Amber noted. "Beck usually scored me pretty high but I didn't do as well with her on that one."

"Still, a *great* accomplishment making it into Intermediate. We all knew you had it in you," Victoria smiled from across the table. "You're going to really take off now."

The sentiment seemed to be unanimous and after a few more words of encouragement, the six still remaining at the table, who just so happened to be the prime suspects in Myrick's investigation, accordingly got up and said their last pleasantries to each other, soon to depart to their various hometowns once again.

Claire walked out of the restaurant first, notably staying close to Kendall, as if clinging to her most prized possession. Jonathan lingered at the table longer than the others, but eventually followed behind as well. Myrick noted that he now appeared visibly upset, as if he felt left out and perhaps was suddenly becoming aware that there was something different about the dynamics of the room. And Myrick did spot that

Kendall made no attempt to look back at Jonathan to see if he was doing okay.

Ellen was the last to leave. Thanking the detective profusely, and perhaps more than was necessary. She then offered to pay for Myrick's meal, but Myrick graciously refused. The waiter was just bringing a plate of eggs, sunny-side up, with a side of bacon to the table. Finally turning to take a seat at the now empty table, Myrick said goodbye to Ellen and then watched as she walked off as well, allowing himself to dwell on the uncanny nature of the entire setting.

As if unaware that time was not something he had at the moment, Myrick took a slow, determined sip from his coffee cup. He then carefully sliced along the edges of the eggs and bacon, mixing them together, and then eating them both with his fork, just the way he liked. By the time he was done, he felt certain he was ready to begin the last phase of the investigation, although blind to the fact that an entirely unexpected development was on the horizon.

CHAPTER TWENTY
Seek Feedback From the Judges

"Good morning, Mr. Mitchell," Bradley spoke, sitting across the table from Deion. They were in an uninviting box-shaped room with no windows. In the corner of the room, high above and affixed to the ceiling, was a small, discreet camera positioned facing toward Deion. Present in the room to interview their suspect were Lieutenant Bradley and a second detective who'd been assisting throughout the investigation - Detective West. The two had strategized beforehand, deciding that Bradley would play good cop and West would assume the role of bad cop. They were certain those two roles would work to perfection on getting the information they needed out of their interviewee.

"Good morning," Deion replied, glancing down at his watch as he spoke, hopeful that the interview wouldn't take long. "It's Detective Bradley, correct?"

"Yes. And this is my partner - Detective West. We'd just like to ask you a few questions." Bradley was clearly ready to get down to the heart of the matter. They had a full day of interviews lined up, and a limited time to work with, given the dancers had flights to catch. Meanwhile, Deion had shown up ten minutes late, and that hadn't made a very good initial impression with Bradley. She was starting to suspect it would be hard to keep up a "good cop" type demeanor with him.

"I'll tell you everything I know."

"I appreciate that. Fortunately, I've already been given a good rundown on things from Detective Myrick with the Colorado Springs PD. I believe you know him."

"I do. I've spoken to him a couple of times."

"Well, he's actually present also. We're recording everything." Bradley looked up at the camera in the corner of the room, wanting her suspect to know of its presence. "Detective Myrick is in the booth watching everything live and we'll be able to check with him if you say anything that doesn't quite add up. Fortunately, based on what he's told us so far," Bradley went right into her "good cop" role, "I'm confident you'll be truthful and transparent with us as well."

"Of course."

"Good, then let's start off with a few questions about your relationship with one of the recent victims - Sacha Arnauld. How did you get along with him?"

"Okay I guess... better than most. He kept to himself. But we actually spent a lot of time hanging out. He and I have been pros for a long time, and we'd frequent the same parties, events, etcetera. We were pretty much on the same travel circuit. If he was brought in to teach, I was usually on the roster also."

"And that would include Sacramento, Boston and Colorado Springs too?" Bradley paused before continuing. "The places where Lavigne, Beck, Steyn... and even your competition partner - Jill McKenna - were all found murdered also."

"I know where you're going with this detective... and I don't blame you. But I didn't kill anyone. I had nothing to do with any of their deaths."

"My understanding from Detective Myrick and others is that you haven't exactly shown much remorse over Jill McKenna's death."

"Everyone grieves differently. I'm sure you've seen that in your line of work."

"I admit, I have. I even interviewed one woman whose defense mechanism was reactionary laughter when she was genuinely nervous or scared. Trust me, I've seen it all."

"Then I'm sure you could tell if I was faking my emotions."

"Are you faking your emotions?" Detective West jumped in on the conversation, seizing on the opportunity. "Because unlike my partner, I'm not entirely sold on your act."

"Don't try me like that, Detective!" Deion immediately spit back, his change of persona so stark that it even caught Bradley a bit by surprise. "Jill meant the world to me. We may not have been able to keep competing together... nothing stays the same forever... I know Isabelle has thrown a monkey wrench into all our plans... but Jill is... *was*... the best dancer I've ever worked with. I'm going to miss her more than you'll ever know."

Deion's words were forceful and there was a sudden moment of tense silence as he let them sink in. Meanwhile, Bradley felt that it was time for her to break back into the conversation and smooth things out, understanding West had done his job and proven that Deion's calm demeanor hid something more fiery lurking just beneath the surface.

"I apologize, Mr. Mitchell. That question," Bradley looked over at Detective West with feigned disappointment before continuing, "could have been worded better."

"Yeah, it could have," Deion agreed, apparently grateful that Bradley had voiced what he was clearly thinking.

Bradley could see that her comment had worked, and so she turned to her next question. "You were planning to meet with Jill McKenna that exact morning. We saw the text on her phone. I assume you were on the way down soon to go meet up with her?"

"That was the plan. I had a big group in my room. We'd all been drinking. It's just part of the weekend's festivities. But I was done with those antics and ready to get serious again. Jill and I still were practice partners. Everyone knew that."

"Of course."

"And of course, with so many people in my room, I'm pretty sure you also agree that's a rock solid alibi."

"Sort of," Bradley responded, careful not to drift out of her lane and reveal too much. "But of course, we can only place the time of death to within an hour or so of when Jill was found. A lot can happen in an hour. Your room was on the same floor as Jill McKenna's. And you admit everyone was drinking heavily. It wouldn't be hard to slip out of the room, undetected, for a few minutes. So, while I believe you... because I can't imagine you'd do a thing to someone like this... not to someone I can tell you *did* care deeply about... we do have to do our jobs, Mr. Mitchell. Your alibi is certainly a consideration. But we're going to conduct a thorough investigation regardless. You'd want us to do that for your friend."

"I do want you to catch the person who murdered Jill. I want her to be held accountable for what she's done!"

Bradley immediately caught Deion's use of pronouns, and decided to follow up on it.

"So you believe the killer to be a woman?"

"Likely." Deion paused, then decided to offer up some background on things. "Sacha thought the same thing. He even muttered something to that effect... in the midst of his drunken stupor... the night of his death. That's where the infighting has been going on in dance lately. That's where Jill's biggest enemies seemed to lie. Kendall, Claire, Jayde, Victoria... yes, even Ellen, they all had their reasons to hate Jill."

"Ellen *brought* Jill to the competition as a paid judge," Bradley decided to emphasize the glaring hole she saw in Deion's conjecture. "Why would she choose to do that if she secretly wished her dead?"

"Ellen had a two-year contract with Jill. She'd signed it back when Jill and I were teaching more together. It's why Jill and I kept leading workshops even while Isabelle was competing with me. That was the deal. Jill and I had to live up to our end of the bargain for at least another fourteen more months. In turn, Ellen was obligated to keep paying us for that same amount of time. I'm sure Ellen wasn't thrilled about that fact. There are lots of pros to choose from, and she probably wished she could free up some money to hire a couple that was on better terms."

"Interesting," was all Bradley said in return. She was considering Deion's point, when West decided to jump in again.

"They say that you were the one who prepared the jello shots on the night of Beck's death."

"I did."

"The coroner's report says she had a blood alcohol level of .204," West paused before continuing. "And that there was heroin in her system.

"Beck was struggling with her demons. No surprise she downed so many shots... or that she was dabbling in drugs. I certainly didn't lace the jello shots with a narcotic if that's what you're trying to insinuate."

"Not trying to insinuate anything," West shrugged, but his tone was still aggressive. He noticed that Deion's demeanor was once again defensive, and it appeared he did not appreciate being challenged. "But her inebriated state... and her presence along the balcony... seems that could create an easy situation for someone who knew how intoxicated she was to push her over the side... make it seem like an accidental fall."

"It would, wouldn't it? You probably should use that information to find the person who killed her then, Detective. Stop wasting your time with those who are innocent."

"Like you."

"Exactly."

Despite the best efforts of their good cop/bad cop routine, Bradley could see that they weren't going to be able to get a confession out of Deion. Still, they'd learned a lot and there was more to a successful interview than just getting a suspect to admit a crime. The key was to confirm as many facts on the record as possible before the person being interrogated lawyered up... which it was clear Deion was on the verge of doing. Aware of that, Bradley wanted to get confirmation of a few more details before he did so and the interview abruptly stopped.

"I hear where you're coming from, Mr. Mitchell," Bradley chimed in. "And I promise we'll catch the person who did this to your friend. I know she meant a great deal to you."

"They all did," Deion added, his tone passionate. "Warren, Trisha, Sacha... all of them were my friends. They were like family to me."

"Then help us with a few last details, and hopefully we can turn our focus elsewhere."

Deion's arms were now crossed over his chest, and Bradley could see that his posture had become more guarded than ever. Still, he nodded his head as if to indicate Bradley was free to continue her questioning - for now.

"Myrick told me that you think Kendall Callaway might have had something to do with this. And we're going to be interviewing both her and her mother in just a few minutes to follow up on your concerns. But I want to return to something Detective Myrick told us you mentioned about Ellen earlier as well... that she was overusing the volunteers. Do you think she was going through financial problems? Maybe you and Jill weren't the only contract she wanted to get out from under?"

"Ellen's always been tight with money. And she was a genius at cutting costs using volunteers. Jill trusted Ellen but I thought we were limiting our potential signing with her again. We were her top draw for the conventions, and she paid us about the same rate as the newer instructors. Jill was finally coming around to seeing what I always had. She did all the negotiating for us with Ellen. But it was no secret that this was the last contract we'd be signing with her. Maybe Jill said something to Ellen to set her off. Who knows?"

"That's one of my theories also," Bradley agreed. "But I do wonder... the current contract required the two of you to teach as a couple. But if one of you wasn't alive to do so anymore, wouldn't that potentially negate the contract, allowing you the freedom to finally sign with someone else?"

Deion didn't like the question. He'd been cooperative to a point, but this was now the *third* time it had been insinuated in some form or fashion that he might have a motive to kill Jill and he'd reached his breaking point, regardless of Bradley's appeasing tone.

"Are you going to arrest me, Detective?" Deion looked with frustration at Bradley first and then over to West as well.

There was a moment of tense silence, as if Bradley was pondering her next move. "No," she finally answered back. "We're not yet done with our investigation."

"Then I'm free to go, right?" Deion glanced down at his watch once again, noticing the time and wanting (for many reasons) to make sure he didn't miss his flight out of New Mexico, and to be done with the Santa Fe Sheriff's Office.

"Detective West," Bradley turned to her co-investigator on the case, "would you mind stepping out to speak with me for a second?"

Bradley then got up from her chair, and West took the cue to do the same. Neither made any attempt to answer Deion's question as they did so; and as they left the room, Deion had an anguished expression on his face, frustrated that he was going to be left in the dark and waiting for a reply. Deion, though, would be getting his answer soon enough, and with it, his fate would be finally be decided.

CHAPTER TWENTY-ONE
Practice In Front of a Mirror

Myrick was staring at the black and white image of Deion on the video screen. It was almost as if the two were eye-to-eye, even if Deion was unaware of it. Bradley had actually offered Myrick the opportunity to be in the interview room, but Myrick had declined, voicing his concern that too many officers in the room might cause Deion to feel overwhelmed and more hesitant to talk. But, in truth, there was another reason why Myrick had remained behind. He completely trusted that Bradley could extract the information they needed without his help, and he was far more interested at this point in studying Deion's non-verbal reactions to see if his read on him had been correct - and it turned out that it indeed was.

"Nice work, Lieutenant," Myrick commented, his eyes still on the image of Deion on the video screen, even as he became aware of Bradley and West entering the smallish recording area.

"Anything else you think we should follow up on?" Bradley asked.

"No, I think you've about covered it."

"You know we're going to have to let him go. We don't have nearly enough to make an arrest."

"That's fine. He's not our killer," Myrick revealed, turning away from the video screen as he did so that he was now looking Bradley square in the eye.

"You sure? He's got quite a motive. Jill presented a lot of obstacles for Deion and Isabelle's relationship. He had much to gain by getting rid of her, especially getting out of that contract. Our jail is full of stories of men who committed crimes to appease a lover."

"He cared for Jill too much to do that. I can see it in his eyes. Jill never stopped being an important part of his life. He literally signed that contract with Ellen in deference to her. That's how much he trusted and cared about Jill. He may want to keep Isabelle happy. But Jill had a place in his heart also."

"Maybe that's true," Bradley acknowledged. "But maybe not. Intuition only goes so far toward proving guilt or innocence."

"But we've known from the very beginning of this case that Deion couldn't have been the killer. I really was more interested in seeing if he could help shore up some unanswered questions on why Sacha was murdered... which I believe he's now done for us."

"And how can you be so certain of that fact?" West chimed in, not entirely persuaded that the quirky outsider from Colorado Springs should have so much say in their investigation.

"Deion Mitchell is 6'2"... per the autopsy, the bullet that killed Jill hit her in her midsection and then traveled through her in an upward trajectory. Based on the confrontation at Jill's hotel room door, and the gun powder present on her body, the shot had been fired at very close proximity. It's highly unlikely that Mr. Mitchell, who is a good six inches taller than her, would've fired a bullet that traveled upward from her midsection to her upper spine. Our shooter is considerably shorter than Deion Mitchell."

West's expression changed as he considered Myrick's point, apparently persuaded by its logic. He seemed a bit defeated as well, as if they were now back to square one in the investigation.

"You think he's got anything else to tell us?" Bradley interrupted.

"No, I think we can be through with Deion Mitchell," Myrick concluded, confidently.

"Then I'm going to tell him he's free to go at this point," Bradley pointed out, and even as she did so, it became clear that West was having second thoughts about whether they were making the right decision. Bradley, though, was the lead and it was her call to make; and more importantly she didn't see what, if any, authority she had to keep him at this point regardless. Deion's flight was due to leave soon and he was entitled to be on it.

As the two detectives made their way out of the recording area, Myrick turned his attention back to the black and white feed and the image of Deion on the screen. He noted that Deion had his head down, his face sunken into his hands, and he seemed defeated, barely lifting his head as Bradley and West re-entered the room.

Myrick listened as the two detectives finally answered Deion's lingering question, explaining that he was indeed free to leave, but that he needed to stay in contact if new information arose and police had any follow up. Deion agreed to keep those lines of communication open, never once threatening to retain a lawyer or insisting on his right to remain silent. He then stood up from his metal chair in the midst of the sparse setting, walked somberly over to the door and out of the room, disappearing from Myrick's view; and there was a level of finality to it, as Myrick suspected the two would never cross paths again.

*****

Kendall and Claire were sitting alone in a row of chairs in the police station lobby when Deion walked out, his head sunken low, and he seemed spent both physically and mentally. Claire then whispered inaudibly over to her daughter as Deion approached, remarking on how he'd likely be the first to turn on his friends to save his own hide. Interestingly, there was no attempt by any of them at a greeting. Deion continued past them without stopping and walked out into the cool morning air, eager to catch his flight back home.

"Ms. Callaway?" West asked as he walked over to the two women sitting in the chairs.

"Yes," both Kendall and Claire answered back, simultaneously.

"I'm sorry," West clarified. "Kendall Callaway. We'd like to go ahead and meet with you first if that's okay?"

"I'd like to be in there with her," Claire interjected quickly, an air of protectiveness in her tone.

"Unfortunately, we can't allow that. We'll need to meet with you individually at this point."

West noticed immediately that Claire seemed to be pondering her next words carefully, not certain if she didn't need to take steps to protect her daughter.

"Are we entitled to a lawyer at this point?" Claire asked, wisely.

"Yes, you are," West explained, dutifully. "It always looks better when you cooperate. But yes, you do have that right."

The situation was now at a crossroads. Bradley had emphasized to West just how important the Callaway interviews would be, and it would throw quite a monkey wrench into their progress, which was on a *tight* timeline to begin with, if everything was put on hold while they sought out and potentially retained an attorney. West was aware a process like that could take days, and then once a lawyer was involved, it changed the interrogation process completely, as the police had lost most, if not all, of their leverage in obtaining a direct confession.

Claire turned slightly as if to say something to her daughter, then stopped herself mid-sentence, changing her decision at the last second and going against her instincts.

"I think... that'll be fine," Claire conceded to the detective. "We have nothing to hide," she said flatly, not because she wanted to actually aid in the investigation, but more so because she wasn't from the Santa Fe area and imagined she'd be spending a fortune obtaining the services of an out-of-state lawyer. She also surmised that she'd be able to change things up if the interview went south and intended to use the time while Kendall was in her interview calling around to law firms to find out what consultation fees were or if any firms provided a free one.

"Thank you for being so cooperative with us," West answered Claire pleasantly, although Claire made no attempt to reciprocate, her arms crossed over her chest. "I promise this won't take long.

"Good," said Claire. "Our flight leaves at 4:50 and we still haven't finished packing."

"We'll have you out of here in plenty of time to handle those things," West returned, although his words weren't actually a true guarantee either Claire or her daughter would be given the green light to return back home.

Leading Kendall back down the hallway of the police station and through a secure door, West was aware that Bradley had formulated a different interview plan for Kendall than had been used with Deion. Myrick had also been consulted and he agreed that this was the perfect opportunity to employ that particular interrogation technique. Meanwhile, once again, Myrick took a backseat, remaining in the recording room to simply observe as Bradley and West went to work.

"Good morning, Kendall," Bradley stood and smiled in greeting, extending a warm handshake to Kendall as she entered the room.

"Um, good morning," Kendall fumbled, appearing a bit perplexed by the situation and nervous about being interviewed.

"It's okay," Bradley quickly assured her, sensing Kendall's apprehension, and genuinely wanting to alleviate her fears. "This won't be a stressful experience. We don't have many questions for you."

"My mom," Kendall again fumbled with her words, "is there a reason she can't be in here with me?"

"I'll tell you what," Bradley answered, prepared for Kendall's question and almost glad that she asked it, "at the end, she can come in here and make sure you're doing okay. Like I said, we're only wanting to help."

Kendall seemed hesitant as she tried to process the detective's words and their import, but she dutifully took a seat in a chair across from Bradley. She then glanced over to see that West was leaving the room, closing the door behind him as he did so, leaving Bradley alone to talk with Kendall.

"I see that you're nineteen years old. Is that correct?"

"Yes, ma'am."

"You're quite accomplished for a nineteen year old. My understanding is that you're already on the verge of professional status as a dancer. I certainly didn't have your level of focus at that age. It must've been quite demanding to balance both education and a potential career."

"It was. People think it came easy, but it didn't. I had to give up *so much*. I'm either at school studying or I'm competing at an event."

"Not much time for a social life, huh?"

"Not really. I mean dance is a social life. But West Coast Swing is more work for me at this point than anything. I come in... hopefully compete well... and then fly back to college."

"Is this what you wanted?" Bradley threw the question out there, already knowing what the response would be.

"Sort of. More so it's what my mom wants. But she has the best of intentions. She knows that the sacrifice now will pay off on the back end. I do get it. If I can establish myself while I'm young, that'll set me up for success down the road."

"*If* you want a career in dance." Bradley wisely added.

"Yes, if that's what I decide to do with my life."

"Because I see from your college transcripts that you're enrolled in both biology and chemistry. Those are tough courses for a first year... the type of track that a student with Pre-Med ambitions might take. If so, that's quite a lofty and admirable goal. It's very demanding also."

"I know. College has been a wakeup call. The competition to get into a good medical school is going to be steep. I feel a little behind the eight ball too. It's hard to juggle so much."

"Does your mom know you don't really want to follow in her footsteps?" Bradley offered up this question knowingly, practically voicing the words that she sensed Kendall wanted to express, almost as if she was in her mind already.

"What makes you so sure I don't want to be a dancer?"

"Because I was once in your position too. My parents didn't want me to be a police officer. They thought it was too dangerous. They had their own plans and dreams mapped out for me. I was supposed to be an engineer... work at the same prestigious architectural firm as my father. Instead, I chose the police academy. I'd actually enrolled in it, even before letting them know. Kind of like you're dead set on a career in medicine and then breaking that news to your mom on the back end."

"The way I see it, all I have to do is make it to the All-Star ranks. Then I can take a break from dancing and focus on college. Once I have that designation, I'll have paid my dues and proven myself, and I can always come back to it again later. Sure, mom wouldn't be thrilled. But she'd at least be happy that I was already an established pro and could come back to it when... or *if*... I changed my mind."

"And the faster you achieved pro status, the better, right?"

"Sure. Who wouldn't want that to happen?"

"There were some obstacles in the way that had to have frustrated you. Jill, for one. She didn't seem to be in your corner as far as I can tell."

"That's true. Jill didn't score me high in competitions," Kendall paused for a moment, trying to be careful with her words and evidencing a maturity and intellect above her age level. "But Jill gave low scores to a lot of us. Take Jayde for example... she's one of the best I've ever competed against. Jill still hardly ever scored her high. There was always some technical reason for Jayde taking a hit. And I know that really tore at Jayde too."

"But of course, there's also the situation with Warren Steyn. I heard that he'd recently decided to no longer fund most of your events."

"I didn't need his help. I never wanted it to begin with. I can make it on my own."

Bradley listened to Kendall's answer, picking up on the frustration in her words, believing that Kendall did have the ambition and ability to do just fine without Warren's help. That, though, brought up a new complex problem... because it was clearly Kendall's mom pulling the strings to ensure that her daughter *was* given every advantage possible. Perhaps, Kendall may not have wanted these things for herself... but she did seem to care about living up to her mother's expectations, possibly no matter what the cost to get there, *especially* if it meant she could then finally move on with her own life ambitions.

"Let's talk about Jayde then. You brought her up and I get the feeling that there was a rivalry between you two."

"Not by choice. It was almost forced on us. I could tell that we were being played against each other, but I don't think we're as different as people think."

"Well, maybe you don't feel that way. But it's possible Jayde does. She certainly doesn't have the same family advantages you do. She's not a legacy."

Bradley could see that Kendall was immediately taken aback by the statement, and there was a measure of sadness in her expression, as if her sense of self-worth had been diminished; and Bradley regretted her last words to a degree, hoping to perhaps take some of the edge off them.

"Having family in your corner is a real blessing," Bradley explained. "I can't tell you how many people come into this police station with no family to speak of... or worse, family that wants to hurt them. I'm not saying your mom has gone about this the right way... you shouldn't live vicariously through your children... but she's at least on your side and wanting the best for you."

"Maybe," Kendall meekly returned, apparently not entirely convinced of that fact.

There was a moment of quiet consideration, and then Bradley decided to change the direction of the investigation.

"I'll tell you what," Bradley finally broke the silence. "I'm going to give you some time alone to speak with your mom. This investigation is important... but so is repairing your relationship with her. And it sounds like that's something you *need* to do," Bradley paused for a moment as she stood up from her chair and decided to add one more suggestion. "You should probably be honest with her about Jonathan too. That's if she hasn't already figured it out."

Rather than wait for an answer, Bradley knew her words had the intended effect and so she decided now was the time to pause the conversation. Sliding her chair back under the table, she then turned to leave. "I'm going to get your mom. I'll send her back to talk with you. Be truthful with her... she deserves that."

After closing the door shut, Bradley stopped in her tracks just on the other side of it, West standing there waiting for her. He seemed pleased with the interview so far. Bradley, however, was less enthused, as she'd unexpectedly bonded with the girl, having realized just how similar their lives were and the difficult obstacles they'd faced to pursue their own dreams.

"Should I go get Ms. Callaway and bring her back here?"

"Yes," Bradley answered, still convinced this was the best course, although feeling a bit of remorse for not being entirely truthful with Kendall. "Let's go ahead and get the two of them in there together. I've set the tone. They're going to have to have it out at this point."

West turned to go get Claire. Meanwhile, Bradley made her way over to the recording room. They'd watch from there as Kendall and her mom talked. Bradley was certain that they'd learn more simply listening to the two of them than anything Bradley could've pried out of Claire by way of interviewing techniques. And by the point the mother and daughter were done with their talk, Bradley would have all the information she would need regarding their potential involvement in the murders.

CHAPTER TWENTY-TWO
Don't Criticize While on the Dance Floor

Watching the video feed on the screen, Myrick was intrigued as he observed the long silence between Kendall and Claire, wondering who would be the first to speak. Claire had hugged her daughter when she'd entered the room, but the weak effort to reciprocate by Kendall told her mother volumes, and she guessed that Kendall had possibly revealed more about family affairs than she should have.

"You know how much I love you," Claire finally offered up, her words drifting as if spoken in a vacuum.

"I do," Kendall allowed, somberly.

"I wouldn't do anything to hurt you."

"But you sometimes do," Kendall replied honestly, no longer willing to put up a pretense.

For a second, it appeared as though Claire would rebuke her daughter over the comment. Her demeanor, however, noticeably changed, as her shoulders sagged a bit and her face took on a look of regret. After another brief and awkward silence, Claire decided to make a confession of sorts, "I found out about Jonathan finally… I just wish you'd have been the one to tell me?"

"I couldn't," Kendall fumbled back, caught off guard by her mother's statement, and immediately feeling terrible that her secret had come to light. "I knew you'd disapprove."

"I would have, but only because I love you." Claire paused in contemplation. "Jonathan's got no future. He's not right for you."

"You mean he's not right for *you*… for what *you* want the daughter of the legendary Claire Callaway to achieve. These are all your hopes and dreams… not mine. This isn't what I want for my life. I don't want to end up like you. I don't want to spend the rest of my life with a man who treats me like an old trophy, putting on a facade so that the world can't see how broken I am inside."

"Warren and I loved each other," Claire forced out, almost trying to convince herself of that truth more so than to persuade her daughter. "We were everyone's dream couple back in the day. You just weren't there to see it. Unfortunately, when you get to the top, there's a lot of people trying to tear you down."

"That's because dance is your everything." Kendall paused before continuing, her tone softer but still determined. "But not mine. It never has been. And when I met Jonathan, he got that about me. I don't know if Jonathan is the one for me long term… but I do know that I'm not meant to follow in your footsteps. And I won't do it any longer."

Once again, Kendall's words hit Claire hard. The thought of all her dreams going down the drain… of losing Warren… and then her daughter… and all her aging connections to the dance world was almost impossible to fathom. On impulse, Claire decided to reveal more than she knew she should have in a last ditch effort to dissuade Kendall and help her understand how foolish she was being.

"You don't know Jonathan," Claire explained, her words solemn. "I mean, you don't know the *real* him. But I do. I was the one who gave him his first opportunity to work an event. He's a charity case, Kendall. His father is in prison. His mother is a dope addict and disappeared from his life long ago. But we gave him a family here. Turns out he does have a gift... just not as a dancer. He's a talented videographer... and thankfully that's provided him a steady stream of income. But this is the most Jonathan will *ever* be. Can't you see that? You were meant for so much more - Kendall Callaway. We... you... can be all those things. You just have to trust me... I can help you go so much higher in life than I ever did. You won't end up like me," there was a profound sadness as Claire professed her truth verbally for the first time ever. "There are so many examples of happy people in the dance world who *do* make it. You'll have one of those storybook lives... I'll do whatever I can to make sure of that."

The two women stared at each other and there was a lasting silence as they each contemplated what would come next. Even the detectives in the other room, watching by video, couldn't entirely predict what Kendall's reaction would be. So, when she did speak, it surprised everyone listening, especially Claire.

"And how far would you go to ensure my success?" Kendall finally pressed, a strange detached nature to her words. "How far would you be willing to go to make sure I reached the top?"

"What are you trying to say?" Claire stammered in return. "You don't honestly believe I'd do something like that?"

"I don't know anymore. I don't feel like I know you at all."

Bradley was listening with bated breath as the video, which was being recorded in real-time, played out before her eyes. Just as she'd predicted, Kendall was doing the hard work for her. Bradley knew there was no way she'd get Claire to talk. The mere fact that she'd already mentioned the potential of retaining a lawyer clued her in to how impossible it was going to be for a detective to get anything of substance out of her... let alone confess to a murder. But with the assistance of her own daughter, and during a moment of weakness, with the two of them alone, perhaps - just perhaps - the truth would come out.

"I'm so sorry for the things I've done," Claire finally began, her eyes red and watery... a tear flowing down her cheek. She was gazing directly at her daughter as she spoke, but almost as though she was looking at someone she knew she'd lost forever. "I'm sorry for living my life through you. I know it was wrong. I think I've known for some time now that I'd made a mistake and that this day of reckoning was inevitable." Claire paused for a long moment, seemingly staring a little bit deeper into Kendall's eyes and into her soul. "I might even be a monster... but not the type you must see me as... not the type that could deliberately hurt the people I love. No, Kendall... I did not kill Warren... or anyone else. You're wrong to believe that about me."

"I didn't mean..." Kendall tried to get out, only to be cut off.

"Yes… yes, you did. And maybe I'm even getting what I deserve for what I've done. It's true that I stoked the flames between Sacha and Alexander. I wanted Natasha out of the picture to clear the path for you. It's also true that I despised Jill for the low scores she gave you, as if she was hell-bent on proving that my say had no importance anymore. I deserve to pay for what I did to their lives. And trust me when I say that I'm going to suffer for the rest of my life now that I've lost both the loves of my life… Warren… and now you."

Bradley had heard enough. Claire had confessed her motives and her misdeeds, but she wasn't going to admit the ultimate fact. The plan had worked, and it was possible Claire had even further inculpatory statements to make, but Bradley's protective side was winning out and she wasn't going to allow Claire's cruel words toward her daughter to continue, unabated, any longer.

"I apologize for interrupting," Bradley explained as she quickly entered the room.

Claire's eyes turned to meet her, and they had an almost lifeless appearance to them, as if she'd gone dead inside. Meanwhile, Kendall's gaze remained downcast and she didn't even attempt to look up as Bradley spoke.

"Kendall, I'm going to need you to come with me," Bradley explained, putting her hand gingerly on Kendall's shoulder, attempting to get her attention.

Eventually, as Bradley remained there, aware of Claire's intense stare but willing to be patient for Kendall's sake, Kendall looked up at her and stood from her chair. Bradley then led her out of the room without saying a word. On the other side of the door, there was a woman waiting, an advocate with the Sheriff's

Office, and Bradley asked her to take good care of Kendall while she went back in to continue her interrogation of Claire.

Struggling to switch between the compassion she felt for Kendall and the disdain she felt for Claire, Bradley re-entered the room and sat down at the table across from her suspect. Strangely, it was as if the two had switched roles, and now Claire was about to become the interrogator, as she was already geared up with questions for Bradley.

"You knew that was going to happen, didn't you?" Claire pressed.

"Maybe not to that level. But yes, to a degree I did expect that," Bradley truthfully revealed, wisely realizing that the only way she'd get Claire to continue to talk was if it was motivated by anger. And Bradley could tell that Claire possessed the ability to harbor extreme resentment toward someone. She was quickly getting a taste of what that might look like in its most unbridled form.

"You used my only daughter against me!"

"I didn't make you... or her... say anything that wasn't already needing to be voiced between the two of you. It was happening whether you were here or the confrontation happened someplace else."

"And that was my decision to make."

"Was it?" Bradley wondered aloud. "Because it doesn't seem like your daughter wants you making decisions for her anymore." Bradley paused to let her words sink in. "And she did ask a compelling question... one I'd like to delve further into. Did you kill them?"

Fire brimmed in Claire's eyes. She was on the verge of revealing more than she should. Even in her rage, Claire knew what a mistake that would be. One of the great gifts dance had taught Claire was the ability to have a thick skin and bite your tongue, even while those around you were given the opportunity to size you - and your very worth as a person - up.

Taking a deep breath in, Claire closed her eyes as if in a desperate search to find some sort of inner peace. When she opened them again, she appeared an entirely different person. There was an eerie lack of emotion in her words when she went to speak finally.

"I'd like a lawyer," she simply stated.

"Of course," Bradley understood that her interview was over the moment those words were spoken, regardless of what other questions she had or how close she'd felt to gaining a confession. Still, there was evident disappointment in her eyes as she understood that she'd pushed too hard. "Have you already retained one? Is there someone I could speak to and that could help us continue this conversation?"

"No, I don't have the money to do that right now. But I know I'm entitled to a lawyer. I want the judge to assign me one. I have a right to remain silent."

"You do," Bradley agreed with the other fundamental constitutional right that Claire had just voiced. "I'm going to step out of the room for a minute. I'll be right back," she assured her.

Almost as soon as she was out of the interview room, she spotted both West and Myrick waiting in the hallway.

"I blew it," she spoke, disappointment in her voice.

"Blew what?" Myrick asked, sincerely, apparently not having come to the same conclusion as she had.

"I almost had her talking. I thought maybe if I got her to hate me she'd fess up."

"She told you everything you needed to know."

"Except that she killed those people," Bradley noted the obvious.

"Which she didn't do," Myrick insisted. "Whoever shot Jill did so while keeping the door open with one foot, requiring a leg strength that literally left a significant scuff mark on the base of the door. But even more importantly, the killer had to be strong enough to drag a body and place it up in the rafters of the pool shed. Claire couldn't have done that alone. The only possibility was that she'd been in this together with her daughter."

"Her daughter didn't kill anyone. I'm positive about that."

"Exactly. Your interviewing technique worked brilliantly and proved her innocence. It just so happens I can prove Claire's as well… even if she isn't exactly mother of the year."

Bradley appreciated what Myrick said. She knew she'd allowed her disdain for Claire to cloud her judgment, but now that she was thinking more clearly, it was also true that Claire couldn't have committed the murders without some level of help. And the only one seemingly willing to do so would have been Kendall.

"So we can now cross three suspects off the list," West interjected. "Not a bad morning."

"Who's up next?" Myrick asked.

"Victoria," West answered quickly.

"It's about lunchtime," Bradley remarked, glancing down at her watch. "I'm going to need fifteen minutes or so to reset before the next one. That last interview took a lot out of me."

"Well, if you don't mind, I actually have a suggestion. I'd like to talk to Victoria myself."

"That's fine. Detective West will assist you. Maybe I'll kick back and down a coffee while I watch you do the heavy lifting."

"That's the other thing. I'd actually like to talk to her in a less confrontational setting. I think she'll be more open with me if the interview wasn't conducted here at the police station."

Bradley seemed a bit taken aback by Myrick's suggestion, and so he attempted to throw in an additional layer of reasoning to hopefully gain her support for this unconventional idea.

"Worst case, what I get out of her isn't what you needed to know. Meanwhile, you at least get a much-needed break to collect your thoughts… and after I get back, you can follow up later with your own set of questions for Ms. Monroe. Really, you've got nothing to lose by letting me take a shot at this. I don't think I've let you down yet. I'm not going to this time either."

"That actually might help too with the tight timeline we're on," West jumped in. We have Alexander Kozlov, Jonathan Scott, Ellen Cromwel, Jayde Ch'en and Amber St. James all lined up back-to-back-to-back, and all are scrambling to make flights out of here this afternoon or early tonight. I don't see how we're going to pull it all off. My guess is we'll be making trips around the country for follow up if we don't start streamlining things."

Considering the situation, Bradley eyed Myrick for a long moment and then finally spoke, "I want to know *everything* she tells you. I know you've got your own cases to solve. We've all got a lot at stake in this. Don't make me regret this decision."

"I appreciate your faith in me... and the accompanying ultimatum. Let's hope I play my cards right... because if I do then we'll be arresting a murderer before nightfall."

"I'm going to hold you to your word, Detective. So go do your job before I change my mind. Your suspect is out in the lobby... find out everything she knows. West and I will start up with Alexander Kozlov's interview if you're not back in time for it."

Bradley finished her statement by adding a wry, intuitive smile to the end of it, as if to let Myrick know that she didn't believe for a second that he was revealing all that he'd uncovered about their case so far. Still, he'd been an invaluable asset throughout her investigation and she was developing a tremendous amount of respect for his investigative skills; and she was equally certain that he'd come back with more information that would help them pull off a miracle and solve the case. Only, unfortunately, she'd also soon learn that the decision to let Myrick conduct this one interview alone would have unintended consequences, setting in motion a domino effect that would force the killer to strike once again.

CHAPTER TWENTY-THREE
Perfect Your Stretch & Anchor

Victoria watched as a barista handed two steaming hot beverages in white cups over the counter to Myrick. He turned and walked back over toward the table, offering one of the two drinks to Victoria, then sitting down just across from her. The two of them were essentially alone in the quaint coffee shop; the only other patron sitting at a far away table and reading a book familiar to Myrick, *Eternity*, and written by one of his favorite authors, James Nealis.

"You know, I would've said yes to going for a coffee, regardless of being one of your suspects," Victoria offered, as her mouth inched northward in a slight smile.

"Well, this is a first for me also. I usually bring my suspects to less upscale places where they mostly serve moldy bologna sandwiches on stale bread."

"In that case, I'm particularly grateful you introduced me to this charming establishment," Victoria glanced from their table over to a green and red neon sign affixed high on a brick wall which read, "Cafeblanca". The rest of her surroundings had a French-Moroccan, old world flair to it, complete with original pictures of an Arabic port town on the walls, and even the old-timey jazz music that was playing fit the mood nicely as Victoria took a sip of her espresso. "You could definitely charm a girl here... or get her to confess to a crime."

"And have you committed any that I need to know about?"

"I'm guilty of a lot of things," Victoria quipped, her large blue eyes looking up from the coffee mug she was drinking, steam rising from it, drawing attention to her mouth as she spoke, "but mostly only of doing things... making poor decisions that have ended up hurting *me* in the long run."

"I think we're all guilty of that."

"What about you, Detective?"

"What about me?"

"Are you guilty of that also? It sounds like you found true love. Most of us would kill... no pun intended... for something like that."

"Riley was the best decision in my life. But I could've done a better job with the time I had with her. I can't change the past though... we all have to move forward."

"Moving forward though is scary."

"You don't have to tell me that... everything seemed different once Riley was gone. The only solace I found was in my work. That part still made sense."

"That's what dance is to me. It's an escape. But unfortunately, it's also a reminder of past relationships. It's like a *Catch 22*... I love dance... I love it even more when I'm experiencing it with someone who means something to me... but when work and relationships combine, that causes problems."

"Yeah, I can actually understand that. Cops spend a lot of time together and form bonds that others don't understand because of how grueling an occupation it can be. Unfortunately, when two officers hit it off and start dating that tends to be when things go south. It's hard when two people both carry the same stresses and burdens back home with them. Makes it near impossible to distinguish when work ends and our life outside it begins."

Victoria listened to Myrick and couldn't help but appreciate the fact that he seemed to understand her situation in ways that so many others didn't. She wanted romance, but it just didn't appear to be in the cards for her. If she dated a competitive dancer, the demands on both to try to make it to the top together were overwhelming. If she went the other direction and dated a non-dancer, it seemingly caused even more problems. Her chosen profession required endless travel, hours upon hours of grueling training so that she could perform with a partner... and then social dancing at conferences with everyone *but* the man she actually wanted most to be spending her time with. It was nearly impossible to navigate, and it had gotten to the point that Victoria had given up on love entirely.

Myrick was handsome. She liked his smile and his calm, unwavering confidence. There was something incredibly attractive in a man that was secure in who he was. She was also charmed by the fact that he'd tried dancing with her, even if it didn't exactly come naturally to him. She didn't care, she just appreciated that he was willing to give it a try. And Victoria couldn't help but wonder if there wasn't possibly something there - a small spark; maybe even a chance at spending time with someone who was only in dance for the fun of it but not completely invested in it as a career. Perhaps that was the type of man she was looking for.

"So, um, aren't you kind of blurring the lines by taking me here?"

"This is just an interview."

Victoria nodded that she understood, although it was difficult to accept that this was once again only a case-related discussion; and even though she knew that was how it *had* to be, the reality of it disappointed her more than she let on.

"Of course, but I can't imagine that you've interviewed too many suspects in a coffee shop."

"No," Myrick conceded. "This is definitely a first."

"Then why here?"

Myrick tried not to laugh. It felt as though the tables had been turned once again and she was already hijacking the direction of the conversation. Her questions were good too, and he had to admit he was having a hard time navigating them. Myrick knew in moments like this, the truth was always the best course.

"Because I suspected you wouldn't be completely open and honest with me if it was conducted at the police station. This seemed like a less imposing setting to find out from you the entire story."

"Hmmmm," Victoria replied, her eyes slightly seductive as she pondered Myrick's point. She took another sip of her espresso and spoke, "You're right. I wasn't thrilled about being in the police station. I wanted out of there. But even so, shouldn't you be playing this by the books? You don't seem the type to skirt the rules, crossing into the gray areas."

"I've got three months left till retirement from police work. Maybe I'll hang a shingle and dabble in some PI work... but this is probably one of my last high profile cases. I'd like to solve it. I don't mind thinking outside the box, if that's what it takes."

"Well..." Victoria glanced around her, taking in the noir type decor. "This... this is definitely more my style. More like the place I'd be willing to confess my guilt.

"I know you didn't do this," Myrick suddenly revealed, then paused. "But I also believe you're protecting someone who might have."

"I wouldn't protect someone who hurt a friend. Sacha... Warren... Jill... each of us had our differences, but make no mistake, I loved each and every one of them like family. I wouldn't have allowed *anyone* to hurt them."

"I don't think you did it on purpose. I do, however, know you're keeping things from me. Things that you might suspect... even if you can't ultimately prove them."

"So what exactly do you believe that to be?" Victoria continued the role of asking the questions, unaware that Myrick was subtly keeping the conversation where he wanted it to be, almost like he was back leading it.

"Ellen mentioned that you've mentored some of the other dancers."

"Several of them actually."

"Kendall?"

"Yes, but she doesn't have her heart in it. She's got her mother's talent, but skill alone will only get you so far. There's plenty of talented dancers out there... it's the ones who work hard that are set apart."

"Jonathan?"

"Kendall asked me to help him so I have. He's sort of the opposite case as her... hard worker... but not sure if that's going to be enough. I really like the kid though. I'm rooting for him."

"Kendall is too, I'd imagine."

"Yes, she'd do just about anything for him."

"And do you think Jonathan would do anything for her also?"

"I know he adores her. They've kept things secret of course. But I teach them both so it was impossible for them to keep their relationship from me."

"How well do you know Jonathan outside of dance?"

"I know that he comes from a tough upbringing. But he doesn't talk much about himself. All I really know about him is what Kendall told me."

"And you never told Claire about their relationship?"

"It was not my place to. She never asked. And so I never brought it up. Are you trying to accuse me of something?"

"No," Myrick thought for a moment, considering whether it was better to change the subject at this point. "No, I have no interest in judging you. How about Jayde? Did you mentor her?"

"Sure, that's no secret. Jayde's a gifted dancer. She may even surpass us all one day. Probably already would've if not for the fact that the deck was so stacked against her. There's no real reason to help her reach the top... there's no incentive to score her high... if anything she's just going to eventually steal the limelight from some of the other pros. But there's no stopping someone with that much talent... and that much drive.

Sometimes I think I'm learning as much from her as she is from me."

"Like, what for instance?"

"Nothing seems to phase her. All of the infighting and backstabbing... it all seems so inconsequential to her. She doesn't engage in any of it. It's like she sees the goal and the rest is mostly inconsequential... white noise... distractions. It's why she's been the perfect mentor to other dancers who've struggled like Jonathan. Someone like Amber is another good example."

"Amber has really taken to Jayde, I can see," Myrick knew his comment was an understatement.

"That was my idea. Amber was struggling to get out of Novice and on the verge of quitting. I could tell Jayde would be the perfect mentor... and I guess I was right. Amber probably took it a bit too far, but the two hit it off and it did seem to work. I just didn't mean for Amber to become a carbon copy of Jayde in the process."

"You don't like that she changed so much just to fit in, do you?"

"No, that's not what I meant to happen."

"Makes you wonder what else she might be willing to do just to fit in, doesn't it?"

"If you're insinuating she did this, then I don't believe it. She's too good a kid."

"I'm pretty certain you'd say that about all your friends in dance. You're very protective of them... and that's a noble quality. Unfortunately, it's flawed in this instance."

"Then are you saying Amber did this?"

"Maybe. Or perhaps she was helping someone?"

"Like a pro that was helping her get to the top? Or someone like Ellen who could pull strings for her? Because that seems really farfetched to me."

"Well, someone is guilty of the crimes, wouldn't you agree?"

"Someone, yes," Victoria paused. "But none of the people you mentioned."

"Hmmmm." Myrick dipped a coffee stick in his cup and stirred it around three times, forming an almost perfect circle each time.

"You know who else is really intuitive?" Victoria finally spoke again, wanting to alleviate some of the tension in the conversation.

"Who?"

"Jayde."

"I have noticed that."

"She picks up on things. Chemistry between people."

"I noticed that too."

"Do you think?" Victoria paused to consider how to phrase her words before continuing. "Do you think once you solve this case... once you retire and move on to private investigator work... that you'll be ready for a new chapter in other aspects of your life?"

Myrick understood Victoria's question, and it was indeed a good one and one that Myrick had considered himself. If asked to sum himself up, Myrick would have explained there were only three things he'd really desired from life: a tangible relationship with God... growing old with Riley... and a career in law enforcement. In just a few months, only one of those three defining traits would remain as a part of the equation. He would always love Riley, but she existed solely as a memory now. Police work was coming to an end. The one constant, and the one he knew would always be there was his God, and if God was anything like Myrick imagined Him, Myrick was certain God would want him to live out and experience all the good things life had to offer.

But knowing what he needed to do and actually carrying it out were two entirely different things. While Myrick could envision starting a private investigative firm, he had no idea how to let go of the past and move forward in any other aspect of his life. Victoria represented that possibility, and it was almost impossible for him not to grapple with both the fact that he found her so attractive; and that she clearly felt the same about him.

"I think eventually I will," Myrick was honest in his reply to Victoria.

Victoria had gotten the only answer she wanted from Myrick. There was no more that she needed to know from him. And so she did him a favor, seeing how conflicted the question had made him, and directed the conversation back on track by relating things to dance.

"It seems like all of us... myself included... we've all had to push forward in different ways. It's what makes life interesting. If we never experienced the hard times, how would we even know what the moments to savor were."

Myrick smiled warmly at Victoria. She'd voiced a thought and a belief he'd kept securely in his heart for the past few years. The loss of Riley had been impossible to bear. He'd experienced the depths of despair like few others had, but he hadn't lost faith. And he did know what the good looked like. And talking with Victoria felt like the good things in life.

"I think about that all the time," Myrick agreed.

Glancing over Myrick's shoulder at the clock on the far wall, Victoria noticed the time. "We should go soon," she noted, partly so Myrick could know that it was now or never if he wanted to ask a few more questions before she had to head to the airport.

"I've got nothing left to ask. Believe me, I wish there was."

"I know you wouldn't have told me I wasn't your suspect if you hadn't already figured out who the killer was," Victoria wisely responded. "Hopefully what I've told you helps shore things up."

"It does."

"Then go solve your case. Do what you were meant to do... so that the rest of us don't have to live in this fear of who's going to be next anymore."

Listening to Victoria's words brought back a sudden rush of memories. Riley had been his fiercest champion. She'd always known what to say at just the right moment to get him to finish a case strong. Victoria's words now were having the same profound effect on him, and Myrick wasn't sure exactly how to process what that meant.

Victoria knew what to do. She took a last sip of the warm espresso, placed the empty cup back on the table, smiled softly and then began to stand up. Myrick, despite understanding the cue, lingered a little longer, but ultimately did the same. The two parted ways; Victoria to catch her flight back home and Myrick to go solve his case. Or, at least, that's what they both believed was going to happen next.

CHAPTER TWENTY-FOUR
Wear Loose Attire & Smooth-Soled Shoes

Myrick was surprised to see Ellen in the interview room when he returned to the station, wondering if he'd just lost track of time at the coffee shop and had missed Alexander's entire interrogation. Fortunately, Bradley stepped out of the interview room at the same instant, leaving West to continue with questions, and giving her an opportunity to get Myrick caught up on developments.

"Did Kozlov not show?" Myrick asked of Bradley.

"He did. Ellen brought him with her. But he's a mess."

"You don't think it's an act, do you?"

"No, I've seen every faked display in the playbook. This was raw emotion. His fiancé isn't doing well post-surgery. Alexander has all the signs of a broken man."

"I'm really sorry to hear that."

"We tried getting some information out of him. He's angry and despondent... and just doesn't seem to have any ability to assist us in the investigation. You're welcome to try if you want. We can get him back in here after Ellen is done with her interview. But he's cancelled his flight. He's staying here for as long as it takes for his fiancé to recover. Although, I don't think that's going to happen."

"Our killer is leaving a trail of devastation."

"That's not all. We've got another problem too. Jonathan's a no show. He called to say he was having a hard time getting his computer equipment all packed up and would just have to head straight to the airport. Nothing we could do, we don't have enough PC to detain anyone yet."

"Let's interview him at the airport then."

"Way ahead of you. There's a Customs Agency room all set up with interview equipment. We called over and secured it. Although he didn't seem too thrilled with the idea, Jonathan agreed to meet us at the airport. We had Jayde set up for an interview here, but she agreed to talk with us at the airport also so we could pull things all together. Amber's flight isn't until much later so we can deal with her back at the police station once we're done. I think it'd be wise for hers to take place here, if possible."

"Really great work, Detective Bradley. It's been a privilege to get to work with you and your team. I'm impressed."

"Likewise," Bradley agreed, but then paused. "But I do need to bring up one concern. Ellen mentioned that Victoria told her all about dancing with you last night. She said there was a sort of connection between you two. We're all human. I hope you aren't letting emotions influence your judgment."

Bradley felt conflicted about voicing this, but she had a job to do. Fortunately, she could see that Myrick hadn't taken the comment personally, but rather seemed to appreciate the professionalism in it. Myrick knew Bradley was right. There was always an inherent danger in getting too close to anyone in an investigation. It was hard to separate the job from emotions, and it was entirely possible for *anyone* to make the mistake of misjudgment, even Myrick.

"I don't believe she's your killer," Myrick explained. "But I understand if you want to speak with her also. She's cooperative. I can instruct her to meet with us earlier at the airport as well."

"I'd appreciate that. I completely trust you've done your job. But this is still my jurisdiction, and I'm responsible for covering all the bases."

Myrick nodded his respect for Bradley. He had his theories but it was always wise to get a second pair of eyes on things, especially someone intuitive enough to pick up on the potential conflict of interest that *did* exist between Myrick and his suspect.

"Do you mind if I sit in on your interview with Ellen?"

"Don't mind at all. She's a very friendly woman. Speaks highly of you."

"She is friendly. She's also an event director and the most connected and knowledgeable of any of our suspects," Myrick revealed, betraying how much he'd learned from immersing himself in dance.

"Nice tip," Bradley arched an eyebrow, impressed that he was aware of such a fact.

Bradley pointed over to the door, and Myrick entered the room, Bradley following close behind. There were only three seats in the room, West and Ellen occupying two of them, and Myrick stepped aside so that Bradley could return to the seat she'd earlier occupied. Meanwhile, Myrick purposefully stepped to the side corner of the smallish space, not wanting to be imposing on the investigation. His efforts to remain inconspicuous, though, were quickly made complicated.

"Hello, Detective," Ellen smiled as Myrick entered the room. "I was confused why you weren't here."

"I was conducting a different interview."

"Let me guess, with Victoria," Ellen offered slyly, and Myrick wondered if she'd done so solely to stir up a bit of drama with the other detectives in the room.

"Very impressive. Yes, of Victoria."

"Oh, she must've wanted to tell you about her run-in with Kendall this morning... just after breakfast."

Hearing Ellen's statement, Myrick wasn't sure if she was being genuinely helpful with information or if this was a way for Ellen to deflect the conversation away from her and toward someone else. If it was the latter, her strategy was certainly working, as a good offense was always the best defense.

"No, unfortunately she hadn't mentioned that," Myrick responded, and he noticed, just as he'd suspected, a judgmental glance over at him from Bradley, who no doubt felt her suspicions confirmed; and that his emotions had colored his interrogation of that particular suspect.

"I'm surprised to hear that. I just happened to be close enough to overhear bits and pieces of their conversation. Victoria seemed quite fed up to have been placed in the middle of such a difficult situation. And you couldn't miss the cold shoulder Kendall was giving both her mother *and* Jonathan at the breakfast table. We could all tell something was up."

"Why don't you fill us in on exactly what you overheard Victoria say?" Bradley jumped into the conversation, her eyes still trained on Myrick as if disappointed she'd trusted him.

"Sure, but she really didn't go into much detail. You'd have to know Victoria to know that she isn't the confrontational type. But as far as I could tell she'd been caught in the middle of Kendall and Jonathan's relationship for a while... which was unfair because she's also a close friend of Claire's. They'd asked her to keep quiet for their sake, and I'm guessing, based on the exasperated tone of Victoria's voice, that had taken quite a toll on her."

"So Victoria was the only one who knew about Kendall and Jonathan."

"No, not at all. Most of us had already figured it out long ago. You can't spend entire weekends with people and not notice signs. Claire, though, was in denial. It's funny how the mind works. She wanted to believe that Kendall did things exactly as she'd mapped out, but there were plenty of clues to the rest of us that Kendall was rebelling against her mom. I was just waiting for the other shoe to drop at any moment. Most of us were quite intrigued to see how that ultimately turned out. Victoria though was the one being caught in the middle and I'm guessing that she'd had enough and needed to finally vent. I also heard Kendall apologize and promise that today would finally be the day that she told her mom the truth."

"And it was. We actually got to watch it unfold right here at the police station. I guess she decided this was the best and safest place to do so," Bradley added, much to Ellen's astonishment.

"Always good to do those types of things in front of witnesses," Ellen jested back.

"That's indeed good advice," Myrick chimed in. "In fact, you've given me a lot of good advice and direction throughout this investigation. I'm glad I listened to you and allowed Jayde to show me the ropes. Thank you for freeing her up time-wise to do that."

"Of course. You took a risk and learned how to dance. Now, you're part of the family in a lot of ways. We all look out for each other. It's why I try to stick around and be the last to leave the hotel. Just in case one of the dancers has a last minute issue or anything. I'm also going to help Jayde get over to the airport in time for her flight."

"Could you let Victoria know we'd like to speak to her again at the airport as well?" Bradley interjected.

"Of course."

"And we'll be meeting with Jonathan and Jayde at the Customs Office. Victoria can come to that same location."

"I'll make sure she gets there. Same with Jayde. Jonathan's riding with Kendall and Claire though. I'm sure that'll be an interesting trip. Would *love* to be a fly on the wall for that one."

"So it was just Kendall and Victoria talking this morning when it got intense?" Myrick asked, curious if anyone else had been present, still on that particular train of thought.

"I saw Jonathan eventually walk over, as if he wanted to find out what was wrong. Jonathan didn't like the idea of saying something to Claire yet. I was surprised by how heated he was about it... he thought it was unfair of them to make that decision as if he had no say in it. I get the feeling he figured it would cause problems if it was brought up at the end of the weekend and then they went their separate ways, leaving him in limbo."

"You think Jonathan was resentful of the situation with Kendall and Claire?"

"Who wouldn't be?" Ellen returned quickly. "I always felt pretty bad for him. He had to know that he was looked at as something less than the others, and not good enough in Claire's estimation. My understanding is she thought Kendall should be with someone like Sacha. He was young... and talented... and single; and she was quite vocal about what a catch he was."

"You think she might have mentioned something like that to Warren?"

"Oh, he had to have known. But Warren was just the opposite of her. I think he wasn't fond of relationships between dancers. He would've been against it. He might've even told Sacha what a distraction that would be. I want to say Jill even once said she'd overheard something like that."

Myrick was particularly intrigued with the information Ellen was providing. Despite the interview being recorded, he was back to writing notes in his little notepad. But, had Ellen seen what he was writing, she would've been quite perplexed at his interpretation of things.

After recording a few more thoughts in his notepad, Myrick closed it up. He then whispered a few words in Bradley's ear, as Ellen watched curiously; and then he excused himself from the room, explaining that he had a few more matters to follow up on before everyone left town.

"Thank you again for all your hospitality, Ellen. I really appreciate it."

"No trouble at all, Detective. I just hope I've been helpful to your investigation."

"You definitely have been," Myrick answered.

Turning toward the door, Myrick left the room and made his way out of the patrol building. Ellen had indeed been helpful.

Her information provided some key details that only solidified his theory of the case. Still, there were a few unresolved issues remaining that Myrick wanted to follow up on and so he made one final trip back to the hotel, curious to see if yet another of his notions would pay off, which he'd soon find out he was right about.

*****

The first thing Myrick spotted when he got back to the hotel was Jonathan and Claire talking just outside the carport of the hotel and by a block-shaped rental van. As Myrick passed by, he went unnoticed, which was just the way he wanted it, preferring sometimes not to be seen. From a distance, he picked up on the fact that their conversation appeared relatively forced, their body language revealing an underlying awkwardness to it.

A pile of stacked luggage, in various different sizes and shapes, lay just outside the back of the open doors to the van. Myrick guessed that this was all of Jonathan's video equipment, which he could see would be quite a chore to get all packed up and loaded into the vehicle in time to get to the airport. Jonathan's story of why he couldn't make it to the police station, at least by appearances, seemed to add up.

Kendall was nowhere to be seen, leaving Myrick somewhat curious as to her whereabouts. He'd figured, now that the cat was out of the bag, Kendall would want to stay relatively close by, not wanting Jonathan to bear the brunt of Claire's frustration alone. Her absence, however, was a question Myrick wasn't likely to get an answer to at the moment, and so he continued on into the hotel and toward the checkout desk.

The receptionist was pleasant, and was apologetic toward Myrick about the chaos of the weekend, apparently thinking he was one of the hotel guests and not a detective there to investigate. Myrick made no attempt to explain otherwise, and simply insisted that it was no trouble and, if anything, only added a level of mystery and intrigue to his stay, making it an experience he would not soon forget, which was entirely true. He then found out, much like he'd expected, that Ellen had gotten the room comped, and that that he was all checked out.

In turn, Myrick nodded his tweed cap at the receptionist. But instead of walking back out the exit doors, he turned toward the conference area one last time. The doorway to the ballroom was eerily quiet and empty, a strange contrast to the bustling nature of it when the dance convention had been taking place. He made his way through the ballroom and toward the back room where Sacha Arnaud had been found stabbed. The room was darkened and so he flipped the light switch, and then glanced around one last time until he found what he was looking for. The room had a partitioned divider wall that was secured on a sliding track. In order to move the wall over, all Myrick had to do was pull down on a side handle and it slid over easily enough, creating an opening to a narrow hallway behind it. Myrick guessed this was a maintenance walk-through that the hotel closed up with the divider wall for appearance's sake. The hallway was likely used if heavy production equipment had to be brought into the ballroom, including the video and audio equipment that had been used for the event.

Slipping though the opening in the partition wall, Myrick stepped into the narrow passageway and made his way along it. Eventually he reached a doorway, opening it so that he could see that he was in the back of the hotel and outside facing the pool deck. This had, no doubt, been where the killer had unexpectedly crossed paths with Nicole. If she'd assisted in bringing in the DJ equipment, she would certainly be aware of the narrow hallway and how it led to the side hospitality room. Her boyfriend had mentioned that she'd been in a search of a late night snack and she would've known about the cheese tray that had been set up for the pro dancers to enjoy. Unfortunately for Nicole, her decision must've been ill-timed, in Myrick's estimation, and she would've run into the murderer, who was using that same narrow hallway for an escape route.

Given the concealed space and the music playing in the ballroom, no one would've heard Nicole's cries, if any, while she was attacked. Meanwhile, her assailant could then easily drag her to a more inconspicuous location where hotel staff were unlikely to frequent - the pool hut, thinking that the body wouldn't be found there until weeks later. This also explained why Nicole's death didn't appear to be pre-planned, as she'd never been an intended target, only a victim of unfortunate circumstance.

There was a chill in the air outside, and a gust of cool wind caught Myrick as he stepped into it, so he zipped up his coat all the way toward his neckline. The wind cut across the pool, causing the water to ripple amidst it and there was a peculiarly tranquil feel about the setting. Myrick could see that the pool deck was empty, save for one person sitting on a lounge chair tucked along the side. Walking over, he immediately recognized the girl sitting there, although this time he was wise enough to make sure it was actually *her*, aware that he'd twice made that mistaken assumption already.

"Hello, Jayde. How's your arm?"

"It's doing okay," said Jayde, an emotionless look on her face as she replied. She held up the cast to show Myrick how it encompassed her entire forearm and elbow.

"You alright?"

"I will be. Just going to be hard for a while. Doc says I'll have this cast on it for a few months. It was a bad break. And that obviously means no dancing. I'm not sure what I'm going to do with myself. Dance is my only real outlet. I'm going to feel sort of lost without it."

"I understand. I'm really sorry to hear that."

"At least I got to show you a few things before this happened," Jayde weakly smiled.

"And I got to show you a few of my detective tricks," Myrick returned.

"We made a good team."

"We sure did."

"I hope you're going to stick with dance after all this. I'll always be around if you need any more lessons... although it appears I'll be the one a little stiff around the edges."

"You know, I do think I'll keep trying my hand at it. I'm surprised at how much it grew on me... how much I enjoyed it."

"Told you," Jayde smiled knowingly, taking a puff of her cigarette, which had a light air of minty aroma to it, adding a nostalgic feel to the breezy nighttime setting.

The context of things felt a bit surreal as the two talked, almost as if they were longtime friends catching up, which was quite interesting given their age differences and completely different life experiences. Still, Jayde was an old soul and she genuinely seemed to get Myrick. In turn, Myrick seemed to have an even better read on Jayde, knowing that she would indeed suffer without dancing, and he felt sorry to see her saddened state, knowing it was probably eating her up inside even worse than she was letting on. Jayde had a hardened exterior, but Myrick had long since learned those were often the ones who harbored the most pain hidden inside.

"I heard Ellen's going to give you a ride to the airport," Myrick finally broke the silence.

"Yeah, but I was kind of hoping you were here to offer me a ride instead. She's quite a chatterbox, especially since all this has been going on. And I'm not really much in the mood for small talk."

"Unfortunately, I've still got some loose ends to follow up on, otherwise I would've definitely given you a lift. Would've been helpful to bounce a few last ideas off you about the case. Maybe we can do that at the airport."

"Oh, so you will be there for my meeting with Detective Bradley?" Jayde seemed a tad surprised but glad to hear the news.

"Yes, Bradley told me about interviewing you... and Jonathan... and Victoria there. I'll probably sit in for some of it."

"Ok, well that's good," Jayde then paused pensively. "You have any leads on who did all this?" she asked. "I'm sure Ellen's going to shut things down for awhile until you get it all figured out."

"I do have some theories. Hard to say for certain, of course."

"Crazy to think you may have to let a serial murderer fly home."

"It is," Myrick shook his head, emphasizing his consternation. He then smiled over at Jayde, grateful for their one final talk, as he stood up from his bar side chair. "I'll see you at the airport."

"Okay," was all Jayde said in reply, curiously watching as Myrick walked over toward the maintenance shed.

Lifting up the caution tape, Myrick reached for the handle of the door, remembering that the lock on it was broken. He then pushed it open, stepped under the caution tape and proceeded inside, disappearing from Jayde's sight.

Myrick turned on his flashlight, walking around and haphazardly kicking items to and fro with his shoe, as if searching for something. He was incredibly curious as to whether he'd find one last key piece of evidence that he'd unfortunately just now realized he should've thought to look for originally.

Peering up at the rafters, Myrick judged that the *only* way to get a body up there was probably to stand along the stairwell and push it up into it, using the stairwell for added height and leverage. As he ascended the steps, Myrick guessed that the third step provided the best vantage point to do so. He then wondered to himself where the killer would've gone next after such a secretive and exhausting effort. It wouldn't be entirely wise to emerge from the supply shed until knowing for absolute certain the coast was clear, even if on a tight timeline to pull things off, unnoticed.

Myrick took a few more steps upward and finally got to the top, where there was more light from the one window on the far side. It was daylight streaming in this time, as opposed to the moonlight from the night earlier, but it still only lit the top floor up, the bottom remaining mostly dark. As Myrick took a seat on the top step, half of his body was bathed in light and the bottom half was shaded by a persisting darkness.

Glancing down at his feet, Myrick scuffed them back and forth, realizing that one particular part of the stairwell felt a bit smoother than the rest. Leaning over, and upon closer inspection, Myrick spotted black and white specks of ash had fallen in the crevices of the boards. There was barely a hint of it, but that was all Myrick needed. Taking his flashlight out, he pointed it downward, between the steps and toward the floor below, scanning the flashlight slowly from side to side, searching for one final clue. And when he found it, he knew instantly that yet another of his assumptions had turned out to be correct.

CHAPTER TWENTY-FIVE
Accentuate the Finality of the Music

Myrick arrived at the airport just before three o'clock. He was aware of the various flight schedules and knew that he and Bradley had only an hour or so until the first of the suspects - Victoria Monroe - flew out, but Bradley had made it clear that she and West were planning to conduct that particular interview alone and so Myrick took his time at the airport, going by the check-in desk, explaining that he was a detective investigating a series of homicides and then requesting to speak to the luggage handlers. After thirty minutes or so there, he began making his way over to the security area. Showing his badge, he was then allowed to pass through and he made his way toward a side office that had what appeared to be an image of a customs officer on it with a sash across his shoulder and lettering that read, "CBP Primary Processing and Baggage Inspection Area".

Opening the door, Myrick proceeded into a room that was marked by distinctive blue-colored walls. On the far wall was the image of an airplane as it circled the globe and just in front of that image was a modern-designed receptionist desk. Behind the desk was an agent, and so Myrick walked over to her, showed his badge once again and indicated that he was there to assist in the interviews.

"Lieutenant Bradley is still in there with one of them. Would you like me to lead you back there?" the pleasant agent asked.

"No, that's okay. Is there a waiting room?"

"Yes," the agent pointed toward the only wall that wasn't a bright blue color, "just through that door. The others are waiting in there as well."

Myrick thanked the agent and made his way through the door, curious as to what he would see inside. Once he entered, the setting did not disappoint. There were approximately twenty block-shaped, metallic chairs, much like the ones seen throughout the airport tucked along the walls in the spacious area. There was also a solitary, steel-constructed desk in the middle of the room, which was used for baggage to be placed on top of and thoroughly searched.

Glancing around, Myrick was glad to see that the primary suspects he'd hoped and *needed* to be present all were there. Ellen and Jayde were sitting together on one side of the room. Myrick guessed that they'd been the first to arrive, and had chosen seats on the far end of the room, as if somehow that provided them a level of insulation from the matter. Claire, Kendall and Jonathan were there as well. They'd found an area closer to the door to sit down, likely not in a talkative mood and grabbing the first chairs they'd noticed. The tension in the air was thick, a stark contrast to the breakfast that they'd all shared together earlier that morning.

As he walked toward the center of the room, Myrick took off his flat cap and nodded, not actually saying a word, but knowing that he didn't need to, as everyone understood why they were there. He then leaned up against the sturdy desk, his thigh perched just over the side of it, as if he was half sitting on the desk and half standing. Inside the pocket of his heavy overcoat was a round object and he pulled it out. He then began tossing the worn leather baseball up in the air in front of him, as if a common thing to do, although based on the expressions of the others in the room, they clearly found it to be odd behavior, even for the quirky detective. Of course what they didn't completely understand was that this was the most pivotal moment of the investigation, and the habitual tossing of the baseball narrowed his concentration, helping provide laser-like focus to his thoughts.

From his current vantage point, he had a perfect view of the room and an opportunity to get a read on it. Jonathan's predicament stood out in particular. He was sitting on the left side of Kendall. On her right side was her mother. Claire had her arms crossed, as if quite unhappy to be there and ready to be home. Jonathan looked flummoxed and sullen, his eyes downcast. And Kendall sat in the middle, as if she was the arbiter between the two, but unfortunately failing considerably in that role, still unaware that there was far more to Jonathan's nervous nature than he was letting on.

Ellen and Jayde's body language was equally compelling. Ellen seemed completely spent, as if she hadn't slept in days. The elegant, perfectly dressed woman Myrick had met the first day was nowhere to be seen. Instead, the individual before him wore wrinkled slacks, sandals and a baggy sweatshirt. Her makeup had been applied, but not to the same meticulous standards as before, and she had her hair back in a ponytail, not wanting to deal with that hassle either. Ellen made brief eye contact with Myrick, and it was almost as if she was making a plea for finality, ready to be finished with all of this madness. Fortunately, Myrick was relatively certain it would be soon.

Jayde, on the other hand, seemed surprisingly full of life, as if her talk with Myrick earlier had almost uplifted her spirits, solidifying the bond between the two kindred souls with the detective-like instincts. She made subtle eye contact with Myrick, although it was more so a knowing confidence, and she even seemed to nod her head in the direction of where Jonathan, Kendall and Claire were sitting, indicating she had a pretty good read on their situation and was fascinated by the conflict that was unfolding between them as well.

"Thanks again for agreeing to meet with us here," a voice broke through the silence, as a door opened on the other side of the room.

Myrick glanced over to see Victoria emerge through the entryway, followed close behind by Bradley.

"Of course," Victoria said. "Am I free to leave?"

"Almost, let me just have a few words with Detective Myrick first," Bradley turned her eyes to the center of the room having spotted the enigmatic detective from Colorado Springs. She then indicated for Myrick to follow her. "Mr. Scott," Bradley then called over to Jonathan, whose head jerked up slightly as if awoken from a distracted state, "I'll be with you momentarily. Just hang tight for a few minutes."

Jonathan nodded his understanding, and then watched, his eyes tracking Myrick's movement, as Myrick got up from the steel-framed desk and walked over to where Bradley was standing. All the while, Jonathan seemed almost too aware that Myrick held the keys to the fate of everyone in that room.

Bradley led Myrick through the door and then closed it securely behind him. Once on the other side, she walked over to a spacious window, which had appeared opaque from inside the waiting room of the customs office due to the half-silvered surface of it, but was actually clear to see through from the opposite side. Bradley stopped him in front of the now-translucent window; prepared to fill him in on her interview with Victoria while the two detectives watched their suspects, who were completely unaware that they were still being observed at the moment.

"I'm not sure she told you everything she knows," Bradley began.

"I know. I'm not surprised to hear that," Myrick nodded, his confidence unshaken, as he watched Victoria take a seat next to where Ellen and Jayde were sitting.

"You still don't think she's our killer?" Bradley watched Victoria, almost more transfixed on her, as if studying her every move. She noticed that Victoria put her hand on Jayde's shoulder, an apparent bond between the two friends.

"I'm certain she's not. More so than ever, in fact."

Bradley's attention turned from Victoria back over to Myrick, who she could see was studying the interaction between Victoria and Jayde also. He then turned his eyes across the room to where Jonathan was sitting.

"We're going to have to let them all go home after this," Bradley sighed. "We don't have nearly enough yet. And you and I both know this isn't over. Our suspect is only going to be emboldened by getting away once again. You and I will be continuing our investigation... only next time it will be in someone else's jurisdiction."

"Don't be so sure about that," Myrick turned to look at Bradley as he spoke. "Let's go ahead and interview Jonathan. Once we're done with that, I'm betting we'll have all the proof we'll need."

"Let's hope you're right. The interview room is over there." She pointed toward the far end of the hall. "West is already in there waiting for you. I'll go ahead and bring Jonathan back there now as well."

Myrick made his way down the hall, leaving Bradley to her task. He was certain that she'd be reading Jonathan his Rights, and it was best that she do so alone so as not to lose his trust. The last thing they could afford was for Jonathan to refuse to speak now that they were so close to finalizing the last aspects of their case.

West stood and greeted Myrick when he entered the room. The two talked for a moment and Myrick revealed a few of his more nuanced theories to West and why he wanted to assist in talking to Jonathan. In turn, West offered to step out of the room, allowing Myrick to sit second seat to Bradley. The role of bad cop could be played by Myrick, if necessary... and it would.

No sooner had West left the room, then Bradley and Jonathan entered it, and Bradley indicated for Jonathan to take a seat across the table. There was a brief moment of silent tension as she placed a thick brown folder on the desk and then pulled out a few documents that'd been neatly tucked inside of it. After glancing through them one more time, Bradley decided to break the silence.

"So we do know about the situation between you and Kendall," she began.

"I think everyone does now," Jonathan replied, embarrassment evident in his voice.

"Whose idea was that? Whose idea was it to keep your relationship a secret?"

"Kendall's. She thought it would be best to wait before we said anything."

"Did you agree with that decision?"

"Not really," Jonathan's eyes seemed to turn downcast a bit as he spoke. "It's hard to be the one behind the scenes, as is. I tend to disappear at these things. Out of sight, out of mind."

"So why did you go along with it?"

"Because I loved her."

"Interesting word choice," Bradley caught the past-tensed use of Jonathan's words and Myrick's eyes raised a bit, impressed with how quickly Bradley had seized on the small but important detail. "Have things changed?"

"I honestly don't know. I trusted she knew what she was doing. But it didn't turn out so good... at least not for me. She wants to please everyone, but I'm not going to stick around while she plays both sides of the fence between me and her mother."

"I'll bet the car ride down here to the airport created a lot of tension as well. Claire seems to be a fiery one," Bradley offered up in an attempt to bond with Jonathan.

"She definitely isn't pulling any punches with me. I don't see any point trying to change Claire's mind either. That's between her and Kendall. Pros overall can be really cold sometimes if they don't like you. You've never experienced anything until you've been around someone that they've decided doesn't belong in their community any more."

"I've noticed that too. It probably was hard to work in an environment like that. You created the videos that they needed to promote themselves. I'm not certain they'd be nearly as well-known without you."

"It's true. They use my stuff to promote themselves all over social media... everywhere."

"But then you weren't good enough to be in their ranks were you?" Bradley suddenly cut to the chase.

"What do you mean?" Jonathan stuttered a bit, somewhat confused by the comment.

"Well, you competed in dance also right? You've been doing so for years now. But without much to show for it."

"Not everyone is good enough to make it. Trust me, I've seen plenty of dancers with potential fall short. They come in all excited, then flame out just as fast. You wouldn't believe all the people that I've watched come and go over the years."

"Still, that's got to be a tough blow."

"It was," Jonathan paused before continuing, his eyes meeting Bradley's stare for the first time. "But not so tough that I'd *kill* someone."

There was a moment of quiet tension between the two, and then Myrick decided it might be a good time to jump in and change the subject.

"Do you mind if I ask a few questions?" Myrick asked.

"Of course not. Go ahead."

"Jayde has a doppelganger of sorts," Myrick began, although he noticed that Jonathan's eyes lingered on Bradley before turning to meet his. "We met at breakfast this morning. Her name is Amber St. James, I believe."

"She does," Jonathan's attention was on Myrick now, confused by the new line of questioning but remembering the awkward moment when Myrick had confused Amber with Jayde. "That's pretty common in dance though. Some of the younger, less experienced dancers find a more advanced competitor they have something in common with and try to mimic that style... and sometimes even look..."

"Yes, but there's a particularly striking resemblance between Jayde and Amber."

"True. That's definitely more than the usual. But you'd be surprised... I've seen others take it to the extreme too."

"I was told you competed with Amber at one point."

"I did... early on. But we were both new to it at the time and struggled. In hindsight, we both should have been more patient. We pushed too hard and didn't understand why things didn't come easier for us."

"Well, I know from trying dance now how difficult that can be. Competing in West Coast Swing, I'd imagine, is definitely not for the timid."

Jonathan's eyes perked up, as he appreciated the detective's sentiment. Even Bradley seemed taken aback that he was able to add that commonality with Jonathan. It had paid off already, and was about to pay off yet again as Jonathan replied, "So you can understand why I got so frustrated and pretty much just gave up on the competition circuit."

"I do," Myrick returned, genuinely. "But what about Amber? Did she give up?"

"No, just the opposite… she seemed to want it more than ever. But wanting something and actually *getting* it are two entirely different things. She really struggled just in the Novice stage. That's when she decided to change things up. That's when she reinvented her style… even her hair color… to match up with Jayde's."

"Because she's actually a blonde, correct?"

"Yeah, that's her natural color. I liked it better that way too."

"You said that Amber struggled, but this morning… at breakfast… you were celebrating that she made it into Intermediate. That's a little like a minor league baseball player who's been languishing at the Single A level finally being called up to Double A," Myrick enjoyed getting to make the analogy to baseball, as that was a sport he'd played often growing up. "She must've been doing something right."

"I guess," Jonathan shrugged his shoulders. "It's like she caught fire all of the sudden. She could do no wrong in these last few comps. I think she finished first in all of them."

"Quite a turn around."

"It really was."

"What about Jayde?"

"What about her?" Jonathan replied, confused.

"Was she as excited for Amber?"

"I don't know," Jonathan seemed confused by the question. "I mean, I don't even remember Jayde being around for *any* of Amber's competitions. These dance events are huge though. You're asking me a question I really don't know the answer to."

"Of course, that was a little unfair of me. But I think it's safe to say that Jayde was far more advanced than Amber. To use my baseball analogy again, Jayde was at the Triple A level essentially... and practically on the cusp of being called up to the Major Leagues. A dancer like Amber would be no threat to her."

"No, it's safe to say that Amber was never going to be in Jayde's league. Jayde was on a whole different level. She's the most determined dancer I've ever known actually. And when you're the cameraman, you're actually in the best position to see how things go down. That Jayde couldn't break into the All-Star level has always been fascinating to me. I was starting to wonder if they were ever going to let her into their inner circle."

"Interesting," Myrick wrote a few more thoughts in his notepad, then folded it back up and placed it neatly in his pocket, pausing briefly to glance over at Bradley. "I don't really have anything else to ask at this point," Myrick indicated that he was turning the interrogation back over to Bradley, which she readily accepted, having formulated several more questions of her own and grateful that Myrick had brought to light the fascinating new details regarding their case.

"Did Kendall know that you and Amber had dated?" Bradley asked, deciding to delve into the subject a little more.

Myrick made no effort to interrupt but instead stood silently to the side, allowing Bradley to pursue things from there. In fact, he didn't interject himself back into the conversation the entire rest of the interrogation, already certain he'd found out everything he needed to and equally assured he'd effectively set up Bradley to ask the questions that she felt pertinent.

By the time Bradley was finished and Jonathan's interview concluded, Myrick had also nailed down the last details of his theory, now confident that he had enough proof, supported by both direct and circumstantial evidence, for an arrest to be made. Unfortunately, for him, the killer had one last surprise in store for everyone… and the spree of violence wasn't over quite yet.

CHAPTER TWENTY-SIX
Focus on Balance & Remain Grounded

"You sure you don't want to interview Jayde first?" Bradley asked, a bit stunned by Myrick's revelation, but having seen enough that she trusted his intuition. After Jonathan's interview, Myrick had filled her in entirely on his deduction of the matter and, while his methods were unorthodox, all Bradley cared about was shoring up the case, getting to make an arrest and preventing any other deaths from taking place.

"I'm certain," Myrick returned. "And I'm equally certain once I'm done explaining things, you'll get your confession as well."

Bradley sized up Myrick one last time and then indicated for them all to proceed into the waiting room, Bradley and West standing by the door as if to guard any exit out of the room; meanwhile, Myrick proceeded to the center of the room, leaning up against the steel-framed desk, just as he'd done before, the leather baseball back in his hand as if an aid to help him process his thoughts.

There was a moment of quiet tension as he glanced around at the room, not yet ready to speak. Ellen, Jayde, Kendall,

Claire, Jonathan and Victoria were waiting with bated breath; all of Myrick's main suspects were there, save one - Amber. But Myrick felt confident he could proceed with this part even in her absence. Bradley and her team were already working on corralling Amber up and bringing her in for questions, her involvement in the case tangential but still critical.

After tossing the ball three times up in the air, Myrick placed it back in the pocket of his thick overcoat, fishing out the small notebook in its stead. "This has been perhaps the most intriguing case of my career," he began, glancing down at the cryptic writing on the notepad. "And I must admit, I've learned some new tricks along the way."

"I think it's safe to say we all have," Jayde jested, breaking the nervous tension.

"Yes," Myrick glanced up at Jayde, then around the room, curiously reading the expressions of those around him. He could see that even Bradley and West seemed on edge about what would come next. "Well, I do appreciate everyone's help in solving this mystery… and particularly yours," Myrick's eyes returned back to Jayde. "I couldn't have solved this case without you."

Jayde smiled back, although it was equally evident that she seemed more than a little confused by the cryptic comment.

"So are we free to go?" Jonathan finally asked the most pressing question.

"Some of you. But not all." Myrick turned his eyes toward Bradley to make sure she had secured any exit points. The mood turned somber as he did.

"Then who exactly is not free to go?" Claire demanded.

"Well, how about we start with you," Myrick turned his attention to Claire. "You did have the motive to kill, didn't you, Ms. Callaway?"

"What are you talking about? I'm offended by the accusation."

"Much like you're offended by your daughter's secret relationship with Jonathan or your waning influence over the direction of the West Coast Swing community, perhaps?"

"Nonsense."

"She's right," Kendall jumped into the conversation, "my mom would never do something so terrible."

"But your mom *is* capable of using her influence to get what she wants, wouldn't you agree?"

"Of course not," Kendall stammered back, the words forced out. She then glanced over at Jonathan, almost apologetic as she voiced what she clearly didn't believe. "I mean, there's no way she'd commit murder."

"Well, what about you then? Would you commit murder just to get yourself out from underneath your mother's shadow? Or, better yet, would you help someone who did commit murder just to protect someone you love?" Myrick turned his attention over to Jonathan as he spoke.

"I... I wouldn't," Kendall stuttered even more so.

"Look, I know you think I did this, Detective," Jonathan cut into the conversation. "I know you've got it out for me. So does Lieutenant Bradley," Jonathan turned his eyes over to the lead detective across the room for emphasis, then continued speaking. "But leave Kendall out of this. She's not the type to get involved in things," Jonathan attempted to defend her, although there was also a subtle jab... *and truth* to his words.

"I agree. Kendall didn't kill anyone. She was on the dance floor with Deion and there wouldn't have been sufficient opportunity for her to have killed Sacha... let alone Nicole... without being seen."

"And I didn't do it either, if that's what you're insinuating by the 'covering for a loved one' comment," Claire interjected.

"No, I know it wasn't you either. The person who attacked me was young and nimble, literally diving over and around objects in that pool supply room. You're past your prime in dance, Ms. Callaway... and in the potential to execute acrobatic maneuvers."

Claire then glanced over at Jonathan, accusingly. "I knew you were bad news. How could you bring my daughter into something so horrible?"

"Relax, Ms. Callaway. Jonathan isn't the killer either. He was running video during Warren's death. No matter what his technical skills were, he couldn't have shot the dart that killed Warren. *If anything,* I'm saying that Jonathan is something of a victim in all this, himself," Myrick stared down Claire as he related his point.

After an awkward moment of silence, a voice echoed from behind him, "So then you must think it's one of us?" Ellen spoke, her voice trembling as if afraid of what Myrick's response would be.

"One of you is certainly the guilty party, it would seem," Myrick spoke without yet turning around. There was a brief pause as he looked back at Jayde, "or maybe it was someone who isn't in this room with us. Someone who I once mistook for Jayde, their appearances are so similar. I believe her name is

Amber St. James... and she does have quite an interest in being like you, doesn't she?"

"She does," Jayde admitted. "She's made no secret of that."

"True, that part was no secret, but the pact that you made with her was."

"I don't know what you're talking about."

"You do," Myrick paused momentarily for emphasis then spoke again, "And I believe Victoria does too, don't you?" He turned his attention to the red-headed vixen in the chair next to Jayde.

"It's, um..." Victoria glanced over at Jayde as she stammered with her words. "I did figure it out also. I'm sorry," Victoria looked over at Ellen apologetically. "I should have told you. I guess I was just impressed that the bonds of dance were so strong that Jayde would step in for a friend. But I did know. I *did* figure it out. Jayde has been competing in Amber's stead recently."

Jayde's eyes lit up in disbelief as Victoria spoke. She then glared over at her, almost accusatory. "Why would you say that about me?"

"Because I know you, Jayde. I know your style of dance. I know Amber's too. I've trained *both* of you. Amber couldn't have done those things. It was you. It had to have been you all along. It scares me to say this, but I think Trisha Beck figured that out too. I remember her giving Amber those low scores in Sacramento and wondering why because she clearly had a soft spot for Amber. I sometimes wonder if she'd been disappointed with what was happening... but I never got a chance to ask her..."

There was an incredible moment of tension in the room as these astonishing facts came to light. Bradley stood amazed, not just at the revelation, but at how masterfully Myrick was playing the room, getting everyone to admit the facts without him actually accusing anyone of the crime yet. She knew that she could interject at any time - this was *her* jurisdiction - but she didn't dare do so, just as intrigued as everyone else to find out the last details of how the murders had been committed... and if Myrick would get his promised confession.

"Okay fine," Jayde shot back. "Let's assume you're right about that. Maybe I didn't want everyone in the dance world to know I had a soft spot for what Amber was going through. But I know what it's like to have to fight against impossible odds to make it in this tough environment... I couldn't watch Amber suffer in silence anymore. She deserved better. I knew I could help her."

"Did you?" Myrick interjected at just the right moment. "Or were you using her for your own ends? Because it appears to be the latter from where I'm sitting," Myrick wasn't pulling punches anymore. "Perhaps, it's best for me to explain."

"Yes, please explain," Ellen interjected, not believing that Jayde could be guilty of such a crime, and equally upset that one of her dancers was being accused in such a speculative manner. Ellen's motherly instincts had kicked in and none too soon for Jayde.

"One of the biggest holes in my case was that you weren't in Sacramento. You couldn't have been involved in Lavigne's death. It was easy to eliminate you as a suspect. Maybe too easy. But then I realized... Amber was your perfect alibi. You could volunteer to help her make it through Novice.

She'd be intensely grateful and entirely indebted to you for it. And of course, you could be certain that she'd *never* say anything, not wanting to jeopardize her own progress. Her silence was guaranteed, even if people did suspect she was getting a little assistance along the way."

"Helping a friend, doesn't make me a killer," Jayde fought back in defense of herself. "I was with Deion and the others the entire time in the dance room. I certainly couldn't have killed Sacha."

"Actually, it was Sacha's death that was the turning point in my investigation. I remember when we first met you weren't wearing shoes. It was raining. You were outside. I thought that was quite bizarre. But then I learned that dancers wear special soled shoes... and are *very* protective of them... and always take off their shoes when outside the ballroom. So it suddenly made sense why you wouldn't have them on, especially in cold, rainy weather."

"Exactly, the suede would've been damaged on them." Victoria cut in. "*None* of us walk around in our dance shoes. That fact doesn't make Jayde any different than the rest of us."

"You sound like you're grasping for straws," Jayde's confidence picked back up and there was notable defiance in her tone.

"Only when I saw you that same morning of Sacha's death... getting coffee... you *did* still have your dance shoes on. You wore them all the way down the hallway... into the lobby... they must've collected quite a bit of debris. Why would you risk that? And then, when I watched you switching out into your regular shoes back in the ballroom afterward, it hit me - you had *no* choice. You had to hurry out of the room after killing Sacha.

You needed a second alibi. And what better one than to be seen on lobby cameras getting coffee. Then to run into me, that just sweetened your alibi, didn't it?"

"This is all pure conjecture. I've seen you play detective. I know that's what you do."

"I've learned a lot about you as well... more than I think you realize. When we first met, I remember you emphasized that your name was spelled Jayde with a 'y'..." Myrick pulled out his faded notebook as he spoke, flipping to the page where he'd recorded that particular detail. That's a unique name and when I ran it through the database, nothing noteworthy came up. You were squeaky clean."

"We run our own background checks as well, detective," Ellen interjected, almost indignant. "Jayde has volunteered many times at events in different states... and not once has a police agency returned any red flags."

"Of course not," Myrick conceded. "You gave the name Jayde provided you, never once questioning it. And why would you? She'd been giving it to you with the same spelling for the three years she's been competing in your events. It's the same each time on her registration paperwork. But..." Myrick paused briefly. "It wasn't always spelled that way... and she spent the first half of her life being known as Jade without that additional 'y' added in. So I got curious as to why you would insist it always be spelled a certain way, and decided to try the more traditional spelling of it: J-A-D-E." Myrick was looking directly at Jayde as he spoke. "And a young girl with a lengthy juvenile record popped up in the system out of Fernley, Nevada, including a very violent Aggravated Assault on her own mother... which I'm guessing was the final straw for a child tragically forced to deal all alone with a parent coping with severe PTSD and who must've believed the system had turned its back on her."

"Everyone has a past they aren't proud of detective... everyone," Jade glanced around the room as she spoke, aware of many of the hidden skeletons of the others in the room. "Most of us would like to forget them also. Maybe I didn't chose the best way to do so, but I'm not the person I once was," Jade's eyes were on Ellen as she emphasized her last words. Ellen, in turn, stared back, a conflicted expression on her face, as if she was struggling to process the ramifications of what she was suddenly learning.

"But how could you move on when there were people in power that toyed with your life... such as Warren Steyn? He made it no secret that you weren't what he was looking for at the next level. You had to have known that as long as he was alive, you were going to be stuck on the outside looking in. Talented enough to make it to the Big Leagues... but not sophisticated enough for the ones who actually had a say in the outcome. I can only imagine the hurt and frustration that stirred up in you. Feelings that you kept hidden deep inside, which only caused them to fester even worse. Your fate was entirely in someone else's hands... forcing you to choose between giving up what you loved most or continuing to pursue something out of your reach... and that understandably must've created anger and resentment."

"Again, you're wrong about me. I didn't care. Warren's opinion of me was the least of my concerns."

"And the low scores that Yves Lavigne was starting to give you... or the possibility that his relationship with Warren was affecting those... his opinion of you didn't matter either?"

"Nope. I know I was going to get to the top with or without anyone else's help."

"Did you know that I also found a cigarette butt of yours... in the pool maintenance room... underneath the stairs? Same unique menthol brand. Same distinctive black lipstick on the end of it." Myrick decided to reveal more intriguing details from his investigation.

"You know how many times I went out to that pool area to smoke? You know how easy it would've been for a maintenance person or someone else to get one of those cigarette butts stuck on a shoe and track that into there?" Jade retorted, although her voice cracked for the first time, finally realizing how dire her situation had gotten. Myrick was far more perceptive than she'd understood.

"You're ignoring some of the facts though, detective," Ellen fortunately came to Jade's aid once more. "I know they found poison in Natasha's system. Are you telling me that Jade is the reason she's in the hospital? Because we all know that Jade thought the world of Natasha. That was her role model. She made no secret of that fact. You couldn't convince me that she'd hurt her friend."

"I don't believe she would either... not purposefully. But maybe this is a good time to explain my theory. I believe," Myrick turned his attention to Jade as he spoke, "That you never meant to hurt Natasha. That drink... the one with the poison in it... that was meant for Sacha. You couldn't have known that Natasha would take it from him. It's why you seemed so genuinely concerned for her wellbeing when she was placed in the ambulance… and why you knew her situation was far worse than it seemed."

"But again," Ellen interjected. "Why hurt Sacha? The two have very little interaction with each other that I'm aware of."

"Sacha made an interesting comment to Jade when we talked at the hotel. He said that they knew dark secrets about each other. I uncovered early on the secret Jade was holding over him… his affair with Natasha. In turn, it's my guess that the secret he was holding over Jade had to do with her filling in and competing on behalf of Amber. If he'd have told me or anyone in law enforcement that important bit of information, which he seemed willing to do, it would've changed the entire course of our investigation, diminishing Jade's seemingly rock solid alibi. And Jade couldn't allow that."

"But she was in the dance room with us just a few minutes before Sacha was killed," Jonathan interjected. "I saw her."

"You did. I also remember you mentioned that she had a cheese plate in her hand. The same girl that had just told me she didn't put milk in her coffee because it was a dairy product, allowed herself to be seen eating cheese from the hospitality area earlier that same night. My guess is she needed an excuse for why her prints would be on the chef's knife… which was also the murder weapon of choice."

"All of what you're saying is just based on speculation," Jade interjected. Her voice cracking a bit and her confident veneer almost completely gone. "I'm sure I could do the same and make it seem like anyone in this room had the motive and opportunity to kill."

"Maybe. But then there's one final piece of the puzzle that became evident. It worked out well that Detective Bradley chose customs for this interview. You turned your luggage in to be checked, correct?"

Jade looked at Myrick with a sideways glance, making no attempt to answer, then noticing for the first time an opaque plastic bag in Myrick's hands, appearing like police evidence packaging. She watched concerned as Myrick placed the bag on the steel-framed table, suddenly coming to grips with what she guessed might be inside.

"I believe you were wearing a costume the night of Sacha Arnaud's death... a Halloween costume," Myrick pulled a rolled up shirt from the bag as he spoke. "This one, correct?"

Jade sized up the shirt and then finally spoke, "Yes, but what's your point."

"Well, there's blood stains on it."

"Of course there are. It's part of the costume."

"Is it?" Myrick noted, not entirely convinced by Jade's answer.

"I remember when I first saw you wearing this shirt, it had bright red stains all along the torso and chest, as if a glossy red spray paint had been used along with scissor cuts to make it look like the indie band's image on the front of it had suffered a particularly gruesome attack. It was a creative homemade costume, bloodied and tattered... and well-suited for a Halloween-themed event. Only later, when I ran into you getting coffee that morning, there was a distinct new reddish-brown patch along the shoulder of the shirt," Myrick unrolled the graphic tee and pointed to a darkened stain along the upper seam of the sleeve. The color is flat, which happens as blood dries on a porous material like cotton... and while subtle, its different appearance still caught my eye. But of course there was no blood at the scene of Sacha's death... and it wasn't until much later that we realized a second victim had been brutally murdered that same night... and that someone had dragged her bloody body to a place of concealment..."

Myrick could see that Jade's eyes were growing wider with every word he spoke, now aware of where he was going with his line of logic, and trying *desperately* to think up an answer for what was coming; only there wasn't going to be a good one. Myrick was on the verge of putting a final nail in the coffin of his case and Jade was becoming increasingly helpless to stop him.

"I'm pretty sure when the blood on this shirt is tested it will come back, not as yours, but matching up to one of the victims... Nicole Whitlock. Although, my guess is you never *meant* to kill Nicole... you didn't know that she'd snuck off with her boyfriend earlier... or that she was going to reenter the room through the same side passage that you were using to steal away unseen. Fortunately for you... you must've heard the footsteps coming... giving you time to ambush her... slicing her throat with a knife. Afterwards you disposed of her body in the one place you knew no one would frequent... because you were out there each day smoking cigarettes and would be aware that the pool shed wasn't being used during the winter time... and so you hid the body inside, figuring no one would find it until you were long gone."

"Then if you knew. Why wouldn't you have just arrested her back then?" Claire chimed into the conversation, "You could've protected us all from a lot of danger."

"Well, I wasn't completely sure, but I did have a pretty good suspicion. So I came up with an idea, I planted the seed in Jade's head that I was on the verge of catching my killer... and that I was going to stake out the killer from the second floor of the supply hut. I wanted Jade to suspect I might be on to her... and I wanted her to take the bait and follow me into there, thinking I'd catch her red-handed. Jade's more agile than I gave her credit for though," Myrick turned his attention away from Claire and back toward Jade, who was fiddling with the cast on her arm, nervously rubbing her hand along the soft cotton padding that lined the plastered edge of it.

"Only someone who was trained in acrobatic-like maneuvers could escape the way she did. *Maybe* someone who was raised by two parents in the military and who spent years having those skills pressed upon her? And that same person *might* even think they could pull off the precarious six-foot leap over to the edge of the pool. Unfortunately, you came up short on the attempt, badly injuring your arm, didn't you?" Myrick glanced at the cast, noting that Jade was still fiddling with it, apprehensively. "My guess is it took everything in you to pull yourself out of that pool, hurry down to the far reaches of the hotel property and scale the fence before I had any chance to catch up with you."

"She made me believe she was a victim," Jonathan spoke, completely in shock. "She used me. I had Jade's blood on my hands." He peered down at his palms in disbelief, as if reliving that terrible moment but now seeing it from a different perspective.

"Jade would've known she had to get back in the hotel. If she wasn't in her room when we searched for her, by process of elimination we'd know she was the killer. More importantly, she needed an explanation for her arm. As for her head, well I'm pretty certain she did that to herself... the hole in the drywall had two distinct lines of demarkation, as if it had suffered two impacts. My guess is Jade was wise enough to first soften up that particular area of the wall with a blow from an object to break it up slightly... then slammed her own head against it, widening the hole... and also creating the necessary gash to her forehead... *without* actually fracturing her own skull."

Ellen glanced over at Jade, no longer sure what to make of the person she *thought* she knew, but still wanting answers for the things that didn't add up in her mind. "Even if it's true that it was Jade... and not Amber in Sacramento," Ellen voiced her confusion, "it still doesn't make sense that she killed Warren... she was on the floor competing when it happened."

"It does when you consider that was also the perfect cover for her to pull it off... in front of hundreds of witnesses... and seemingly have the perfect alibi. Jade, as she revealed rather plainly to me, was trained in the use of weapons. So I did a little research. Her mother was stationed in Laos in the late 80s as part of the US government's investigation into POW/MIA cases. Both Vietnam and Laos prohibited the use of firearms. To ward off rats and other unpleasant animals, small poison needle-like darts became commonplace. They were silent but potent weapons for killing. They are also incredibly accurate. My guess is Jade knew that. And that she knew she could easily conceal a small trigger release using a wrist attachment concealed neatly underneath her shirt. When the music stopped, she fired the poison-tipped needle. No one would be the wiser.

"That would be nearly impossible to pull off," Jade fumbled back, defiantly.

"For some, perhaps. But not for the person who so swiftly caught my cap mid-dance and never missed a beat. And of course the poison dart was shot just at the exact end of a 32 count phrase… & while you would've had a brief pause… making the execution of it that much more ideal. You have incredible reflexes, Jade… that's a gift… although this time around it's proven your curse also." Myrick paused for a moment to let the facts sink in, but then voiced one last thought. "There's really only one thing I haven't figured out - what happened to the knife you used to kill Nicole? We determined that you used the cutting blade from the cheese board already on Sacha Arnaud, it was still wedged into his back. So where did you get a second knife to kill Nicole."

"Oh, you mean this," Jade's fingers had slipped inside the edge of her cast and when she pulled them out again, a three-inch blade materialized as well. In the time it took for Myrick to realize what was in her hand, Jade moved so swiftly that even he didn't have time to react. Jade swung the knife up against Victoria's throat, a mixture of desperation and fury on Jade's face. "Don't make me use this!" she quickly demanded.

Out of the corner of her eye, Jade caught a glimpse of Bradley stealing toward her. She dug the knife a little deeper into Victoria's throat, and a slight hint of blood trickled down, emphasizing for all to see that she wouldn't hesitate to kill… *yet again*. The consequence of taking another life was the least of

Jade's concerns at this point, and there was certainly no point protesting her innocence. Her only hope now was to take a gamble on a last ditch escape.

"Back up!" Jade demanded as she pulled Victoria to a standing position. "And slide over the gun in your hand!" she demanded of Detective West.

West turned his eyes to Bradley, as if to plead for direction. Bradley, in turn, nodded that he should comply and so West slid his firearm over to Jade, who pressed down on Victoria to crouch toward the floor. As the two stooped low, Jade deftly dropped the knife and picked up the pistol. In a flash, she had the police-issued Glock pointed at Myrick, and then all around the room, warning that she knew both how to handle the gun *and* use it.

"Same thing to the two of you," Jade demanded of Myrick and Bradley, "weapons on the ground!"

Both Myrick and Bradley complied, carefully placing their firearms on the floor and then standing back up slowly, hands in the air, wanting to make sure they weren't considered a danger or that Jade would do anything drastic. Victoria's life lay in the balance, and one wrong move could cost her it.

Jade had the firearm jabbed into the midsection of Victoria's back, using it to forcefully direct her hostage out of the room, but as she got closer to the door, she swung it to the side and trained it specifically at Myrick. Jade was good with a weapon, her parents had trained her well; and she was about to show everyone how comfortable she was with a firearm in her hand.

"I missed in the maintenance shed," Jade's eyes penetrated Myrick as she spoke, "I won't miss again."

Myrick understood in an instant that Jade was going to shoot him. In the blink of an eye, he lurched away just as her finger pulled against the trigger, firing off a shot that echoed through the room; and the bullet ripped into Myrick's flesh as he hit the floor.

Jade wisely had more than one reason for shooting Myrick. She did want revenge for him solving the case, but she also knew that shooting him would create a distraction in the room, allowing her to make her escape with her hostage while the other detectives tended to a wounded Myrick. Jade didn't wait to see what would happen next; instead, she jammed the gun violently into the back of her captive again, causing Victoria's eyes to go wide in disbelief, and then the two women disappeared out the door.

Bradley, meanwhile, had raced over to Myrick's side on the floor, simultaneously signaling for West to go after Jade. West sprung to life, hurrying toward the doorway, leaving Bradley to tend to Myrick. Only Myrick was stubbornly pulling himself up from the floor, a layer of dark blood soaking through his jacket along his upper shoulder. Myrick had bladed his body as he dove to safety, fortunately protecting any vital organs, giving Jade a shot at only his right arm and shoulder. She'd hit the mark, but the wound was unlikely to be a mortal one.

"I'll be alright," Myrick immediately shot over to Bradley, brushing away her concerns over the injury. "You take the side door and circle around. I'll see if I can distract her long enough so that you can get the jump on her."

Bradley glanced at the thick blood stain enveloping his shoulder line, a look of hesitation on her face, but then she nodded her agreement and turned to go toward the back corridor which she knew led to a side door out of the facility. Myrick pulled himself to his feet, his right arm draped down and practically useless to him. Snatching up his firearm off the ground with his non-dominant left hand, he then hurried his way in the same direction that he'd seen Jade, Victoria and West go.

On the other side of the door, he heard the panicked words of the customs agent calling for backup over an emergency line. As Myrick hurried by, the customs agent pointed in the direction that she'd seen the others go, while still speaking excitedly into the phone, alerting other officers as to the danger inside the airport. Suddenly, Myrick heard more gunfire, and darted off in the direction of it.

As he exited the door of the customs office, a bullet whizzed just by his head and lodged into the frame of the door. Myrick ducked back inside, blading his body behind the edge of the wall, so that he couldn't see Jade or Victoria... although he did have a line of sight toward Detective West, who had also found cover and was hiding behind a circular column. Myrick spotted two bullet holes wedged in the column; evidently Jade had taken shots at West and narrowly missed him as well.

The gun that West had slid over to Jade was a Glock 17. Myrick had counted six shots so far, and so he guessed she had *at most* eleven bullets left in the magazine. He could try to get her to waste those shots attempting to take him out, but he also suspected Jade was way too smart to make that mistake. His only hope was to stall and keep Jade within the vicinity long enough for Bradley to come around and stop her.

"Jade, listen to me! I can help!"

There was a brief moment of tense silence and then Jade's voice cut through it, "You don't understand I have nothing left. My life is over." There was a profound hopelessness in Jade's words as she came to grips with the fact that she'd somehow convinced herself to destroy everything that was important to her. Her eyes darted from side to side as if taking in her surroundings for the last time.

In the midst of her desperation, and as the tension grew, another voice spoke. But it wasn't Jade or Myrick who ventured a response... it was Victoria... and her words were full of deep emotion, "There's always hope, Jade," she explained through a voice that quivered. "Nobody is beyond salvation. *Nobody*."

Jade had the gun placed hard against Victoria's temple, but she released her finger from the trigger so that it didn't appear that she was on the verge of shooting the fatal shot. Still, although the danger was lessened slightly, it was clear the situation could change at any moment, and so no one dared move.

Myrick, meanwhile, was more nervous than he'd been at any point in the situation. He'd been in his fair share of hostage crisis situations and he knew the worst thing someone being held captive could do was interject themselves into the dialogue; that's when tragic things tended to happen. Myrick was stunned by Victoria's bravery, but he had no desire to watch her sacrifice herself. *Maybe Jade's life could be redeemed?* Regardless, Myrick was determined it not come at Victoria's cost; and that new variable had a tremendous influence on what Myrick decided should be his next calculated negotiation tactic.

"Let's make a switch. I have a vehicle here," Myrick insisted. "We aren't far from the border. You let Victoria go and take me in her stead, and I'll help you get out of here."

Again, there was silence and Myrick could tell Jade was considering her options. This was his one and *only* time to act. Myrick reached his hands around the doorway in surrender, placing the firearm on the ground where Jade could see it. He then moved his entire body through the doorframe, his hands up in the air; and proceeded carefully out into the open. Myrick was now completely defenseless. The next shot from Jade would surely be fatal.

Now able to get a clear look at both Jade and Victoria, Myrick could see that they had inched over to a nearby escalator... about to descend it. Only Jade had to have known by now that there would be airport agents covering every conceivable exit by this point and there was *no* escape. While she'd loosened her grip on Victoria momentarily, the hopelessness of her situation had kicked back in and now the gun was pointed directly at Myrick, just as it had been when she shot him the first time. Myrick could see that her finger was starting to squeeze on the trigger yet again.

"Just trust me," Myrick reiterated. "I can get you out of here."

Jade seemed to listen to his words, and he could see that, despite her actions, there *was* a fair amount of confusion and hesitancy in her eyes. She glanced from side to side and then even over her shoulder and down toward the bottom of the escalator, hearing the heavy footsteps of officers rushing toward them from off in the distance. In a flash, however, panic consumed her and suppressed any chance at reasoning. Her eyes wide, terrified about what was to come next, she turned them toward Myrick, raising the gun one more time so that it was trained right at his heart.

A shot rang out, and Myrick braced for the bullet. But instead, he saw Jade double over in pain, stumbling simultaneously backward. Her balance off, she lost her footing at the edge of the escalator and then fell perilously down it. Myrick immediately raced over, just in time to see Jade hit the bottom level, her body sprawled out on the ground, and a crowd of on-lookers scurrying over toward it.

In an instant, Bradley was standing by Myrick at the top of the escalator also. He could see that she still had her firearm in her hand and he could smell the familiar scent of spent gunpowder. Bradley's shot had saved both his and Victoria's lives, but it had forever changed Jade's. While she was still alive, and medics would find a way to save her, she'd also suffered the type of horrific outcome that her actions had long ago set in motion and she would spend the rest of her life behind bars, never to dance again. And that, to Jade, was a fate almost worse than death.

EPILOGUE
Don't Be Afraid to Try New Dances

"You flying out there again *already?*" Ox pressed, a confounded expression on his face.

"Yep," Myrick simply answered, as he returned his police vehicle for the last time, readying himself for retirement.

Today was Myrick's last day with the Department. He was going to miss it tremendously. He'd been preparing for this moment forever it seemed, practically counting down the days, but now that it was here, the impact was hitting him harder than he'd expected. There was no replacing the people and friendships of those he worked with in law enforcement. They all shared a common bond. There was a truth to the brotherhood of the thin blue line. And there were few true friends like Ox and the others he'd worked with as a detective.

"You aren't going to spend your *entire* pension visiting that girl are you?" Ox pressed, jokingly.

"It's not like that. We're just friends."

"For now," Ox laughed as he replied knowingly.

"We'll see," Myrick conceded.

"Then why do you keep going out there, brother?"

"Dance lessons. She's my instructor. Victoria's helping me get ready for a new profession."

Ox was speechless, perhaps for the first time in his life, as he heard Myrick's words. He didn't know whether to congratulate the man or warn him about the *seriously* ill-considered decision he was making. Still, Ox was a wise and good enough friend to know that he should simply encourage his buddy's happiness, regardless of the foolish nature of it. There were plenty of cops who put in their 20-25 years then struggled to find meaning in retirement. Ox could tell that wasn't going to be a problem for Myrick.

"Well, I believe in you man."

"I'm glad *someone* does," Myrick jested back. "But I'm no fool, I think I'll find myself a day job too just in case."

"You gonna work security at a retail center or something? I hear there's good money and even insurance benefits in that."

"No," Myrick paused briefly in contemplation. "No, I think I may take a few months off... maybe travel... hit up a few dance conferences," he winked. "But then expect me back here. I may just hang up my own shingle. Evann Myrick, Private Investigator, has a good ring to it, don't you think?"

Ox smiled widely, excited to hear his friend's idea. "I do," he replied, but then he paused in contemplation for a moment, as if he'd had a better suggestion, "But you need something with a little more pizzazz. How about Evann Myrick... private investigator... *and* dance instructor?"

Myrick thought for a moment. The idea did have a good ring to it. His cheeks then raised slightly and his eyes squinted in apparent amusement. "Nah," he finally answered back. "I think that's taking it too far." He laughed, heartily.

"Maybe so," Ox returned, amusement pasted all over his face. "You gonna be back this way anytime soon?"

"Eventually. Victoria's got us going to Santa Fe at the end of the month. We'll be meeting up with a few of the other dancers... Ellen, Kendall, Jonathan, Claire..."

"Really?" Ox cut Myrick off, suddenly perplexed. "I thought for sure you'd want to stay as far away from that place as possible. Can't be too many good memories there for *any* of you guys. I heard your suspect pled guilty already and was sentenced to life in prison. There won't be any trial or any need for you to be there to testify, right?"

"Yeah, Jade did plea up and take responsibility for what she did. She knows she's already caused enough harm. She didn't want to put the families through any more."

"That's not gonna bring her victims back though," Ox pointed out.

"True," Myrick conceded, pausing briefly before continuing. "But no amount of all-consuming anger toward Jade will either. Better at least that the families get some sort of closure and can move on. There isn't much left of Jade anyway. She suffered a pretty terrible spinal fracture. I doubt she'll ever walk again."

"Then, back to my original question... why go out there? Shouldn't you be traveling the world? You're finally semi-retired... go enjoy life for a while."

"Oh I will. But this was Victoria's idea and I respect it. Jade matters to her. I can't really explain it... and Victoria probably couldn't either... but she wants to be there to mentor

Jade. She talked the others into doing the same. They made some sort of pact. The dance community has bonds that the rest of us don't totally understand and they don't give up on each other easily. Jade will pay her price for what she's done... she can't hurt anyone ever again... but there's a longer term consequence to decisions. The prison system is a scary place for anyone to be, let alone someone as young as Jade. I think Victoria just wants her to know that her ultimate destiny hasn't been decided yet and that she can still make choices that affect it."

"Pretty amazing of her to get all of you together like that," Ox smiled, grateful to know that the Victoria's of the world still existed. "You sure she's not the one?" he pressed one last time, a slanted look in his eyes, not yet willing to concede the point.

"Unfortunately I think the two of us were meant more to be friends. There was really only one girl for me anyway. And I'm good with that... I'll see her again eventually," Myrick expressed with complete assuredness.

The two friends continued saying their goodbyes and Myrick explained that he had to hurry off to the airport before he missed his flight. Victoria was planning to pick him up and he didn't want have to break the news that he'd somehow been delayed. It was the beginning of a new day for Myrick. The future was indeed exciting. But he wasn't going to let go of his past either. Riley, police work... and all the treasured experiences up to this point in his life... *those* were the things that made him who he was. God had done a good work in Myrick. He was definitely one of kind. And it wouldn't be long until he realized that his work had only begun. A killer would soon be on the loose in the dance world yet again, and there was only one man qualified enough to unravel the mystery.

- END OF BOOK #1.

DANCE TIPS AS RECORDED IN DET. MYRICK'S NOTES

- In starter position, keep feet about shoulder length apart
- Knees should be slightly bent
- Engage lat muscles (??)
- Maintain a good frame
- Don't look down at feet!
- Counting aloud to get rhythm is ok
- Lead starts with left foot, follow with right
- Complete weight transfers with each step
- Roll thru the feet
- Work on stretch/anchor & maintain connection
- Anchor step is really just 3 steps in place
- Practice basics (Sugar Push, Left/Right Side Pass, Tuck Turn)
- Remember to breathe!!

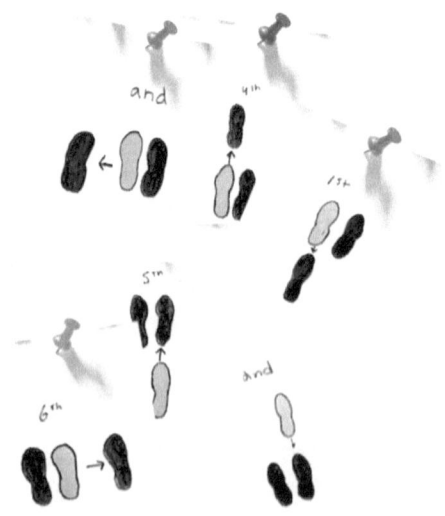

Coming Soon!

A Quick Quick Slow . . . DEATH
An Introduction to Country 2-Step...
And a Murder Mystery

BOOK #3 IN THE ADVENTURES
OF DETECTIVE EVANN MYRICK

A new novel by

DOUG DORSEY

Available in 2026 from Studio 15 Publications, Inc.

A WORD FROM THE AUTHOR: Thanks for reading *Kick Ball Slay*! I would love to hear your input on the novel. Please send me an email (ddorsey@Studio15inc.com) or connect with me online (Facebook, Instagram, Threads or LinkedIn). In addition, if you're in the Florida area and want to get some West Coast Swing dancing in, here are some of the groups/locations I highly recommend: Jax Westies, Floorplay WCS & Country, Goldcoast WCS, District Dance Academy, O-Town West Coast Swing, Monarch Ballroom, HonkyTonk Hammerheads and Jacksonville Country & Swing Dancing. And of course, there's also my absolute favorite place to dance - The Dance Shack (www.TheDanceShack.com). Save some dances for me!!!

ABOUT THE AUTHOR

DOUG DORSEY** is the author of *Kick Ball Slay: An Introduction to West Coast Swing... <u>And</u> a Murder Mystery, Never Alone, Broken Hero, The Deception, The Red Ledger, The Betrayal* and *Rock Step, Triple Homicide: An Introduction to Lindy Hop... <u>And</u> a Murder Mystery.* For more information on his books, visit him at www.Studio15inc.com. And if you want to learn more about dance in general, tune in on Spotify to *The Dance Shack Podcast*, which is co-hosted by Eddie Laski & Doug Dorsey!